W9-ACZ-175

Ben stared down at Emily

He could see the freckles dotting her shoulders in the morning light. Was he ready to rejoin the world now, for her? Could they possibly have a future together?

A whimper from another part of the house made him ease out of bed. Covering Emily with a blanket, he slipped on his clothes and went out to the main living area. It was so her. Big, overstuffed couches covered in fabrics that resembled watercolors, high ceilings, warm wood floors. Chic but cozy.

Lady was scratching at the door that led to the foyer. "Hey, girl, need to go out?" Ben glanced over at the dog's bed by the fieldstone fireplace—her puppies were out for the count.

After letting the dog out into the yard, he went into the kitchen to put on the coffee. While it brewed he studied the large, airy space. Granite countertops, brick walls hung with pots and pans, an island counter in the middle of the floor, a huge refrigerator covered with pictures. Smiling, he crossed the room to get a glimpse into Emily's life. There was a photo of her and Lady, one of a dark-haired woman in dance wear, one of Emily and a man, arms linked.

Ben frowned. *A boyfriend?* No. The guy was too old. He moved in closer to get a better look. "What the hell...?"

Dear Reader,

Welcome to my new Superromance novel. I hope you enjoy this look at an urban soup kitchen. For years I've volunteered at a kitchen very similar to Cassidy Place, and I'm continually amazed at the staff's hard work and belief that it's our responsibility to help people less fortunate than we are. It's truly a wonderful organization, and I'm glad I'm able to help out.

Several years ago I thought, "Wow, I'd like to set a book here." How could I craft a hero who's a guest at the kitchen, though, and a heroine who volunteers there? It took me a while, but I managed to create Ben, a formerly prosperous businessman, who's lost his company and his self-esteem. At the soup kitchen he meets Emily, who has a connection to him that neither of them knows about. Before they discover it they're involved, and nothing—even such a big surprise—is going to break them apart.

Emily and Ben are basically decent people caught in circumstances not of their making. It was a challenge to play out their journey to happily-ever-after. I liked both of these characters from the outset, and I hope you do, too. Though I don't agree with some of their choices or actions—that makes for good conflict, right?—I do appreciate the predicament they're in.

Please let me know what you think of the book. You can reach me at kshayweb@rochester.rr.com or P.O. Box 24288, Rochester, NY 14624. Also, visit my Web site for updates on my work at www.kathrynshay.com or www.superauthors.com.

Kathryn Shay

A TIME TO GIVE
Kathryn Shay

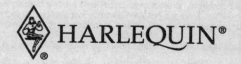

TORONTO • NEW YORK • LONDON
AMSTERDAM • PARIS • SYDNEY • HAMBURG
STOCKHOLM • ATHENS • TOKYO • MILAN • MADRID
PRAGUE • WARSAW • BUDAPEST • AUCKLAND

If you purchased this book without a cover you should be aware
that this book is stolen property. It was reported as "unsold and
destroyed" to the publisher, and neither the author nor the
publisher has received any payment for this "stripped book."

ISBN 0-373-71315-0

A TIME TO GIVE

Copyright © 2005 by Mary Catherine Schaefer.

All rights reserved. Except for use in any review, the reproduction or
utilization of this work in whole or in part in any form by any electronic,
mechanical or other means, now known or hereafter invented, including
xerography, photocopying and recording, or in any information storage
or retrieval system, is forbidden without the written permission of the
publisher, Harlequin Enterprises Limited, 225 Duncan Mill Road,
Don Mills, Ontario, Canada M3B 3K9.

All characters in this book have no existence outside the imagination of
the author and have no relation whatsoever to anyone bearing the same
name or names. They are not even distantly inspired by any individual
known or unknown to the author, and all incidents are pure invention.

This edition published by arrangement with Harlequin Books S.A.

® and TM are trademarks of the publisher. Trademarks indicated with
® are registered in the United States Patent and Trademark Office, the
Canadian Trade Marks Office and in other countries.

www.eHarlequin.com

Printed in U.S.A.

Books by Kathryn Shay

HARLEQUIN SUPERROMANCE

Don't miss any of our special offers. Write to us at the
following address for information on our newest releases.

Harlequin Reader Service
U.S.: 3010 Walden Ave., P.O. Box 1325, Buffalo, NY 14269
Canadian: P.O. Box 609, Fort Erie, Ont. L2A 5X3

To the staff and volunteers at Salem Soup Kitchen, in
acknowledgment of your dedication
and desire to help those in need.

CHAPTER ONE

STARING ACROSS THE DINING HALL, Emily watched the tall, muscular man stop and look up at the picture over the entryway. "I wonder what his last name is," she muttered to herself.

"Best you get your mind off that one." Alice Smith, the administrator who ran the Cassidy Place soup kitchen where Emily volunteered three nights a week, tossed out the warning as she refilled creamers and sugars. At 7:30 p.m., they were ready to close up for the night.

Emily liked this down-to-earth woman with her sturdy build, a tidy bun corralling her coarse gray hair. Though Alice worked tirelessly at feeding the impoverished, she could be tough when one of the guests got out of line, or the volunteers grumbled too much.

Emily's grin was sheepish. "I didn't realize I said that aloud."

"You did. Anyway, what you were thinking is written all over your face." Alice tucked a strand of hair that had escaped from Emily's braid behind her ear. "For as long as he's been coming here, he's fascinated you."

Emily turned her gaze back to Ben. "I guess he has. He's different from the others."

"Yeah, he is. He broods a lot, but I like that he pitches in around here. Most guests just eat and take off."

"But, it's more than his helping out. There's just something about him that doesn't quite fit." She nodded across the room. "He always does that."

Alice started to wipe the counter. "Does what?"

"Stares at that picture of Mick Cassidy over the entrance. Every Monday night when he comes in, he stops at it. His expression is almost sentimental. Nostalgic."

"Odd. The old guy's been dead for years."

Emily changed the topic. She was all too familiar with what had happened to Mick Cassidy and his son, the one who'd founded the soup kitchen as a memorial to his father—not to mention the fate of the workers from Cassidy Industries who used to volunteer here.

Making small talk, she surreptitiously watched Ben as he approached one of the twenty long tables that were in rows. "He's sitting down. I'll go wait on him." She grabbed a place setting and rushed off.

"Time's almost up," Alice called after her.

"I know. I'll hurry." She crossed the dining hall. The room was as huge as a gymnasium, with big windows, a high ceiling and scuffed hardwood flooring. Cassidy Place was housed in a wing of a beautiful old church on St. Paul Street and had character. "Hello, Ben," she said when she reached him.

His gray eyes lit up when he saw her. Ringed with dark black, they were accented by thick lashes. After a moment, though, the light went out in them, like it always did. "Hello, Emily."

She set silverware and a place mat on the table in front of him. "You're later than usual."

"Am I?"

"Hmm." She fussed with the knife and fork, wishing she could crack that facade of his. "Busy today?"

Forcefully he shook out his paper. "Uh-huh."

"At a job?"

"Yes." He looked down and began reading.

"Where do you work, Ben? You've never mentioned it."

He hesitated. "Construction jobs here and there."

Since he'd finally answered a question about his circumstances, she dared another. "Then you can afford a place to live?" She'd worried he was homeless, like many who came to Cassidy Place. "You don't..."

"Live on the street? No, not anymore."

He raised the paper and stuck his nose in it, signaling he was done talking. Well, at least she'd gotten this far tonight. Over the past year, she'd had to drag any personal information out of him. When he did talk to her, he seemed so lonely it broke her heart.

She scurried back to the kitchen where the aroma of

cooking meat and fresh bread permeated the air, contrary to the smell out in the dining area. Guests at shelters like this weren't always clean. "One more," she said and smiled at the older woman who dished up food in front of the huge industrial stove. "It's for Ben."

"Ah, that one. Let's give him a hefty portion. He needs meat on his bones."

He's got nice meat on his bones already. Blushing at the thought, Emily transferred her gaze to the windows that lined the wall above the king-size dishwasher. More than once she'd checked out *his bones.* He wore tattered shirts and threadbare jeans, revealing the muscles beneath them—from the construction work he did, she guessed. Now that it was spring, those muscles were vividly defined beneath his T-shirts.

Sliding his plate and a dessert onto a tray, she hurried back to the table. Alice had served him milk and coffee, which he drank slowly, precisely, like he did everything. He seemed to savor each drop. "Here you go." She set his meal in front of him.

He gave her what passed for a smile. "Thank you."

She glanced around. "Can I sit with you a while?"

"All right." As he ate, she studied him. His features were square cut and angular. Right now, his jaw sported about a two-day beard. In addition to being sexy, it was somewhat sinister. "You look tired, Emily," he finally said, scrutinizing her face.

Another disagreement with her father. "Do I? I'm not sleeping well."

He hesitated. "You're not sick are you?"

"No. Family problems." He glanced at her hand, her left hand, but said nothing.

"Are you married, Ben?"

He'd forked in a mouthful of meat and now he almost choked on it. The volunteers at Cassidy Place were friendly but they usually kept a professional distance from the guests.

He cleared his throat. "No, I'm not married."

"Ever been?"

"No." And then, he added, "Came close, though." Still, he didn't ask her.

"I was married. I've been divorced for almost three years." And the breakup had done serious damage to her self-esteem. Sometimes when she tried to sleep at night, she could still hear Paul hurl insults at her, see his face suffused with disgust.

Again, Ben studied her. He ate some potatoes, then wiped his lips with his napkin. They were nice lips. "The divorce was tough?"

"That's an understatement. You know, I just don't understand intentional cruelty."

"Me, either. Any kids?"

Her hand went to her stomach. "No, I...can't. I wish we had some, though. I'd have a baseball team if I could."

He laughed.

Emily cocked her head. "Why does the conversation always revert to me when I finally get you to talk?"

The corners of his mouth turned up. "Because you're more interesting."

"No way. Come on, tell me more about yourself. Do you have brothers or sisters? A father or mother living?"

"No. No living relatives." He shook his head. "Alice need help tonight?"

She felt frustrated with the change of topic. "Probably with stacking the chairs and folding up the tables so the janitor can get in here tomorrow morning. He has a fit if that's not done."

From across the room, the one other guest left at a table yelled, "I need something here."

She stood. "I'd better go talk to Hugo. He's not very happy tonight."

Ben nodded and looked back to his plate.

But when Emily rose and crossed the room, she could feel him watching her. Hmm, he was definitely different. And she liked him. She wished he'd pay more attention to her. Oh, well. The story of her life. She'd always wanted the attention of a mother, but hers had left home when Emily was five. For years, she'd craved more attention outside of work from her father. And, of course Paul, who'd walked out on her, had said outright she wasn't worth anybody's attention.

He was wrong, though. Emily was worth all of those things. She knew it, and she wondered if the man behind her, whom she'd been having these stilted conversations with for almost a year, would recognize it too. If he ever got to know her.

SURREPTITIOUSLY, BEN WATCHED her like a hawk. It was his only vice these days. Once every week, he allowed himself to feast on the sight of Emily Erickson. She had strawberry-blond hair, which right now escaped from her braid, and when she got close, he could see wisps framing her face, probably from the heat of the kitchen. She had the most flawless skin he'd ever seen, lips just a bit pouty, a cute nose...but it was her eyes that really got to him—they were a mixture of browns and greens and reminded him of a forest in the fall. As she walked away, she glanced over her shoulder and smiled.

He didn't return it; instead, he shifted in the straight-back chair and picked up the newspaper to block her from his sight. Best not to encourage her. For almost a year, he'd been trying to keep his distance, though she'd done anything but cooperate and they'd gotten closer than was good for her. She was always sitting with him, asking him questions, paying extra attention to him. And too often he succumbed to spending time with her. Invariably he regretted it. When he was with her, Ben felt like a man starved for food, but when a banquet was set out in front of him, he was forbidden to eat. There was a time when he'd have gone after a woman like her with all he had, and gotten her, too. But that part of his life was over.

"Ain't you got none left?" he heard Hugo, a regular, snap at her.

Ben looked over the top of the paper in time to see Emily step back. She seemed more vulnerable in the leotard and tights she wore under a filmy black skirt. She told him once that she took a dance class after her stint at the soup kitchen.

She spoke softly to Hugo, who then swore. Ben set down his paper and crossed the room.

He came up to them just as Emily let Hugo have it. "That language won't be tolerated here. If you want to eat, you'll behave yourself. Meanwhile, I'll see if I can find more chicken for you." She glanced at Ben, nodded and walked away.

He grinned safely behind her back; from beneath that cream-puff exterior, he'd often seen her tough side emerge. The contrast continually amazed him, and sometimes he wanted to plumb those depths— thoroughly.

Ben dropped into a chair. "Hey, Hugo, what's going on?"

Desperate eyes leveled on him. Ben knew the expression intimately, had seen it in his mirror often over the past two years. "Aw, Ben, I didn't mean to yell at that girl." He shook his head then rubbed his hands over his eyes. "I wanna bring food to Josie, and Emily said they were done serving."

"Cassidy Place doesn't send home doggy bags, Hugo, you know that. Josie has to come here if she wants to eat."

"She's sick." Translated, she's either stoned or drunk.

Familiar with the latter, Ben laid a hand on Hugo's bony shoulder. "There are free clinics to help her, man."

Hugo's body sagged beneath the old work shirt. "I dunno what to do."

"Talk to Alice. She's got names of places to help Josie."

"Yeah, maybe."

"And apologize to Emily. She didn't do anything to you."

He returned to his seat before Emily came back, but he couldn't focus on the paper. He was remembering when he'd needed one of those places that reformed drunks....

Ben had been on a long binge, and that night, dashing under a bridge to escape the rain, he'd slipped and fallen, and then passed out. He'd woken up with his face in a puddle of slime, a cop standing over him.

"Get up. You're drunk."

Ben had stared up at the officer through bleary eyes. His father had been a bum, often cornered by the police like this. And now Ben was the same. He'd struggled to his feet.

In a surprising move, the cop had pulled out a card. "This is a clinic to help you sober up, if you want to be more than a drunken bum."

Something about the taste of slime in his mouth, the epithet of the cop, hell, maybe it was finally hitting bottom, had made Ben take stock and had given him the impetus to make changes. It had been a long road back....

Picking up the paper, he shook off the memories and turned to the business section, scrolling down the front page. When he found what he was looking for, his hand fisted, crumpling the edge of the paper. Mackenzie Enterprises' stock was up another five points, credited to its hostile takeover two years ago of a company that made monitoring equipment for public utilities. That business was now flourishing. Earning money again. A lot of money. Ben's hand started to hurt. Consciously, he forced himself to relax. Breathe deeply. That kind of tension would drive him back to the bottle and, though he'd lost everything, he wouldn't go there again. Over the top of the paper, his gaze strayed again to the photo that graced the entrance. Mick Cassidy smiled down from the one and only picture Ben had managed to save of his father. Their nomadic travels from city to city, house to house, had made it difficult to keep mementos. Lost in thought, Ben missed Emily approaching his table.

"Thanks for calming down Hugo, Ben."

He lowered the paper. "No thanks necessary, ma'am. Just take it as payment for my dinner."

Again, that smile that could stop a truck in its tracks. "You pay for your dinner ten times over. And please, don't call me ma'am—it makes me sound like my grandmother."

He suppressed a grin.

She nodded to the paper. "Anything interesting in there?"

Sometimes, when he was feeling particularly lonely, he talked about current events with her. On occasion, he let her help him with the crossword puzzle.

"Not much." Unless she wanted to discuss the business world's corporate shark. If it was the last thing he did, Ben would get even with that man. He'd never been vindictive, cold and callous—until Lammon Mackenzie had entered his life. He hated the man most for that.

"Ben, is something wrong?"

Only my whole life. "No, why?"

"You look angry."

"Nah. Just wish the economy was better." He nodded over her head. "Seems Alice is looking for you."

Emily rose when she saw the older woman in the doorway and smiled down at Ben. She squeezed his arm. "Someday, I'm going to get you to tell me more about yourself."

His heartbeat accelerated. "Boring story."

"I doubt it."

He watched her leave. Well, she was right about that. His story was anything but boring. Sad. Infuriating. Stupid. But not boring. It was his own damn fault he'd let Lammon Mackenzie get his company. He'd lost everything to the bastard—everything but this place.

Which was why, once Ben had sobered himself up, he came here every Monday. Cassidy Place, which he'd started ten years ago in memory of his father, and was still solvent because he'd gotten funding from the United Way, was the only thing he had left in his life to prove he'd made a difference, made his mark on the world.

That was why he returned weekly and endured the torture of seeing Emily. In order to stay sane after all that had happened to him, he needed the reinforcement that he was more than an ex-drunk has-been who didn't have the smarts to hold on to the company he'd built from the ground up. And there was no way in hell Emily Erickson was going to find out what a failure he was.

LAMMON MACKENZIE SCOWLED at the cell phone as he listened to the message. "It's me again," he barked after the beep. "Where the hell are you? Call me."

Just as he clicked off, the office door opened. His assistant, Pete Heller, stood in the doorway and nodded to the desk. "There's a call for you from your lawyer, Mac."

"All right." He scowled at Pete. "I suppose you'd like to leave now."

The tall, lanky man arched a brow. "What, at 9:00 p.m.?"

"Funny."

"We human beings need food and sleep."

Mac hid a smile. If the guy wasn't such a shrewd market analyst, he'd fire him for his irreverence. "Get the hell out of here." He picked up the phone. "Jacob, nice of you to get back to me."

"It's only been a few hours since you called. I have clients other than you, Mac."

"Nobody who pays you as much."

"Well, you've got me now. What can I do for you?"

He knocked his knuckles against the paper. "I'm ready to sell off Rockford Instruments." Formerly known as Cassidy Industries.

"Wow, that was fast. I had no idea this move would come so soon."

"I'm *that* good at turning things around, Jacob."

Of course this time, he'd had help. Cassidy Industries had been in bad shape when he'd snatched it out from under Benedict Cassidy. The guy was too fair, too optimistic and too foolish to make it in the business world. It had been child's play, really, to take the company from him. Even easier to build it back up again.

"All right, I'll start the paperwork." Jacob hesitated. "What will you do now?"

"I have a line on another business that might be fun

to court." Man, he liked the thrill of the chase. The kill, when the time came.

"You have a lot of energy, Mac."

"For a man in his late fifties, not bad. Get in touch when you've got this rolling."

He disconnected and leaned back in his plush leather chair. Propping his feet up, he linked his hands behind his head and closed his eyes. At least he'd have something to look forward to. Aside from his daughter, work was the only thing in his life. He preferred it that way. He didn't have to tolerate a nagging wife who wished he was home more, friends who disagreed with his tactics. He didn't have to explain himself to anybody.

So there was no reason why he opened the left drawer of his custom-built granite-topped desk. No reason to pull out the picture of the man, woman and child. Still, he did it.

A lump clogged his throat as he stared at the images. Mac was young, only twenty-six. He had dark hair then, not this mop of gray. He was thinner, too, and more relaxed. The little girl was stunning, just like her mother. God, his wife had been beautiful. And fragile. She'd never stood a chance with him. He could still remember her laughter… *Lammon, you're home early, I love it when you surprise me like this…* Lying beside him… *You're so good in here*—she'd tap his naked chest over his heart—*why can't you let others see that? See what I see…* Her face when she'd held out their child to him for the first time… *It's all right that you weren't here for the birth, darling. Isn't she beautiful?*

But then, as always happened when he thought of Anna, bad memories followed like the furies chasing prey. *I can't believe you did what the paper says… Tell me these are vicious rumors… I won't leave her with a man like you….*

Abruptly he dropped his feet to the floor, shoved the picture back in its hiding place and bolted out of his chair. He strode to the sideboard and poured himself a hefty scotch. When it didn't take the sting away, he gulped back another. Finally, that numbed him.

He studied the office—the oak ceiling, the grass-cloth walls, furniture that had cost more than some people's houses. They were all testaments to his success, and that comforted him. The clock caught his eye. Ten o'clock. He scowled at the phone. Stalking to the desk, he picked up his cell and punched Redial.

The answering machine clicked on again. "This is Emily Erickson. Leave a message at the beep."

"Emily, this is your father. Where the hell are you?"

CHAPTER TWO

THE APRIL SUN BEAT DOWN on Ben's shoulders, making him sweat like he used to after an hour in the sauna at his former health club. His T-shirt was more wet than not and his back ached. But he hefted the concrete blocks without complaint. This Saturday-morning stint with its overtime pay would earn him enough money to buy heavy work boots for the winter. Grunting with effort, he was hit with a flashback so quickly he couldn't roadblock this one....

Buy those hand-tooled boots, Benedict, they make you look like a cowboy.

He'd chuckled at Mallory, his model-chic fiancée, and mimed drawing a gun out of an imaginary holster. *Watch it, ma'am, never know what an hombre like me might want from a lady like you.*

She'd laughed and he'd bought the boots. They'd cost almost a thousand bucks and he hadn't blinked at the expense.

"Hey, Cassidy. You got a visitor." The foreman hovered over the hole Ben was in helping to lay the foundation for a small house.

Ben frowned up at him. "Who is it?"

"Didn't ask his name. Take a break. You been goin' nonstop since six this morning."

Ben glanced at the Timex that had replaced his Rolex. It was noon. Who the hell would know he was here? He'd cut off all ties with his old life when he'd lost his company. Puzzled, he climbed the ladder and shaded his eyes against the sun. Trey Thompson, his former lawyer—his former *friend*—stood on the edge of the site looking like the preppy from Yale that he was, in an oxford shirt, khakis and Docksides. As best he could, Ben wiped the sweat off his face with the hem of his shirt and crossed to Trey. "Hey, counselor, how's it going?"

Trey grasped Ben's hand warmly. "Fine, except you had me waste my whole morning chasing you down. Can't you at least return my phone calls?" There was a note of exasperation in his voice. And offense. Ben had forsaken the racquetball games, the lunches and occasional double dates he and Trey had shared for almost a decade.

"Phone calls?"

"Don't bs me, pal. I know you got my messages. Your landlord thinks I'm a handsome devil and assured me she left them under your door."

"Still charming all the ladies, are you?"

His friend snorted. "And she's the one who told me

you were here. Apparently the head of this construction crew lives in your boarding house."

Ben shook his head. "So much for privacy."

Trey nodded to a makeshift bench in the shade. "Can we talk? It's about Cassidy Industries."

"Look, Trey, I appreciate your attempts to stay in touch, but I'm not interested. I wish you could accept that." Every couple of months, Trey contacted him. It was a painful reminder of what Ben had once had.

"You've made that perfectly clear." Trey shot him a blistering look. "And I still resent it. And I still don't understand why you prefer to live like *this*." He swept his arm across the construction site.

"It's an honest living," Ben said defensively.

"Of course it is. I just don't get why you chose it. You're the guy *Fortune* magazine dubbed the most successful, best-liked, self-made man in business. You went to Wharton. You developed a patent for fuel-cell technology and—"

"And lost my shirt." *And my self-confidence and self-esteem.*

"Still, you could have stayed in the business world. Any company in Rockford would hire you."

"Drop it, Trey! I won't rehash this."

His friend clearly fought his anger. "All right. But you'll listen to why I came."

"Fine then."

"Mackenzie's selling off your company. Probably in

pieces. The employees could all lose their jobs if the buyer moves the plant out of Rockford."

"He's selling already?" Ben raked a hand through his hair. "I know that's his MO, but it's only been two years." He mouthed a vicious expletive.

"My sentiments exactly. Now can we talk about this?"

Ben made his way to the bench. He tried hard not to think about the people on staff who'd survived the first round of Mackenzie's cuts, but now would suffer the sword of his greed. Dan, the comptroller, was still there. He'd heard Mackenzie had brought in his own vice president of human resources but had kept Janice, who supported her elderly mother and did the personnel work for Rockford Gas & Electric. His secretary and mother hen, Betty. And all those factory workers in the plant....

Trey sat when they reached the shade and removed his Ray-Bans. "I got a line on something."

Still standing, Ben braced his foot on the bench and draped his arm over his knee. "Trey, I appreciate all this, but I've told you time and again the battle was over the day Lammon Mackenzie outmaneuvered me. Why do you keep after this?"

The lawyer's lazy gaze sharpened. "I'm still involved for a number of reasons. One—" he held up a finger "—you and I were friends as well as colleagues. I'm mad as hell that you ditched me because things went south. Two—" another finger joined the first "—I was your attorney when the sleazebag went after Cassidy Industries and I couldn't stop it, so I owe you." He drew in a breath. "Number three, you won't use the money you got for the business and paid my fees. I put it in a bank account for you, but it just sits there. So that's still an issue."

"Damn right it is. I keep getting notices on it." He straightened. "I don't want the damn money."

"And last," Trey continued as if Ben hadn't spoken, "I think I might have something on the bastard."

"Unless it's something he did illegally when he took over, which you would have found out then, it doesn't matter."

"It's not exactly illegal, but it's unethical and we might be able to claim fraud and possible bribery."

"I—" Ben stopped. "It is? What?"

"Remember when the contracts from Rockford Gas & Electric got stalled?"

"How could I forget?" Ben began to pace. "If we'd gotten those contracts, we wouldn't have had to take Mackenzie on as an investor."

Cassidy Industries made instrumentation for utility companies; the business had gotten in financial trouble because Ben's products had been eroded by software and digital advancements. He'd extended his bank credit and mortgaged his personal assets to keep the company afloat. Finally he'd needed an investor and had made the poor choice of Mackenzie Enterprises.

Negotiations had gone well, but after the honeymoon was over, Mackenzie had started making stipulations on his several-million-dollar loan. Their business relationship had become heated, unfriendly, then downright hostile. In the end, Ben had been forced to agree to the two things that caused him to lose the company: that Cassidy Industries receive the Rockford Gas & Electric contracts, which were in the process of being approved by the utility company's officers, and that the patent on fuel-cell technology, which Ben had developed to take the business to a new level, had to come through within six months. He still remembered that heart-stopping day he'd discovered the contracts had been delayed indefinitely. At that time, the patent had been pending.

Trey's eyes narrowed. "My private investigator thinks maybe Mackenzie paid off the contracts guy at the utility company. He seems to have had an unexpected windfall right as Mackenzie began his pursuit of your business. If I can find a connection between this guy and expenditures Mackenzie made at the time, we'll have something. But it's tricky and may take a while. We're also going to check to see if he did anything about the patent that didn't come through until after you sold out." That patent, worth gold now, belonged to Cassidy Industries, not Ben.

"Trey, I don't want you spending money on a private investigator for me."

Trey shook his head. "It's not just for you. I want to know what I did wrong."

"The only thing we did wrong was to fight fair."

"Maybe not. In any case, I owe you."

"Don't start on that again."

"I'll start on that all I want. You hired me fresh out of law school. I became a moving force in the legal world of Rockford because of you."

"At least my debacle didn't hurt you too much."

"It didn't hurt me at all. Do you know how much I earn?" He swore. "Let me spend some of it trying to make sense of what happened."

"You're wasting your money."

"No, I'm not." Trey grabbed his arm. "Just promise me you'll think about this. I won't go any further until I hear from you. But at least return my calls. I hate leaving my girl in bed on Saturday morning to hunt you down."

That got a chuckle out of Ben. Though he couldn't remember the last time he'd had a girl in his bed on a weekend, he did recall it had felt damn good. "I promise I'll think about it. Now get out of here."

Trey nodded and headed the other way.

"Thompson?" Ben called out.

The lawyer looked over his shoulder, his brows raised.

"Thanks. I wish you wouldn't do it, but I appreciate your…caring enough."

Trey smiled. "I'll be in touch."

As Ben trudged back to his job, he squelched the tiny bud of hope inside him. The fact that Trey always engendered this optimism was one of the reasons Ben didn't want to see him. Nothing was going to come out of this newest development. If Trey could have stopped the takeover, he would have done it before.

The war was finished between Ben and Mackenzie. Even if Mackenzie had played dirty, the result was that Ben had lost everything. There was no changing it now.

"WHAT'S THIS ALL ABOUT, Dad?"

Emily's father glanced up from his computer screen. He was a big man, with powerful shoulders. Despite his thick shock of gray hair, he kept himself fit for someone nearing sixty. His perpetual grimace softened somewhat when he saw her. "Good morning to you, too."

She smiled. "Good morning." She held up the FedEx package. "I received this request from Jacob Brill by messenger as soon as I got in. He wants information on the employees. Why?"

"I'm selling off Rockford Instruments."

"What?"

"I'm selling. The stock's up, the climate's good. Gotta strike while the iron's hot, girl."

"Did you, at all, think to tell your vice president of human resources about this decision?"

Lazily he leaned back in his chair. She recognized the casual pose as one of his many tactics to disarm someone who confronted him. "I decided last Monday. I tried to call you that night, but you were out. I flew to Vegas on Tuesday and just got back."

"I have dance class until ten on Mondays."

His smile transformed his rough features, especially when she was the cause of it. "I remember when you started dancing. I thought you might be a ballerina."

Grinning, she shook her head. "I'm not good enough for that."

"Where were you before class?"

"I had dinner with friends." Not exactly a lie. Her father would be furious if he knew she worked at Cassidy Place. Not only had he withdrawn all financial support of the soup kitchen when he'd taken over Cassidy Industries, canceling comp time for workers, too, but he had some grudge against the place that Emily didn't understand. And a contempt for the previous owner that didn't make sense.

Her father shrugged. "In any case, it's time to unload this company."

Emily tried to quell her pique and sank into one of the plush leather seats in front of his desk. "I'm not going to let you do this again." Twice, he'd sold off companies without her knowledge, and had slashed jobs left and right. The last time, she'd threatened to leave Mackenzie Enterprises.

"All right. What do you want?"

"To save the jobs of the workers here." Those who hadn't gotten caught in the layoffs had stayed after Mackenzie Enterprises had taken over because they needed to make a living. But their loyalty had not transferred with them. It was obvious how much they hated the sterile environment her father had created, and how much they disliked him personally. Whereas Cassidy Industries had had a real family atmosphere and the employees had loved Benedict Cassidy. She wondered whatever had happened to him.

"It'll take a good six months to put the word out, find a buyer, or buyers, complete the due diligence. The workers will get something else."

"Buyers?"

"Yes. There might be more money in selling off the inventory, getting rid of this albatross of a building and offering that precious patent to the highest bidder."

The patent for a product that Benedict Cassidy was brilliant enough to develop. "Oh, Dad, you're going to dissolve Cassidy Industries?"

His face flushed. "It's Rockford Instruments now."

"But—"

"Here it comes." Shaking his head, he sighed.

"At least try to keep the company intact." She thought for a minute. "And look for a local buyer so the company isn't moved out of Rockford. That way, the workers would be able to keep their jobs."

"I don't care about all that."

No, of course not. He never did. But she did. "Wait a few months to see if you get a buyer for the whole company. If you can't, then sell it off."

"You always do this."

"Yes, I do. It's the only reason I'm working for you, Dad."

And not doing what I love. After she'd graduated from college, and she'd told her father about her dream to start a dance studio, he'd dismissed it as demeaning. He said if she wasn't going to dance professionally, she shouldn't make teaching her life's work. Since she'd been insecure and looked up to him like a god, she hadn't pursued it. Later, after she'd married Paul and he'd balked at her opening a studio too, she'd given up. When she'd begun to work for her father and had realized she could keep him from cutting too many jobs in his takeovers, even *she'd* dismissed the dream and had convinced herself she was doing good work.

His expression softened. "That's the only reason you work for me?"

She shook her head. Despite his controlling streak, she was his Achilles' heel. His only weak spot. He'd raised her single-handedly and loved her to pieces. Standing, she circled the desk and kissed his cheek. "No, of course not. I love you. I like being around you.

I just wish you cared more about the people whose lives you disrupt."

He grasped her hand, held on. "All right. You have a few months."

"Thanks." She started away.

"Emmy?" Her childhood name. "I'm going to Boston tomorrow. Have dinner with me tonight?"

"Oh, sorry, Dad. I told you I have dance on Mondays. How about when you get back?"

"You got a secret beau you're hiding from me?"

She thought of the soup kitchen and Ben. "No, of course not. I'm meeting Jordan before class for a light dinner and some girl talk."

His gaze hardened. "I don't like that woman."

"Well, she doesn't like you much, either. So you're even." Jordan Turk, her best friend, blamed her father for manipulating her out of starting her dance studio and for encouraging her marriage to Paul. "When will you be back?"

"Thursday."

"We'll do it then."

Emily hurried away, her mind whirling with a thousand thoughts, mostly about how to protect Cassidy Industries employees. When she reached her office, the phone was ringing. "Hello," she said, snatching it up.

"Hey, girl." Jordan was on the other end. "How are you?"

"Speak of the devil. My father and I were just talking about you."

"You've got that right. He's the devil incarnate."

"Be nice."

"Why? He's done vicious things to you. And all in the name of love."

"Jordan."

"I was calling to say I'd be late for dinner, but I'll tell you my good news now, since it's relevant to good old dad. I applied for the loan for my dance studio and found a place for it. The space is available in six months. I hope to open after New Year's."

"Oh, Jordan, I'm so happy for you."

"You remember *your* dream of owning a dance studio, don't you? The one your father and that ass Paul convinced you to give up."

Emily's heartbeat sped up. "I remember. It's good you're going ahead with it, though."

"I could still take on a partner." She paused. "You said you'd think about that."

"Oh, Jordan, I can't commit right now." She explained the immediate situation of her father selling Rockford Instruments.

"He's never going to change. Are you going to spend your whole life cleaning up after him?"

God, she didn't want to do that. "No. But I can help these people."

"It's bad enough he talked you into marrying Paul."

Emily regretted telling Jordan that she'd almost backed out of the wedding. That her father had convinced her to go ahead with it.

"Please, let's not revisit all this."

"Don't you still want a studio, honey?"

"Every day. And I'd love to be your partner in this." Spending her days teaching dance. Working with kids instead of disgruntled employees.

"Well, you won't get your studio unless you stand up to him." Her friend's exasperation sifted through the phone lines like an electrical current. It touched raw nerves. When Emily didn't respond, Jordan said, "Never mind. I'll see you at seven."

After she hung up, Emily sank wearily into her chair. Damn, she felt like a hamster on a wheel. She'd just get to a point where she thought she could leave the company, and her father's actions sucked her back in. Not only that, but the mention of a dance studio made her think about having children. Or more precisely, *not* having them, which was even more depressing than working for her dad. Her hand went to her stomach. She'd give anything to have a child of her own.

It's your fault, you know. Her ex-husband's handsome features had been contorted with frustrated rage as he'd hurled the accusation.

The doctor said both of our tests were inconclusive. You have endometriosis.

I've had surgeries to correct that. Look, Paul, I'm

*not laying blame, but your sperm motility test wasn't
so hot either.*

My sperm is just fine.

Sighing, she turned to her computer. Though she'd
divorced Paul and still hoped to have the dance studio,
she was probably never going to have a baby, given her
medical problems. Besides, she was thirty-four with no
man on the horizon.

But as she called up her e-mail, she wasn't able to
put the thought out of her mind. Could she get pregnant with the right man? And who might that be?

A fleeting image came to mind—of gray eyes the
color of steel, a killer smile and a body to die for. Jeez,
she really needed to get a social life.

WHERE THE HELL WAS SHE? For as long as Ben had been
frequenting Cassidy Place as a guest, Emily had been
a volunteer. She'd only missed three Mondays—and
he'd worried each time if she was sick or had quit or…
had a date.

Disgusted by his reaction to her, he tried to focus on
the crossword. A five-letter word for *beautiful.* Hmm,
Emily? Hell, this wasn't good. A six-letter word for *red.*
Russet, almost the color of her hair. He slapped the
paper down.

"Something unpleasant in there?"

He glanced up to see Alice with a coffeepot in her
hand. "No, my mind's just wandering."

"Want more coffee?"

"Sure." What would it hurt? "I was, um, wondering where Emily is. She usually works on Mondays, doesn't she?"

A knowing gleam lit the older woman's soft brown eyes. "She's here—at the dishwasher because we're short volunteers. Tom, the guy who usually mans it, is sick."

"Why didn't you say something? I would have pitched in."

"I suggested that to Emily. She said you work too hard all day and shouldn't be doing manual labor at night."

He stood. "I don't work that hard. I'm going back, if that's all right."

With Alice's consent, Ben carried his dirty dishes into the kitchen. Guests were required to bring back their own plates. He remembered setting up that edict for Cassidy Place. But some people still often left their mess for the volunteers. Emily didn't usually complain about it, but on occasion he'd seen her confront a customer for his thoughtlessness. The sight of her dragging a big guy back and making him clean up after himself was amusing.

The kitchen was hotter than usual tonight, probably because the April evening was still warm. Volunteers bustled in and out, preparing food or picking up plates. Emily scraped dishes while another worker loaded them into the dishwasher. Ben recognized the man as Jimmy, the guy who ran security on the floor.

Emily looked up as Ben crossed to them and aimed a megawatt smile his way. "Hi, Ben. Finished with your meal?"

He bused his plate, then rolled up his sleeves. "Yes. And I'm going to take over for you. You like being out on the floor better than working inside."

Her smile brightened. "How do you know that?"

"You told me once. Come on, I'll do KP with Jimmy."

She and the other man exchanged a look.

"What?"

"Jimmy has a date. He wasn't supposed to be here this late tonight." She glanced to her helper. "If Ben's going to work, you can leave."

The young, handsome black man shrugged. "You sure?"

"Go." She handed an apron to Ben. "Want to clear or stack?"

"Stack." That way he might not have to see her face, flushed by the heat, or her hands, long and slender. He wondered if she'd blush like that after sex. What her hands would feel like stroking his back. Over the past year, he'd had dreams….

"Ben, are you all right?"

"I'm fine," he said, feeling his body tighten at her nearness. Damn, this *wasn't* good.

Whipping on the white apron—she wore a matching one over her cropped pants and shirt—he began his task. They fell into easy conversation as they always did when he let himself relax with her. "No dance tonight?"

"I left work early for once and went to the four o'clock class. I changed there."

"What kind of dance do you take?"

"Ballet, tap and jazz, all on different days. Though tap gives me some trouble. It always did."

"Always?"

"Uh-huh, I've been taking lessons on and off all my life."

"Nice hobby." He'd like to see her dance.

"How about you? Got any hobbies?"

He used to. He played racquetball with Trey, went running with his dog, liked a game of pool. "No, not really."

She scraped dishes. "Do you live alone, Ben?"

"Um, yeah." He took a plate from her hand. "You?"

"It's just me and my dog."

"You have a dog?" Harriet's shaggy face came out of nowhere. He'd loved that animal so much.

"A cocker spaniel." Emily's expression turned tender. "She's a beauty. She likes to be coddled, so I call her My Lady. Lady for short." She smiled. "*Lady and the Tramp* has always been my favorite story."

"Ah, I should have known you'd like happily-ever-afters."

She started to say something but a rush of people entered the kitchen, clattering dishes in front of her. Emily conversed with the guests who handed over their plates, then continued the conversation with Ben when things slowed down. "Why did you react when I told you about my dog?"

"I had one once." She'd been a stray mutt hanging out at the soup kitchen. Eventually, Ben had taken her home.

"What happened to it?"

"I gave her away when I wasn't able to keep her."

"I'm sorry. That must have left a hole in your life."

He didn't respond. He didn't want to talk about his dog or think about anything else he'd lost. Luckily, things got busy again. In no time, the evening was over. Dishwashers were usually the last to finish, so the place emptied out quickly, leaving him and Emily alone in the kitchen. When the last plate was clean, he whipped off his apron. "I'll go see if Alice needs help out there."

Just then the older woman bustled in. "No, we're done. One of the stragglers stacked the chairs. But there's a mess on the floor from a family with kids that the janitors aren't gonna like."

"I'll get a mop and take care of it."

"That would be great," Alice said.

Emily watched Ben's back as he disappeared through the doorway.

"Have fun tonight?" Alice asked.

Chagrined, she felt herself blush. "I like working with him."

"I like *him*." Alice sat on a stool. "I wonder what his story is."

"Me, too." Emily crossed to the dessert cooler and removed chocolate cake for the two of them. "He seems so smart, so well spoken. He talks like an educated man. I can't believe he needs to come here."

"I was thinking the same thing. His clothes are definitely Salvation Army, though."

"I wonder if he was always poor."

"Maybe not. A lot of people who use Cassidy Place were once better off. Ben has a job, but we don't know how much it pays. Sometimes people just come for the company. Like that Helena who always flirts with Ben."

Helena, the tall, slender woman with mounds of streaked hair. No one had any idea where she came from. She did indeed make cow eyes at Ben.

They ate their treat and discussed some of the other guests until Ben came back to the kitchen. He crossed to a janitor's closet, rinsed out the mop and put the things away. "That's done. I'll be heading out."

Emily watched him. He'd taken off his long-sleeved denim shirt and wore only a black T-shirt. He had such nice shoulders. Great pecs. Flat abs. Paul used to spend hours at the gym and never looked as good.

Alice kicked her under the table. Good thing, or she'd probably start drooling. "Time to close up."

Ben scanned the area. "Nobody's here to walk you out?"

Like most soup kitchens and shelters, Cassidy Place was in a location that could be dangerous after dark.

"No, Jimmy usually does. If not, Tom." Alice grabbed her purse. "No matter. We'll be fine."

"I'll see you to your cars."

Alice smile approvingly. They shut off lights and secured the doors, then went out the back and locked up. Alice's car was closer—thank you, Lord. The older woman drove off as they headed toward Emily's Taurus.

The spring moonlit night was unseasonably warm, but the difference in temperature from the hot kitchen was enough to make Emily shiver.

"Cold?" Ben asked as he shrugged into his denim shirt.

"A bit. I have a sweater in the car." When they reached it, she unlocked the door and grabbed her wrap off the front seat. He watched her as she got stuck putting it on, a button caught in her hair, some of which had come out of the braid. "Ouch," she said, tugging to loosen it.

"Here. I'll get it."

She turned her back to him and he moved in close. His body heat felt wonderful.

"It's twisted up in here. I have to pull out the tie." She felt a bit of pressure, then nothing. "There, I've got it."

Emily stilled. Time seemed to freeze. Then she felt her braid come undone completely. When Ben's hands sifted through her hair, she felt the touch in the pit of her stomach, and lower.

"Ben?" she whispered, her voice throaty.

"Your hair's grown since I last saw it down. The color's so many different shades of red, like a sunset in St. Croix. It's beautiful."

"Th-thank you."

He lifted her sweater so she could slide it on. Once she did, he squeezed her shoulders. *That* touch made her weak in the knees. She leaned back.

Abruptly, he dropped his hands and stepped away. "Best you get in the car, Emily."

She turned to him. His face was awash with moonlight. His features weren't softened by it, though. If anything they were harsher than usual. Without censoring her actions, she squeezed his arm. "You're a nice man, Ben."

He retreated another step out of her reach. "Get in the car," he said tightly.

She angled her head, confused by his reaction, by the force of his words. "All right." The parking lot was deserted. Traffic whizzed by on the street and a firetruck's horn sounded far away. "How will you get home?"

"I don't live too far from here."

"Let me give you a ride."

"Hell, no." His dark eyebrows furrowed. "You shouldn't be offering rides to guests at a soup kitchen."

"You're not just a guest, Ben. We've both known that for a long time."

His shoulders tensed and his hands fisted at his sides. "That's all I am. Now get in the car."

She waited.

"There's danger here, Emily. Don't think anything different."

She gave him a weak smile. "Not from you." Opening the door, she slid in. "Thanks for helping out with the dishes," she said as she fastened her seat belt. "Good night."

"Good night." He shut the door.

Emily started the car and drove off. "I lied, Ben," she confessed into the dimness of the car as she turned onto St. Paul Street and caught sight of him standing where she'd left him, watching after her. "You are dangerous." Tonight when he'd touched her confirmed something she'd suspected for a long time: his attraction to her.

Which, of course, was not a good thing. She knew in her heart Ben would never let anything come of their feelings for each other. Despite his obvious poverty, he was a proud man. Since they were from two different worlds, he'd never let her into his life. Even if she wanted to be a part of it.

You do, girl.

Of course she did. But there were many things she wanted and couldn't have. A baby. A dance studio.

Freedom from self-imposed vigilance of her father. Ben whatever-his-last-name-was was simply another thing to add to that list.

CHAPTER THREE

THE COCKER SPANIEL WAS BEAUTIFUL, with its big soulful eyes, delicate features and golden red fur. When Ben entered Cassidy Place and saw her in the partially enclosed alcove, curled up on a bed of blankets, he couldn't resist kneeling in front of her. "Hey, Lady, what are you doing here?"

The dog stood, barking first before nuzzling into his neck. He held her there a minute, mesmerized by the throb of her body—and the little bodies obviously inside her. "You make me miss my girl, Lady."

"Want a puppy?" He didn't have to turn to see who was behind him. That soft voice and that body had haunted his dreams for two weeks since the night in the parking lot when he'd touched her.

He stood while the dog continued to sniff him. "No can do. But thanks." Emily was dressed for dance class again. This time, the tights and leotard were dark wine under the black skirt. "How are you, Emily?"

"I'm fine. We missed you last week."

"I, um, had something else to do." Which was to

avoid her. He wouldn't have come to the soup kitchen tonight if Trey hadn't called earlier. After he'd hung up, Ben's isolation had become too big for him to handle. "So this is Lady."

"Uh-huh." Emily hugged the dog. "How're you feeling, girl?"

"When's she due?"

"Not for ten days." She looked up at Ben, the scoop of her form-fitting spandex top revealing the top of her breasts. "I leave her alone all day and now, at night, she cries when I go out. Hormones," she said, a twinkle in her beautiful eyes, which were more brown than green tonight. "So I brought her with me."

Hormones were something Ben knew a lot about. Especially these past few weeks. His body had been in hibernation for two years and he was pissed that Emily had woken it up.

"She looks close to ready." He'd delivered his own dog's pups once, so he could read the signs.

"I know. And she was restless tonight." She rose. "Go back and lie down, girl."

The dog obeyed.

Emily folded her arms across her waist. "Have you been well?"

"As well as can be expected."

She cocked her head. "What does that mean?"

He ran a hand through his shaggy dark hair, which

needed a trim. "Nothing." He glanced over her shoulder. "It's slow tonight."

"Yes. Sit at my table. I'll bring your food. It's fried chicken. Your favorite."

Damn, he wished she wouldn't do that—keep track of him, try to please him. It made resisting her all the harder. He took a seat at the table she indicated. Max, who was a recovering alcoholic and on unemployment, nodded. "How's it goin', Ben?"

"Just fine. You?"

"Twenty weeks and countin'." The man sipped his coffee.

Ben gave him the thumbs-up.

Across from Max was Lorena. Every week she sat in the same chair and spoke to no one but Emily. She wore hats no matter what the weather and covered herself, albeit in tattered clothes, from head to foot. She also stowed most of her food in plastic bags, odd containers and napkins. He nodded to her, but she looked away. The only others at the table were a family of five he'd seen here occasionally, but didn't know personally. The man—the father?—had gone to get some giveaways, and the woman was frantically trying to seat her three children. "Here, let me help." Ben hefted one of the toddlers, who appeared to be about two. "What's his name?"

"Mohammed," the woman told him in accented English. Ben guessed they were one of the many refugee families who frequented Cassidy Place. "And this is Anwar and Tidi." The youngest curled into her chest, secured by a long scarf. The woman herself was dressed in matching colorful robes.

Ben seated the boy, who began to bang on the tray.

"Thank you." The woman's smile was weary.

The father returned carrying a plastic bag. Periodically, when the soup kitchen had extra, vegetables and bread were set out for the guests on a long table. When Ben had been in charge, if there had been no donations for a week, he'd supplied them out of his own pocket.

"I was able to obtain bread and carrots and lettuce," the man said.

His wife sighed. Most people had no idea what it was like to live hand to mouth, Ben thought. Many of the impoverished would work but couldn't find jobs. Ben hadn't known any of this, not really, until he'd experienced his own downslide. His heart went out to them.

The meal was served and Ben tried hard not to watch Emily, but his gaze kept tracking her as she glided over the floor like the dancer that she was. He wondered what she did for a living—not dance, he knew that. Did she like her job? Who were her friends? Did she have a guy in her life?

When she brought his meal, her arm brushed against him and he felt it all the way to his toes. "Thanks," he muttered hoarsely.

She placed plates in front of the family and asked what to do with Mohammed's dinner. "Set it here," the mother said. "I'll feed him first."

"No need." Emily pulled up a chair. "I've got a few minutes."

The boy looked up at her. He babbled something in his native language. "Hungry, aren't you, little guy?"

Out of the corner of his eye, Ben could see her cut the boy's food. She fed him some chicken and let him spoon up his own mashed potatoes. The few minutes she spent with the child gave the mother an opportunity to eat. When the second boy, Anwar, started to whine, Ben leaned over. "What do you need, buddy?"

He pointed to his milk.

The mother tried to adjust the baby in the front makeshift knapsack. "Wait for a minute, Ani."

"I'll get it." Ben helped the four-year-old sip. Over the child's head, he caught Emily's gaze. The approval there warmed him. He smiled, genuinely, without holding back. Her eyes darkened and she focused on his mouth.

He glanced away, affected by that look. So when he finished his dessert, he decided to head out. He preferred to wait until the evening was over to help close up, but he needed to get away from Emily. Unfortunately, she caught his arm when he was halfway to the door.

"Leaving already?"

."Yes."

"I wish you'd stay. Talk a while."

"I told you two weeks ago that kind of thing wasn't a good idea."

Her cute little chin tilted. "Says you."

"Yep. Says me. Night, ma'am."

On his way out, he heard some rustling in the alcove where the dog was resting. Lady was up, pacing. Ben frowned. "Hey, girl, you all right?" As he petted her head, he noticed she was shivering. Uh-oh. On the other side of the room, Ben saw Emily at the counter and motioned her over.

She hurried to him. "What's going on?"

He nodded down to the dog, who'd begun to pant. "I think you're about to become a grandmother."

"Oh, dear. It's too early. What should I do?"

"Hopefully, we won't have to do anything. But find some newspapers." He rolled up his sleeves. "It's okay, girl, I'm here. And I've done this before."

EMILY STRETCHED OUT on her couch in the great room of her house and watched Lady feed her five puppies in a nest set up for them by the fireplace. Exhausted, she yawned. She knew she should take a nap, but she didn't want to leave them just yet. What a night! It had taken five hours for the pups to make their debut. And there had been complications. Thankfully Ben was there. He'd had to tug one puppy out and clean two from their sacs.

She knew from what she'd read they could have died without his help.

Alice had stayed, too, and they'd loaded Lady and her pups into Emily's car at about 3:00 a.m.

Before she'd left, Emily had stood by her Taurus in the parking lot with Ben. For the first time since she'd known him, he looked truly happy.

"I'm glad I was here." He leaned against the side of the car, a genuine smile on his face. "It's a thrill, isn't it, to see new life into the world?"

"Yes." They shared that bond now. "I wish you'd take one of the puppies when they're weaned."

"I'd like nothing better. But my situation precludes that." There was that extensive vocabulary again.

Apparently riding high from adrenaline, he reached out and squeezed her shoulder. "Take good care of them."

Before she thought better about it, she stood on tiptoes and slid her arms around his neck. He stilled for a minute, then his arms encircled her waist and he drew her closer. He was all muscle and steely strength. His lips brushed her hair. "You'd better go."

She stepped back.

"Good night," he'd said and walked away into the darkness....

Sighing, Emily curled up on her side. The grandfather clock in the foyer chimed ten times, but still, she stayed where she was, fascinated by the pups burrow-

ing into their mother, snoozing, stretching. The doorbell intruded on the moment. Reluctantly she got off
the couch, crossed to the foyer, checked through the
window and opened the door. "Hi, Dad."

"Well, you don't look sick." *He* looked worried.

"I told Donna I wasn't when I called in. Just that I'd
been up all night."

"Why?"

"Come see for yourself." She tugged him through
the foyer, over the Italian marble tile, into her great
room. "Look."

He tracked her gaze. "Harrumph." But she saw his
smile. "I can't believe you kept that bitch after she got
pregnant."

"I love that bitch, Dad. Come look at the babies."

He hesitated and she wondered what was in her father's makeup that always made him resist his soft side.
She knew he'd grown up poor and had been knocked
around by the uncle who'd raised him, but still, a lot of
people overcame those odds. Finally, he knelt in front
of the box. "Hey, girl." He didn't touch the mom or
pups, though. He just watched them and shook his
head. "You used to love that storybook when you were
little. *Lady and the Tramp.*"

"I remember." She waited. "Mother used to read it
to me."

His body tensed but he stayed where he was, studying the dogs. "We had a cocker spaniel."

"I don't remember that."

"It was before you were born." He stood and jammed his hands in the trousers of his suit. "It took us a while to have you so we got a dog in the interim."

"Did she like dogs?"

Her dad got a faraway look in his eyes. "Yes." When he answered, his voice was gruff.

He never talked about her mother. All pictures of the woman who'd given birth to her had been destroyed when she'd left. Emily had no idea why she'd abandoned them; her father would only say she didn't want to be his wife and her mother anymore. A few times, Emily had been tempted to search for her, but she didn't have the courage. What good would it do to look for a woman who'd made it clear she didn't want her young daughter, anyway?

"Do you ever think about her?"

His face flushed. "No."

"I wonder where she is."

"Last I heard she went to New York." He crossed to the bank of windows and stood in the spring sunshine, staring out at the front lawn. "Before we married, she worked in a bookstore." He shook his head. "She loved to read to you."

"Not enough to stick around, apparently."

It seemed as if her dad was about to say something, then he shook himself and checked his watch. "I have to go. I just wanted to make sure you're all right."

"You don't have to escape. Stay for lunch."

"No, I can't. I have a meeting." He kissed her cheek and strode to the door, calling over his shoulder, "I'll see you tomorrow."

Emily sighed as she watched her father leave. She suspected he didn't have a meeting, but that talking about his ex-wife made him uncomfortable. When she thought about her mother, Emily just got sad. She had to fight hard not to dwell on the fact that the woman who'd given her life didn't love her enough to stick around and raise her. She'd never be that way with her kids, if she ever had any.

Slowly Emily sank onto the Aubusson carpet. "You're lucky to have those pups, Lady. I envy you."

Fatigue settled on her like a heavy blanket. How pathetic it was to be jealous of a dog.

BEN SWORE SILENTLY at himself as he rode the bus from the inner city to Corn Hill, where he used to live and where Trey still did. After finishing a day's work that just about broke his thirty-eight-year-old back, coming off a night of no sleep, he couldn't resist the urge to make this trip. He didn't even know if Trey would be home, but after last night, he needed company.

As Ben got off at his stop and covered the few blocks to Trey's upscale condo, he thought about delivering the puppies. He hadn't felt that *needed* in two years.

And then what had happened in the parking lot with

Emily: he hadn't backed away from the hug and couldn't help brushing his lips across her corn-silk soft hair. God, she'd felt good against him. Curvier than she looked. Just the right complement to the hard planes of his body.

A body that had given him grief for hours because of that simple indulgence. Damn it.

He reached the brick building on Hoffman Street where Trey lived and caught sight of the Porsche in the condo's parking lot.

You got a Porsche? What's wrong with you?

Just because you prefer those little Jags....

Their taste in cars had been as dramatically different as their taste in women.

Man, give me a redhead any day, his friend always said.

Not me. I'm a brunette connoisseur.

And he had been. Mallory had worn her black hair short, styled in a careless bob. She'd been rail thin, too, and most of the time she'd looked like she'd just walked out of *Vogue*. Hell, when had he begun to prefer strawberry-blondes with generous curves and freckles?

He slipped into the building along with another couple and made his way to Trey's unit. Punching the doorbell, he forced Emily out of his mind.

Trey answered before he could ring again. "I don't believe it. You haven't been here in two years."

Ben jammed his hands into the pockets of his best jeans. "Hello to you, too."

"Hey, Ben."

"So, are you going to invite me in or not?"

Trey moved aside.

Ben stepped into the living room with its floor-to-ceiling windows and designer furniture. He remembered his own condo and how he'd worked with a decorator—at Mallory's urging—to furnish it. "I forgot how nice this place was."

"Like yours was, buddy." When Ben didn't comment, Trey said, "Sit. Can I get you a beer—" He cut himself off. "Sorry."

"It's okay." Ben hadn't touched a drop of alcohol in over eleven months. "I'll take a soda."

Trey glanced to his own drink on the table in front of a large-screen TV.

"Don't even think about it."

"All right."

Trey got Ben his soda and took a chair facing him. "It's a crime you've never visited me here just because you hit on hard times."

Ben took a swig of the soda. "It was a little more than hard times."

"It didn't have to be. Your life as you knew it didn't have to be over."

"Mallory didn't agree with you."

"What did you expect from a snob like her?"

"She had her good points." And she had. Loyalty just wasn't one of them. Of course, he hadn't given her much choice when he'd drunk himself into the gutter and stayed there for months.

Trey sipped his scotch. "So what brings you here?"

"I delivered pups last night. Five of them." He shook his head. "It reminded me of Harriet. I got thinking about my old life, I guess."

"No kidding? Where was this?"

"At Cassidy Place."

"You still work there?"

"Not exactly. Long story." He glanced around the apartment. "So, how's everything going?"

"Great." Trey's expression intensified. "Since you seem more open tonight, I'm going to ask again if I can help get you out of this funk and back to your real world."

"My real world has no appeal to me anymore." Except for the fact that, if he wasn't a bum, he might be able to go after Emily.

"Come on, Ben. I can help you get a job. A good job. You can start over in the corporate world."

He felt himself weakening. "Nobody's going to hire me after my two-year disappearance."

"You don't know that."

Ben didn't say anything.

Trey studied him. "It's a woman, isn't it?"

He glared at his friend. "What are you talking about?"

"Why you're here."

"I came here to see you." He scanned the living room. "Like I said, I miss sitting around and shooting the breeze with you."

"I think you miss your old life. And I think maybe some female's got you thinking that way."

Ben frowned at the validity of what Trey said.

"I recognize the signs, buddy. I've known you for a long time."

"There's no woman, Trey." He picked threads on a pillow. "But I *have* been thinking about what you said about investigating Mackenzie." Ben wondered if, down deep, that's why he'd come here tonight.

"I haven't done anything more on it, like you said. But I could put out some additional feelers, if you're interested?"

"I guess I am. What harm could there be for you to at least look into it?"

"None that I can see."

He looked at this friend. "And it might help out the employees."

"Just the employees?"

He shook his head. "I'd rather live like I do, than go back to where I went the year after Mackenzie screwed me."

"Is playing it safe worth the price?"

It had been. Until Emily. But he wouldn't tell Trey that, at least not yet. "Yeah, it is."

Trey just waited.

Finally, Ben said, "So, okay, do it. Poke around some. Don't go all out or anything. But see if you can get some dirt on Mackenzie."

CHAPTER FOUR

EMILY PULLED INTO CASSIDY Place's parking lot at five o'clock. The air was still warm and filled with the smell of budding flowers. Since it was Wednesday, she wouldn't see Ben, but she wanted to get her mind off her own issues.

The first thing Emily saw when she entered the building was Alice standing by the stove with Jimmy and the three volunteers who'd come in to cook at four o'clock. The older woman's expression was a mixture of anger and disgust.

"Oh, my God, what happened?" Emily asked, looking past them.

The tables and floor were covered with milk and flour, creating a gooey mass. Ripped apart bread bags, fresh vegetables and frozen meat had been tossed into the mess.

Alice shook her head. "Vandals. They ransacked the kitchen, then left their signature on the walls of the dining hall."

"I don't understand. Why would someone do this?"

Two police officers entered just as she asked the question.

Alice nodded to them. "Maybe they can answer that."

The older cop, stout and stern-looking, crossed to Alice. "This seems like a case of pure vandalism, Mrs. Smith. You're sure nothing's been taken?"

"Not even the food that wasn't destroyed."

"Well, there's no use in dustin' for prints. This place would be a hotbed of suspicious ones. We took pictures and we'll ask around the neighborhood if anybody saw anything, but if I were you, I wouldn't count on findin' out who did this." He glanced at the other volunteers and at Emily. "Meanwhile, you all should be careful about coming and going here. I'll alert patrol cars, but don't walk out alone at night or hang around inside without a lot of people to keep you company." He made some notes on his pad. "And get those locks reinforced. Heavy dead bolts at the top and bottom oughtta do it."

"I've already called the chair of the board," Alice said. "He's going to have a locksmith here tomorrow."

After the police left, Emily faced Alice. "I'm so sorry."

"Damn it." The older woman kicked a nearby stool, then pulled herself together. "Well, no use cryin' over spilled milk—" she rolled her eyes "—pardon the pun. We have to clean up. And somebody has to tell them outside there won't be a meal tonight."

"I will." They all turned to see Ben standing in the doorway. "I heard what the police said. I'm sorry."

Alice gave Ben a grateful smile. "Thanks. I'd appreciate it if you'd tell the guests."

As Ben left, Emily wondered why he was here on a Wednesday, so early in the evening. Shrugging, she rolled up her sleeves. "What can I do?"

Alice surveyed the kitchen. "Might as well start in here. Then we can see about the damage in the dining room."

They began by tossing the trashed food into barrels, and went on to clean up appliances and countertops. They were about half finished when they heard banging in the dining room. "Oh, dear," one of the volunteers said. "Do you think the vandals are back?"

Everybody in the kitchen stood still. Finally, Jimmy crept to the swinging doors, cracked one and peeked through. Smiling, he pushed the door all the way open. "Way to go Ben," he called out.

There were about a dozen men straightening tables and righting chairs. Emily scanned the dining hall where graffiti had been scrawled on walls in ugly black lettering: epithets, four-letter words, boasts including *I Am the King!*

In an hour, both rooms were set to order. Ben entered the kitchen just as they finished mopping the floor. "Alice, got a sec?"

"Sure, Ben, for you."

When she returned a few minutes later, she was grinning like a proud grandma. "He's got a crew organized to stay tomorrow night and paint after we serve dinner."

"How sweet," Emily said. "I'm going to go thank them all." But when she hurried into the dining room, Ben was gone.

The next night, Emily shared a quick meal with her father, and though it wasn't one of her regular shifts to volunteer, she changed into old jeans spattered with paint, a T-shirt she'd bought on a trip to Italy, which read *Ciao, Bella*, and ancient tennis shoes. She arrived at Cassidy Place just after the painting had begun.

Standing in the doorway, she watched Ben direct the cleanup as if he'd been leading men all his life, as if he had experience being in charge. As she reached him, she noticed he wore low-riding jeans, a black T-shirt and battered sneakers, but he might as well have been dressed in a thousand-dollar suit for his commanding presence. "Hi. What can I do?"

He obviously hadn't seen her come in. His smile was brilliant—for a moment—then the Mr. Leave-Me-Alone mask fell into place. "You don't volunteer on Thursdays."

"Not normally. But I knew you were painting so I came to help."

He eyed her outfit. "I see you've had some experience."

"Yep. Put me to work."

"Alice and Pat can use help over in the entryway." He handed her a paintbrush. "Go get 'em, tiger."

His whimsy warmed her as much as his grin—as much as his uncensored reaction to the puppies. Given a different situation, this man would enjoy life. He probably had at one time. More than ever, she wished she knew his background.

There were nearly two dozen workers, so it only took a few hours to give the dining hall a couple of coats of paint. By the time they finished, Emily's shoulders ached. But her heart was full. Humming softly, she cleaned her brush. When she finished, she looked for Alice, who was talking to Ben near the kitchen.

"The place needed a new coat of paint anyway. Looks good, don't you think, Alice?" There was pride in Ben's voice.

"Yep. Don't guess it had been painted since Cassidy Industries did it years ago."

"No, it hadn't been."

Alice focused her shrewd gaze on him. "How do you know that?"

Flushed, Ben caught sight of Emily. "Well, looks like we're all cleaned up. I'll be going." He scanned the room. "Jimmy seeing you to your cars?"

Alice nodded. "Uh-huh."

When he started to walk away, Emily said, "Ben, wait. Let us give you a lift home."

"No thanks," he called over his shoulder. "See you Monday."

She frowned after him. "He shouldn't have to walk home after doing this for us."

Squeezing her shoulder, Alice said, "Watch it girl, you're playing with fire."

Alice's words echoed in Emily's head as she climbed into her car, waved Jimmy off and drove out of the parking lot. Damn Ben. He could at least accept a ride as payment for his help. Annoyed by his foolish pride, she cruised the few blocks near the soup kitchen. Hell, she was thirty-four years old and she could drive downtown if she wanted.

Ten minutes later she was about to give up when she spotted him, stopped for a light at Andrews Street. Emily was touched by the loneliness of the figure, silhouetted in the streetlight. His head was down, his shoulders slumped and his hands were stuffed in his pockets. As she swerved to the curb beside him, he glanced toward her car and did a double take. For a moment, he stood still. Then he stalked to the Taurus. Given his now-rigid stance, she had a fleeting thought that maybe coming after him wasn't such a good idea.

BEN WAITED FOR THE LOCKS to click—at least she'd taken that precaution—then yanked open the door. He slid in, relocked the car from the passenger side and counted to ten. Then he switched off the engine and grabbed her shoulders. "Damn it, Emily. What the *hell* do you think you're doing?"

Wide-eyed, she trembled in his arms. "Looking for you."

"Down here? At this hour of the night?"

"If it's that dangerous, you shouldn't be walking about alone, either."

"I can take care of myself."

"So can I."

"Princess, you don't have a clue." He wanted to shake her and kiss her at the same time. The scent of her hung delicately in the car, and her slender form, under his hands, felt good. Damn, he wouldn't do this. He saw her wince when his grip tightened. Immediately he gentled his hold, but didn't let go.

"Why are you treating me this way?" she asked, her voice throaty. "I was just trying to do something nice for you. Like you did tonight for Cassidy Place with the cleanup and painting. Like you routinely do for everybody there."

"You're *always* trying to do something nice for me. What does a guy have to do to discourage you?"

She sucked in a breath and, in the moonlight, he could see moisture well in those huge eyes. "I—I didn't know I was..." A few renegade drops trickled down her cheeks. She sniffled. "Let me go. I get the point. I didn't realize..." Her words trailed off in sob.

"Aw, shit," he said and drew her to him.

She cuddled into him like she was meant to be there, which she wasn't. She grasped his shirt and buried her nose in his chest. His hand creeping to her hair, he pulled out the tie and tunneled through the heavy mass. Its flowery scent wafted up to him and he breathed her in.

"I'm sorry I made you cry. Please, Emily, stop."

"Okay," she mumbled. Then, after a moment, she added, "I'm embarrassed."

"Why?"

She shook her head, her face hidden in the folds of his shirt.

He set her away so he could look at her. The bright streetlights, combined with the glow from the sliver of moon overhead, gave him a glimpse of her blotchy skin and eyes, red-rimmed. "Why are you embarrassed?"

"Paul said I didn't know men. Didn't know how to read them, please them," she choked out. "I didn't mean to impose myself on you."

His body, taut as a wire, tightened impossibly more. "Paul's your ex, right?"

She straightened her shoulders and nodded. "Leave me some dignity, Ben. I won't bother you anymore."

He couldn't let the comment go. "Listen, lady, and listen good. Paul is an idiot. First off, to let a perfect woman like you go, and second, for filling your head with that nonsense about you and men."

He could tell she didn't believe him. "That's nice of you to say, but you're just being polite."

Polite? Holy hell, his body was about to combust from wanting her and she thought he was being polite. It was all too much. He lowered his mouth to hers. She started and he thought she might pull away.

Then she melted into him. Her body seemed to liquefy as she inched closer. Once Ben had her in his arms, rational thought fled. He was steeped in the feel and scent of her. Easing back into the seat, he tugged her onto his lap. She went willingly. His hand slid to her waist as his lips moved over hers. She responded in kind—opened her mouth and touched her tongue with his. He tasted her as deeply as he could. He caressed her breast; she was full and heavy in his hand. She moaned, and so did he. The kiss, the embrace, got hotter, deeper. A horn beeping and a screech of tires down the road shocked him back to conscious thought. Because he was afraid he might take her right there on Andrews Street in the front seat of her car, because he was afraid she might let him, he tore his mouth away.

"Sweetheart, we have to stop."

"No." She buried her face in the crook of his shoulder.

"Emily, please. You're killing me."

Slowly she drew back and looked at him, owl-eyed. "Really?"

He grinned and tucked her tousled hair behind her

ear. "Really. Do you have any idea how much I want you?"

She smiled Jezebel's smile and shifted on his lap. "Hmm. Some idea."

"We have to stop," he repeated.

"No." The word was forceful, reminding him she could be a tough cookie when needed. He'd witnessed it at the soup kitchen. "Come home with me, Ben. Make love to me there."

His jaw dropped open. He started to object, but months of loneliness silenced him. She was offering him a night's respite from everything that had happened in the past two years.

FOR THE ELEVEN MONTHS he'd been frequenting the soup kitchen, Ben had tried hard to keep from getting to this place. Emotionally and physically. Emily's bedroom was painted a pale peach and filled with finely crafted oak furniture. Impressionist prints decorated the walls and a thick peach-and-blue flowered rug covered most of the plank-wood floor. As Ben waited for Emily to come out of the bathroom, he sank onto her queen-size bed.

Problem was, it felt natural. It felt right to be here. Still, if he was a truly good man, he'd get up and leave before she came out of the bathroom. But he wasn't going to do that because he was no longer the man he used to be. Lammon Mackenzie had seen to that. Instead, Ben unbuttoned his shirt, slid it and his T-shirt off and removed his boots and socks. He'd just gotten the snap of his jeans undone when the bathroom door opened.

Moonlight streamed into the bedroom through slatted blinds, catching Emily in its silvery net. She'd switched on a dresser lamp, and her hair shimmered in the light. Moved by her ethereal beauty, he swallowed hard and stood. Only inches away, she waited. She'd put on a sea-green little slip of a thing with barely there straps. He leaned down and kissed a strap. Her skin was so silky it made his body snap from hungry to voracious. He fisted his hands to gain control.

She didn't help—running her fingers up his chest, licking his nipples. He manacled her wrists to stop her. Instead of devouring her, he planned to taste, to relish, to enjoy with epicurean delight, but his body was thrumming with need and he had to pace himself. When she raised her head, her eyes were wide and luminous.

"Do you have any idea how much I want this?" he whispered softly.

A blush crept up from the scoop of the silk to her neck. "I do, too."

"You are so lovely." His fingers slid from her shoulder to elbow, raising her gooseflesh.

"I want to be, for you."

He lowered his head, starved for this kind of contact, for *her*. Pushing aside the strap, tugging on the top of the gown, he exposed a generous swell of her breast. Then a nipple. He closed his mouth over it. She started before letting out a soft moan. He suckled, fed on her body, let it nourish his soul. Soon though, he became greedy. Less gently, he pulled off the other strap, gave a yank so that she stood there naked, bathed in soft light like a Degas painting.

He forced himself to go slowly, to savor the experience. To that end, he brushed his lips down her throat, over her chest. Kneeling, he tantalized the silken skin of her abdomen. He felt her shiver, tremble with desire, so he linked his hands with hers and continued his slow exploration of the most beautiful female body he'd ever seen.

HE WAS KILLING HER. Emily was so aroused, so sensitized, his ministrations almost hurt. Still, he went slowly, tracing her ribs with his tongue, letting his hands drift to her backside and caressing her there. He gently nipped her hip and soothed it with his tongue. His jaw was scratchy and its abrasion on her skin heightened her response. Her moan was long and low and lusty. She threw her head back and dug her hands into his hair. Never in her life had she felt so cherished. He widened her stance, then his mouth closed over her. It wasn't long before she shattered. When her tremors calmed, he stood. "I have to be inside you."

A satisfied smile spread across her lips. "I want that."

Scooping her off her feet, he cradled her close before laying her on the bed. He unzipped his jeans and eased them and his shorts down. She reached for the pulsing flesh that sprang free, but he stayed her hand. "No, love. It's been a long time. I won't last if you touch me and I want this to be perfect."

"It already is."

Quickly he rolled on a condom she'd gotten earlier from the bathroom; the action sent a ripple of liquid desire through her. Placing one knee on the bed, he bent over to kiss her. Then he lay beside her. Scissoring her legs, he smiled into the dim room. "For better access," he said grazing her curls with his knuckles. She yielded to him completely, brushed her hands over his shoulders, down his pecs. He groaned at her light caresses. His body was steel-hard.

"Now, love," he said as he positioned her. And gently, like the tender man he was, he entered her.

At that moment, Emily experienced a sense of completeness she had never known.

For most of the night, Ben lay awake thinking about her. After a second bout of lovemaking, which was almost as cataclysmic as the first, she nestled into his body and fell asleep. He kept her anchored there in the crook of his arm. He wanted this woman for more than tonight—and that meant changing his life.

You don't have to live like this. You can have your

old life back. Any business in Rockford would be glad to hire you.

Trey hadn't understood that Ben couldn't take that risk again. Losing his company and all that he'd worked for his whole life had practically destroyed him, in more ways than one. He'd believed through the whole process that he'd beat Lammon Mackenzie at his own game. And when Mackenzie had won, the hate, the virulence that had spewed out of Ben was so foreign to him that he hadn't known what to do with it. So he'd drowned himself in a bottle. Once he'd sobered, he'd had a hate so strong, it had left him cold. And vengeful.

Counselors at the clinic where he'd finally ended up had explained why he'd turned to the booze. *It's a common reaction to loss. You escape it any way you can. And truthfully, Ben, because your father was an alcoholic, you probably had a predisposition to it.*

Those counselors had saved his life, though he'd been unable to risk venturing back into the business world.

The beauty in his arms stirred. Their legs entangled, he hugged her tighter, kissed the top of her head, basked in her warmth and loveliness.

I'm hoping someday you'll meet someone who will change your mind about this self-imposed exile, one of the counselors had told him. *Until then, stay sober. Work hard. And think about letting go of your bitter-*

*ness. The kind of hate you're feeling will hurt you much
more than Mackenzie.*

Ben stared down at Emily. He could see her freckles in the morning light. Some dotted her shoulders. Was he ready to rejoin the world now, for her? Could they possibly have a future together?

He knew he had to make a decision before she awoke. And he was pretty sure what that decision would be. Hearing a whimper from another part of the house, he eased out of bed and covered Emily with a blanket. He slipped on his clothes and left the bedroom. The main living area was so her. Big stuffed couches were covered in fabrics that resembled watercolors. High ceilings, warm wood floors and walls painted a light gray completed the chic but cozy space. He found Lady scratching at the door that led to the foyer. "Hey, girl, need to go out?" He glanced over at her bed by the fieldstone fireplace; the puppies were out for the count. He had a vision of leaving Emily with sleeping children and going to work. Instead of taunting him, though, the notion warmed him.

"Whoa, Cassidy, you're getting ahead of yourself."

After taking the dog out to do her business, he went to the kitchen to make coffee. While it brewed, he studied the large, airy space. Granite countertops. Brick walls of light gray with pots and pans hung there and over the angled island counter in the middle of the floor. The refrigerator was huge, with pictures taped to its surface. Smiling, he crossed the room to get a glimpse into her life. There was a photo of her and Lady; one of a dark-haired woman in dancewear like Emily often wore; one of Emily and a man, arms linked, smiling. Ben scowled. A boyfriend? No. The guy was too old. Ben moved in closer to get a better look. And when he did, he froze. "What the hell?"

EMILY WOKE UP TO THE SMELL of coffee. Hmm. Had she set the timer? She buried her face in the pillow. It was the scent there that brought her fully to consciousness—and made her remember.

Last night, Ben had come home with her and they'd made love. She sank back into the mattress, hugging the pillow, recalling his words, his touches, how he'd coaxed her into the most soul-searing pleasure she'd ever experienced. More than once, she thought, smiling.

But it wasn't just sex that had happened between them. They'd connected. They'd found an emotional intimacy that transcended the physical. Then it hit her. *Oh, God,* she thought, she'd made love with a man and didn't even know his last name! Well, that would change. Today she'd find out everything about him. And besides, who cared? She knew him as a man, as a person.

Flinging the covers back, she slid out of bed. After stopping in the bathroom, she slipped into a peach-colored robe and followed the smell to her kitchen. She found him looking out the window at her backyard, a mug of coffee in his hand. She just stared at him in his denim workshirt, at the broad expanse of his back. Desire caught her by surprise. She chuckled, causing him to turn around.

"Good morning," she said, smiling.

She didn't expect his hard glare. His stony silence. Uh-oh.

"Ben?"

"How long have you known?"

His cut-glass tone chilled her. She belted the robe tighter. "Known?"

"My last name."

"I was just thinking that I *don't* know your last name."

"I know yours. Or I thought I did. Erickson. But that was Paul's name, wasn't it?"

"Yes. I use my maiden name—"

"Mackenzie?"

"How did you know that?" When he didn't answer, she crossed to the window and reached out to touch him. He stepped back as if he was afraid of being scorched. "What's going on, Ben? Do you regret what happened?"

His eyes held no sign of his earlier affection. They were a hard, flinty gray. "Honey, you have no idea."

Last night, he'd called her *sweetheart* and *love,* but not with the sarcastic inflection he gave to *honey.*

"Ben, if it's about our situation, we can deal with that."

"You're a piece of work. What was it, some game, some perverted pleasure you got out of seducing me?"

"W-why would you say that?" She wrapped her arms around her waist. "It was nothing like that. You know it wasn't."

"I don't get people like you."

"People like me?"

He slammed the coffee cup down on the table and grabbed her by the shoulders. "Isn't destroying me once enough?"

Her throat tightened. His anger, his brutal hold on her, were in such contrast to what they'd shared hours ago. "Please, tell me what happened to make you talk like this."

He shook her hard. Mouthing a vile expletive, he released her, stalked to the refrigerator and ripped down a picture. "This happened, Emily *Mackenzie.* I saw *this.* All I want to know is why."

"Why *what?*"

"Why you brought me here. Made love with me like you cared."

"I do care."

"Well, if that's even remotely true, Daddy wouldn't be happy with this turn of events."

Her heart began to pound in her chest. Something was very wrong here. "Would you just tell me why you're so angry?"

He went on without answering her question. "And why would you volunteer at Cassidy Place? Are you spying for him? Are you trying to destroy that, too?" He loomed over her. "Because I swear, Emily, I won't let him do that. I won't let him demolish the one good thing left that I've done."

"*You've* done?"

"Of course, *I've* done. I built Cassidy Place from the ground up, just like Cassidy Industries. Your father stole the business away from me and is about to sell it off in pieces, I hear. But I'll kill him before I let him sabotage my soup kitchen."

Tears sprang to Emily's eyes. "Oh, God, no. Your last name is Cassidy? You're *Benedict Cassidy?*"

BEN GOT TWO BLOCKS from Emily's house before he went into a store to find a pay phone. Dialing, he blanked his mind from thoughts of Emily and what they'd shared last night. After three rings, he heard a sleep-slurred "Hello."

"Trey, it's Ben."

"Cripes, buddy, it's seven in the morning."

"Last week, I told you not to go all out on your investigation of Mackenzie. Just to look into it."

"Yeah, I am. I haven't found anything more yet."

"Well, I've changed my mind. I want you to pursue it aggressively. I want to go after Lammon Mackenzie with everything we've got, no matter what the cost." He glanced down the street toward Emily's house. "I want to bury the bastard."

CHAPTER FIVE

Six months later

BEN THREW OPEN THE passenger door to Trey's Porsche and stepped out into the October wind. His light wool Hugo Boss suit kept him warm, though. The woman he'd had dinner with last night had told him the gray pinstripe accented his eyes. He didn't care about that, but he did know it felt good to be back. Everything had fallen into place the past few months.

Trey rounded the front of the car, his briefcase firmly in hand. His friend wore a blue power suit, appropriate lawyer dress for this little mission. "Ready, buddy?"

"More than."

"Remember, Mackenzie thinks this meeting is only with me. He won't appreciate seeing you."

"Like I give a damn."

When Ben started toward the door, Trey grasped his arm. "Think she'll be here?"

Ben had filled Trey in—minus the intimate details—on what had happened between Lammon Mackenzie's daughter and him because Trey needed to know why Ben had had a change of heart. Good businessmen didn't keep secrets from their lawyers. And what they'd discovered about Mackenzie's tactics in the takeover did indeed reveal Ben had been a good businessman. It had also revealed that Mackenzie was a liar, cheater and—*ta-da*—a fraud.

"I'm prepared for that, if she is."

Ben hadn't seen or talked to the illustrious Ms. Mackenzie since that fateful morning at her house. He hadn't been back to Cassidy Place, though he'd had Trey see to it that the soup kitchen was solvent and Mackenzie couldn't harm it in any way. And Ben sure as hell hadn't contacted *her.*

Though he'd hardened his heart and kept a ruthless grip on his emotions since their last encounter, he couldn't stop dreaming about her. It was the only time she was in his mind, since he was unable to control his unconscious. There, he saw her shocked face, listened to her frightened pleas that morning he'd confronted her. And there, he also felt her touch him like she cared. Felt her come alive, and apart, in his arms. Sometimes, because of those images, he questioned his interpretation of what had happened between them. But try as he might, he couldn't come up with any explanation except that she'd worked with her father to keep tabs on him and perhaps undermine Cassidy Place. Though why Mackenzie would want to do either stumped him.

"Maybe you should have talked to Emily when she called me four months ago," Trey commented after they were checked in by the guard and entered the sprawling glass-and-brass building that housed Mackenzie Enterprises.

"Are you kidding?"

"She said she needed to speak to you."

"Forget it. There's no way I'm ringing that bell again."

They traveled up in the elevator to the penthouse where a secretary sat in a spacious reception area, with offices forming a semicircle around her desk. Plush carpet, paneled mahogany walls and expensive furniture shouted wealth. The woman was most likely new, because Ben didn't recognize her from before the takeover.

"Mr. Thompson?" she asked when they approached.

"Yes."

She looked at Ben.

"I brought my associate," Trey told her, turning on the charm. "I hope that's all right."

"Of course." If she noticed the absence of an introduction, she didn't comment. She buzzed the inner sanctum. "Mr. Mackenzie, your ten o'clock is here."

A familiar voice answered curtly. "Send him in."

The woman rose, walked ahead of them to the oak door and opened it. Trey entered first, Ben behind him. The door closed before Mackenzie looked up from his desk. "What can I do—"

Ben stepped out from behind his lawyer and, for a moment, Mackenzie froze.

With faked nonchalance, Ben strode over to the desk and stared down at the man he hated more than anyone in the world. The man who'd used his own daughter to hurt Ben. "Hello, Mackenzie."

"What the hell are you doing here?"

"What's the quote from that movie? Oh, yes, I'm going to be your worst nightmare."

Over the shock, Mackenzie leaned back in his chair and lazily crossed his leg over his knee. His features were a mask of disinterest. Emily resembled him in nose and cheekbones, but she could never look as hard as he did. "I think you've got that wrong, Cassidy. I was yours, remember?"

Trey spoke up beside Ben. "We remember, all too well. However, certain actions you took before the transfer have recently come to light, and the tables, as they say, are about to be turned."

Mackenzie's expression hardened. "I don't have time for this." He reached for the phone. "I'm calling security."

"Fine." Trey whipped out his cell. "We'll call the newspapers to inform them of the fraudulent tactics you used to take over Cassidy Industries."

The man's hand stilled on the phone. Before he could say anything, the door to his office swung open.

"Dad, Donna's on a break and I...."

Trey and Ben turned. Her father stood.

Emily Mackenzie looked up from the papers she held and stopped dead in her tracks.

Her white sweater was stretched across her swollen stomach. When his mind finally started working again, Ben gauged that she was about six months pregnant.

MAC THREW BACK HIS CHAIR and bolted upright. "Emily!"

She said nothing, simply stared at the men before her. Mac wondered how she'd know who they were, but her open-mouthed shock made him suspect his daughter did indeed recognize them. Hell, she'd been furious when he'd snatched the company out from under Cassidy and had laid off more than half of the employees. Now, if she heard this....

Thompson stepped forward. "Ms. Mackenzie, I'm Trey Thompson. We've spoken on the phone."

"Hello, Mr. Thompson." She turned to Cassidy. "Hello, Ben."

"Ms. Mackenzie." Cassidy's voice was frigid and he glared at Emily.

Mac circled the desk. "Emily, I'd like you to leave. This meeting isn't any concern of yours."

His daughter was distracted. She couldn't seem to wrest her gaze from Cassidy.

"Emily? What's wrong with you, girl?"

Finally, she looked at him. "Nothing, Dad. What did you say?"

"This doesn't concern you."

"I think," Cassidy said coldly, "this concerns her very much. As a vice president in Mackenzie Enterprises, you're going to need her to help bail you out of this mess."

Emily frowned. "What's he talking about?"

"Shall we all sit?" Thompson suggested.

"No, we shall not." Mac strode to the door. "Both of you get out of my office right now."

Thompson dropped the polite veneer. "Then you're prepared to answer to our charges publicly? And maybe in the courts, if we decide to go that far?"

"Charges?" Emily asked. "What charges?"

"Emily—"

Thompson set his briefcase on the edge of Mac's desk, unsnapped it and drew out some papers. He handed them to Mackenzie. "These charges."

"What the hell is this?"

Emily crossed to him and they stared down at the papers. The draft read:

"It has come to light that in the acquisition of Cassidy Industries, Lammon Mackenzie used his association with Rockford Gas & Electric to stall contracts that were to be given to Cassidy Industries. Albert Ackerman, then vice president of sales, was also Mackenzie's golf partner at the time of the delay. Ackerman took possession of a condominium in Florida and a Porsche two weeks after the acquisition was final and paid cash for both."

There were more incriminating details.

"Bribery...delaying contracts...fraud?" Emily gripped her father's arm. "Dad, is this true?"

Reading the charges about what they knew, and obviously *didn't* know, gave Mac courage. "Of course not. It's some mealy-mouthed attempt to get Cassidy Industries back." His grin was malicious. "Well, get in line, Cassidy. The company's about to be sold for five times what I paid for it. Too bad you couldn't turn it around like I did." Then he added, "Hey, maybe you could buy it back. But, no, wait. You're a bum now, aren't you? What did you do, borrow those clothes from Thompson?"

Cassidy visibly reined in his temper. He stuck his hands in his suit pants pockets and gave his own version of an evil grin. "Seems like we're on the same page, Mackenzie. I do intend to buy back my company, but at the price you paid me when you stole it from me."

"When hell freezes over. I'll sue you for libel if you pursue these ridiculous charges."

Trey laughed. "Go ahead. We'd welcome the publicity. By the way, the document later mentions that we have sworn testimony from a former employee who worked on the electric company's contracts. He was fired shortly after your actions, and was only too happy to give me the details as to why."

Thompson looked to Cassidy.

It was Cassidy's turn to laugh now. "Let's leave him the documentation, Trey." To Mac, he said, "If we don't hear from you by tomorrow morning, we're going to make this public, warning any other company you want to buy in the future to be vigilant. We'll also sue your ass for fraud. We'll ask for the company back, punitive damages *and* income lost."

Cassidy gave Emily a blistering look and walked out. His lawyer followed.

When they'd gone, Emily turned accusing eyes on Mac. "Oh, Dad. You didn't."

EVERY MUSCLE IN EMILY'S BODY ached as she drove into her garage and switched off the car's engine. She shouldn't have gone to dance class after the emotional exhaustion of the day, but she couldn't bear to come home alone, and she knew venting her frustration through physical exercise would be better for the baby. Sitting in the dim overhead light of the garage, she rubbed her belly. "You're okay, little one, aren't you? I'm sorry we had such a rough day."

She felt a nice strong kick.

"What's that? You're doing fine? Good. Come on, I'll make us some tea."

She entered the kitchen, switched on the light and,

crossing to the cupboard, she removed a teabag. As she picked up the kettle, she thought about Ben in her kitchen that fateful morning, his face a mask of pain and anger. She was still reeling from seeing him today, and from the information he'd brought to light. He looked so different in an expensive blue suit with a stylish haircut and a snarl on his clean-shaven face. She wondered how his circumstances had changed so much in only six months. Where, for instance, had he gotten money? In that, and in his demeanor, he wasn't at all the Ben she'd fallen for at the soup kitchen, the Ben who'd made love to her like she was his last meal. Her emotion welled and caught in her throat. She'd missed him so much and now, she guessed, he was gone forever. For a while she'd held out hope that once he calmed down, he'd talk to her. But knowing exactly what her father had done to him quashed any hope of that. Tears came to her eyes. Since she'd gotten pregnant, she was at the mercy of her hormones. She swiped them away and turned to fill the kettle at the sink.

"Oh!" She slapped her hand over her heart.

Wearing a khaki raincoat, Ben was standing at the entryway from the garage. Frowning. Though he seemed weary, he was still the angry, cold, detached man she'd confronted this afternoon.

"Ben, you scared me."

"You shouldn't leave your garage open at night. No telling who will show up at your house." He shut the door carefully, leaned against it and folded his arms over his chest. "Then again, you were never very good at avoiding the riffraff."

She set the kettle on the counter, hoping he didn't notice how shaken she was. "It's good to see you."

"Is it? Well, I don't return the sentiment."

The comment cut deep, but she'd be damned if she let it show. "Then why are you here?"

He nodded to her belly. "Is it mine?"

"Excuse me?"

"Is that child you're carrying mine? Or did you seduce some other poor sap who believed you were who you said you were?"

Her hand went protectively to her stomach. "Yes, the baby's yours."

Myriad emotions crossed his face. Shock. Resignation. And a tiny flicker of joy.

"But we used a condom…."

"I know. And I was told I couldn't get pregnant. But Paul and I just weren't the right mix, I guess." She said the words more flippantly than she intended, but damn it, no one was going to make her sorry about having a baby. Despite the circumstances, she was elated about this little miracle.

"Were you ever going to tell me?"

She felt angry at the unfairness of the question. "I *tried* to tell you. When I couldn't figure out any way to contact you, I called your lawyer. He succinctly said you had no desire to see or talk to me ever again."

She let that sink in.

"As a matter of fact, that's exactly what you told me when you walked out of here that morning."

After which, she'd dissolved into sobs that had lasted all day and a funk that had taken her two months to overcome. It was only when she'd found out about the baby that she'd begun to feel better. She hadn't been able to forget the contempt on his face, though.

Ben just stared at her. So many things had fallen into place when she'd discovered who he was: his interest in Cassidy Place, how articulate he was, his perpetual sadness. Finally, he said, "I want DNA tests done."

"All right."

His cool slipped a bit. "Damn it, Emily, you're not lying, are you? This baby *is* mine."

"Yes, he's yours."

All the sarcasm, all the rigidity drained out of him. "He? You're having a boy?"

Her grin was wide. "Uh-huh. You should have seen the sonogram, Ben. He was cuddled up sucking his thumb. I have a picture if—"

"Stop!"

She waited.

"I want him."

"Oh, I knew you would. You'll be a wonderful father. I—"

He held up his hand. "Let me finish. I want the child but I don't want you, Emily."

She bit the inside of her cheek to contain her hurt. "I see."

His brow furrowed. "Did you think I would?"

"I don't know. I thought maybe after what we shared that night..." She couldn't go on around the lump in her throat.

"Spare me the drama. We both know your interest in me was because of your father, not because you had feelings for me."

"That's not true!"

He drew papers out of the breast pocket of his raincoat. "I won't listen to any more lies."

Damn him. "Then what do you propose?"

Placing the papers on her kitchen table, he carefully smoothed out the creases. "This is a copy of what I left your father. Read the whole thing. You'll find it's incriminating enough to destroy his reputation."

"What does that have to do with the baby?"

"I could use it to blackmail you into giving me the child."

"That's utterly ludicrous. In any case, you agreed not to report him to the authorities if he sold you back the company."

"That was before I knew you were having my child. I can always change the terms, if you don't agree to my stipulation." He shook his head. "I had you investigated, once I found out who you were. You've aided and abetted your father in all his acquisitions. And let's not forget how you went after me as icing on the cake." Hurt shone in his eyes. "Though I still don't understand what you had to gain from that."

She swallowed hard. "I didn't go after you. I didn't know who you were."

"Our meeting could not possibly have been a coincidence."

"It was Ben, I swear. And it wasn't so much a coincidence. You had reason to be at Cassidy Place, and so did I."

He pounded his fist against the table. "Are you denying you didn't know what he did to me?"

"Of course I didn't. I was in the middle of my divorce when my father became an investor in your company. I had nothing to do with it. Then I was in Europe. When I came back to work, he'd taken over Cassidy Industries and you were gone."

"Maybe that's all true. It would explain why we never met before. But that doesn't mean you didn't find out who I was and what your father had done to me when you went back to work." His anger built. "Don't try to convince me that your last little scheme at the soup kitchen wasn't intentional."

"What could I have hoped to accomplish there, Ben?"

"Keep tabs on me. Hurt Cassidy Place?"

"I'd never be a part of either one of those things."

"I don't believe that. I never will." He drew himself up, as if he was regrouping. "But none of it matters. What matters is the child."

She cradled her stomach. "I feel the same way. As I said, it's preposterous that you'd think I'd give up my own son. But you can have joint custody and see him whenever you want."

"That's not enough. I won't have my child living away from me half the time. My father...never mind."

"What about your father?"

"Let's just say he was in and out of my life as a child. I won't do that to my own son."

"I'm sorry. I know you had a rough past. But if you even remotely meant your earlier threat, I'll fight you every step of the way to keep my son."

"*My* son."

Damn it, she was going to fight for her baby—and for him. "Ben, I know you're angry, and if it's all true, what my father did, I understand why, but please, can't we focus on us?"

"There is no us."

"That's how this little one came about."

"Let me rephrase. There can never be anything between us again. I could never trust you now that I know who you are." He added, "Or love you."

At the stark words, her bravado disappeared. To hide her tears from this man she no longer knew, she sank into a kitchen chair and buried her face in her hands.

After a moment, he tugged them away. "Here, drink this." He'd gotten water. "Try to calm down. Being so upset isn't good for the baby."

She swallowed hard and drank. When she could, she looked up at him. "I'm better, thanks. You're right, this isn't good for him." She placed her hand protectively over her stomach. "What are we going to do, Ben?"

"I have an idea. But you're not going to like it any better than my first one."

"READY?" TREY ASKED BEN as they once again rode the elevator to Lammon Mackenzie's office.

Dressed in his own blue power suit, Ben chuckled. "I've been ready for this for two years." The only thing he hadn't been prepared for was the bomb Emily had dropped on him.

And his emotional reaction to knowing she was pregnant with his child. He'd gone over to her house planning to be cruel and vindictive, just like her father, but in the end he couldn't treat her so badly. Instead, he'd been cold and remote, and completely dismissed any kind of relationship between them. The most he could manage was a compromise of sorts.

This time, the secretary was unfriendly. "Mr. Cassidy, Mr. Thompson. They're waiting for you in Mr. Mackenzie's office."

Trey nodded to her. "Fine." His lawyer expected to see Jacob Brill and Mackenzie at this meeting. He didn't know Emily would attend.

When they entered the spacious office, the tension was tangible. His back to them, Mackenzie stood staring out the window. An older man—Brill—sat at a conference table with papers spread out. Emily stood at one end of the room, facing them, her hand resting on the back of a chair. Today she wore a green suit that accented the roundness of her stomach. It caught Ben off guard. He had to steel himself against the urge to cross the room, put his hands on her belly and feel his child move in her body.

Brill rose. "Mr. Cassidy. Mr. Thompson. Sit down please."

They complied.

"Mac?"

Mackenzie turned and glared at them with an expression of cold rage. He strode to the table and sat at the far end.

Emily smiled politely. Ben stole a glance at her face when she took a chair. It was chalk-white.

Brill cleared his throat before he spoke. "I've asked Mac not to participate in these discussions today. Frankly, I don't even know why Emily is here, except that Mr. Cassidy requested her presence."

Ben only nodded. Trey frowned at him.

Brill continued. "We've read your report. It's preposterous and libelous. We refuse to admit to any wrongdoing. We have our own people researching the source of the complaint."

Ben checked his watch. "Well then, it's all over but the shouting. My time frame doesn't include investigating the charges. Either Mackenzie signs over the company to me today, at the price he paid me originally, or we sue."

"We realize all that," the lawyer told him. "Which is why we're prepared to give you what you want. Mr. Mackenzie's not willing to risk a public scandal."

"And he's guilty as hell, so that helps."

"I'm not, you son of a bitch."

Brill held up a hand. "Mac, please. In any case, you get what you want, Mr. Cassidy. In return, we'll require you to sign a waiver, stating that you will not sue for damages, and the contents of this agreement will be confidential."

They'd known this was coming. Trey said, "We're prepared to do that."

"Then we're in agreement. I have the papers drawn up. If you're ready to sign them, we can get this over with today."

Trey had a big grin on his face. "We are." He looked to Ben. "Right?"

"Yes." Ben glanced at Emily, then zeroed in on her father. He knew in his heart this was the wrong time to make the announcement, but he couldn't resist the opportunity to see Mackenzie's reaction. "There's one more thing you should know, Mackenzie. Your daughter and I are going to be married this week."

They all froze.

Then Mackenzie said, *"What?"*

"You heard me."

Mackenzie turned to Emily. "You didn't agree to this atrocity, did you?"

"Yes, Dad, I did."

"Well, I won't allow it." He stood and slapped his hand on the table. "If you think for one minute, Cassidy, that you can blackmail my daughter into marriage or take her as some sordid spoil of war, you're crazy."

Ben was furious at Mac's assertion. Maybe because it struck too close to the mark. But even though he'd told Emily he could blackmail her, he'd never really meant it. "I didn't have to blackmail her. She wants to marry me. Ask her."

Emily nodded, but she was trembling. "Dad, this baby..." She caressed her belly. "Ben's the father."

"I don't believe it. When you told me you had a fling last summer.... It couldn't have been with Cassidy! You never met him during the takeover. You don't even *know* him."

Ben watched Emily to see how she would handle this situation.

"Dad, please. I know this is the last thing you need right now. And I know it's not what you or I wanted for me out of life. But it's going to be all right."

Emily's placating her father, her worry about *his* needs now, and her implication that Ben wasn't good enough for her, pushed him to a place his saner side told him not to go. Deliberately, he rose and went to stand behind her. Placing a possessive hand on her shoulder, he said smugly, "And you're wrong about us not knowing each other. We obviously do. Intimately. In the biblical sense."

Emily gasped.

Infuriated, Mackenzie pushed back his chair and rounded the table. When he reached Ben, he dragged him away from Emily and drew back his arm. But before he could land his punch, Ben grabbed onto him, and they both went down to the floor.

"Oh, dear Lord!" Emily shouted.

Mackenzie was pulled off by Trey and Brill.

"Calm down, Mac," Brill said when everybody was standing again. "This isn't helping anything."

Ben surveyed the scene. Brill was exasperated, Mackenzie shell-shocked and Trey was silent. Emily seemed stunned. It should have felt wonderful. He had his company back, he had his revenge against the man who'd almost destroyed him and a beautiful woman had agreed to become his wife.

But the hurt in Emily's eyes—she looked at him like David facing down Goliath—made Ben's victory a hollow one.

CHAPTER SIX

"DO YOU TAKE THIS MAN to be your lawful wedded husband, to love and cherish in sickness and health, in good times and bad, till death do you part?"

Emily peered up at the judge with dry eyes and an aching heart. "I do." She practically choked on her words. This was blasphemy. Oh, she wanted to marry Ben. But after the scene with her father that day at the office almost a week ago, Ben's motives were more in question than ever.

As the judge repeated the vow to Ben, Emily thought about what her father had said.

Don't tell me you fell for his ruse.

Until he'd planted the seed, it had never occurred to her that Ben might have known all along who she was, might have wanted her to get pregnant. But he'd been so angry when he'd found the picture on the refrigerator. Her dad had an explanation for that, too....

Cassidy's a good actor, and a lying son of a bitch. It fit his purposes to play the injured party.

In the bright light of the chambers, Emily watched

Ben's stony face as he promised to honor and care for her. He was so handsome with his square-cut jaw, angular features and, of course, in the expensive clothes. She'd seen him only twice since she'd agreed to marry him.

First, he'd still wanted the DNA tests. They'd gone to the hospital together and gotten the results separately. She wondered what he'd felt when he'd seen the incontrovertible evidence that he was indeed the father of this child. Then, he'd dropped by her house yesterday and had told her where and when to show up for the wedding. He'd left his coat on, wouldn't sit down and had given her the information in cold, clipped tones.

She'd stopped him when he was about to leave. "I have a question."

"What?"

"Are you marrying me to punish my father, to get back at him?"

"It's easy to see you and he both think of this marriage as a punishment."

"You seem angrier today than the last time you were here. Why?"

"Look, I don't want this marriage and neither do you, but we agreed on it because of the baby. Let's leave it at that."

He was wrong. Despite his cold remoteness, *she* wanted to marry *him*. She'd come to care a great deal for him by the time they'd made love. Carrying his baby strengthened her feelings for him. Though he was being curt and distant, she knew in her heart his actions were self-protective. Unfortunately, that also made him unable to trust her. Or to love her, he'd said.

"Emily?" He extended his hand, palm up. In it he held a ring.

"Oh." She put out her hand.

He slid the ring on the third finger. Then he squeezed her hand.

She looked up for his ring. Nothing. She had just assumed he'd bought one for himself, too, when she'd asked him about getting them and he'd said he'd take care of it. Obviously he didn't want to wear her wedding band. Damn him, how dare he? Her anger must have shown because he was scowling.

"I now pronounce you husband and wife," the judge said enthusiastically. "You may kiss the bride."

She heard Jordan say from behind her, "Oh, hell."

It was Ben who'd insisted Jordan and Trey be here....

We'll need witnesses. Do you have a friend?

Yes, of course. But she won't be happy about this wedding.

Well, that makes four of us!

Now his hands grasped her shoulders. At least he was gentle, the way he'd been that night they were together. She lifted her face. He tried for a small perfunctory brush of her lips. But she grasped his neck to hold him there and gave him a full, hot kiss that left them both breathless. When he drew back, there was surprise on his face. His stoicism had cracked, and he didn't appear happy about it. She took satisfaction in that.

After the judge congratulated them, Ben led her out of the wood-paneled chambers. "I've made reservations for four at the Rio Bamba at seven," he told them in the hallway.

Trey smiled weakly. "Great."

Jordan's light blue eyes sparked with anger. "What are we celebrating? This is a travesty."

Ben's gaze turned colder. "We're celebrating our wedding." He gestured to Emily's belly. He hadn't touched her yet, hadn't tried to feel their child. "And our baby."

Emily squeezed her friend's arm. "Jordan, let's not make things any more difficult. For my sake, leave the recriminations behind."

Jordan, dressed in a beautiful peach suit, drew herself up to her five-nine height. "For you, Em."

"Well, now that's settled we'll be going. Trey and I will meet you there." Each pair had come in separate cars, with Jordan and Ben driving.

"No." Everyone looked at Emily. "I'll ride with my husband."

Surprised, Ben nevertheless took Emily's arm and guided her out of the courthouse.

The night was cool and she was glad she'd chosen a long-sleeved suit, off-white, with heels to match. They stopped at a sleek silver Jag in the parking lot. "Is this yours?" she asked.

"Yes. I've leased it." He opened the passenger door.

Emily struggled to get into the low-slung vehicle and he had to assist her.

Rounding the hood, he slid into the other side, started the engine and drove away. After a few moments of silence, her nerves were raw and her stomach queasy. "Did you always drive a Jag, you know, before?"

"I did."

"It's a beautiful car."

He grunted.

"No room for a baby seat, though."

In the glare from oncoming headlights, she saw him smile. "Hmm. I'll think about getting something else for then." Glancing over at her, the expression on his face still tender, he asked, "You all right? You looked a little green in there."

"My stomach's off today."

The softness of his features fled like mist in the morning. "The thought of marrying me is enough to make you sick."

She took a deep breath. "Ben, please stop saying that. I wanted to marry you."

His hands gripped the wheel. "Jordan's right, this is a travesty."

He pulled into the Rio and, as they waited for the valet, she turned to him. "Can I ask you something?"

"Does it concern your father?"

"It's something I need to know."

"All right."

"Did you know who I really was at the soup kitchen? When you slept with me?"

"Let me guess. Good old dad put that idea in your head."

Her silence was her answer. It infuriated him.

"I'm not going to keep defending myself to you and especially not to your father. Go ahead and think whatever you like."

"Ben, we need to—"

The passenger door opened suddenly and the valet extended his hand to help her up. Ben, clearly angry at her question, threw open his own door and got out. They were joined at the entrance by Jordan and Trey. Emily pasted a phony smile on her face and greeted their friends.

No one looked ready to celebrate.

AS THEY SAT AT THE BEST TABLE in the Rio, the fanciest restaurant in Rockford, Ben gritted his teeth. This had been a colossal mistake. He'd arranged the dinner with some vague notion of keeping things civil with Emily. It had seemed the right thing to do, to take his bride out to supper. His bride and the mother of his child. But obviously he'd been wrong.

Then again, nothing was working out as he'd planned. First there was the utter joy he'd felt when the results of the DNA tests had confirmed that she was indeed carrying his baby. It had softened him toward her. Then, he'd begun to worry about Emily. He'd tried to curb it, but his natural inclination was to protect her, watch out for her, like a real husband. The push-pull of that and being so angry about the situation made his thinking fuzzy. Still, he couldn't stifle his concern, especially now when she sat next to him, looking like a sapling ready to snap at the slightest wind.

He'd ordered champagne, which Emily couldn't drink, so he'd told the waiter to bring her club soda. The toast was strained, and they chose their food in silence.

"So," Trey asked after they gave back the menus, clearly trying to make small talk, "are you buying another condo or are you going to live at Emily's place?"

Ben had stayed in the spare room of Trey's condo for the past six months. He'd kept his construction job, though, until they were ready to implement their plan to corral Mackenzie. Then he'd quit and dipped into the bank account Trey had set up for him two years ago for clothes and other necessities. With the interest garnered, there had still been enough to buy back Cassidy Industries.

"I'm moving in with Emily tonight."

The seltzer spilled over the edge of her glass. "You are?"

"Yes. I packed some things in the trunk of my Jag. Trey can help me bring over the rest tomorrow."

The color seeped from her cheeks. What the hell?

"What did you expect, Emily?"

"Maybe that you'd have told me your plans." She didn't keep the sarcasm from her voice. Apparently she had no intention of being a doormat in this whole charade.

Thankfully their meals arrived. And then Emily and Jordan began to talk about a dance studio Jordan was opening. Trey asked several questions about the venture, while Ben's mind wandered to Emily's health and state of mind. Stress wasn't good for the baby, he knew that. But how could he ease it, how could he take care of her, and not get suckered in by her again?

He tuned back into the conversation when Jordan asked, "What are your plans work-wise, Em?"

Emily glanced at Ben. "I, um, I'm needed at Mackenzie Enterprises."

"You can't associate yourself with Mackenzie Enterprises," Ben said flatly.

"I work there."

"I won't have my wife work for a company whose CEO tried to destroy me once, and may very well go after me again."

While Emily thought about that, Jordan jumped in. "You won't *have* this? Who the hell do you think you are?"

"Her husband."

Emily stiffened in the chair. "Not my keeper." She held herself rigidly poised. "However, I can understand your not wanting me to work there."

"Emily—" Jordan warned.

Ben held up his hand. "Before this leads to another full-scale argument, isn't it almost a moot point?" He faced his wife. "You won't be working much longer, will you?"

She touched her stomach. "I hadn't thought about that."

His anger sparked. "Maybe you should think more about the baby than your father."

"I wasn't...."

"What? Putting Daddy first again?"

Her face went white and her hand went to her throat. "Excuse me," she said tightly and practically ran out of the room.

Jordan bolted up. "I'll go see if she's all right."

"No you won't." He stood. "She's my wife. I'll take care of her."

Her friend loomed before him like an outraged Valkyrie. "You're doing a wonderful job. Forcing her into this marriage. Making cracks about her father. Can't you see this is all too much for a six-month-pregnant woman? She's about ready to snap."

He said only, "Keep Jordan here, Trey."

When he reached the entrance, there was no sign of Emily. His heart began to beat faster.

The maître d' approached him. "Mr. Cassidy, are you looking for the woman you came with?"

"Yes."

"She's in the ladies' room."

Ben headed for it as the maître d' called out, "Excuse me, you can't go—" The comment was cut off when the door closed behind him.

"Emily?"

He heard her retching and found her in a stall with the door ajar. She must have been too sick to throw the latch. He eased inside. She was down on her knees, vomiting. He knelt behind her and swept her hair off her face. Placing a hand on her back, he rubbed in soothing circles. But he didn't say anything. *He'd* made her sick and he knew it.

Finally she tried to push herself up from the floor but she was too weak. So he scooped her up and carried her out of the stall and over to a huge pink flowered divan. She laid her head against the cushions while he wet some paper towels at the sink. Gently, he bathed her face. Then he poured some water into a cup from the dispenser and brought it to her. "Here, just sip."

Her hands were too shaky to hold the cup, so he put it to her mouth. He was ashamed at how his words and actions had affected her.

After she calmed, he sat back. "I'm sorry I brought this on."

Her eyes still closed, she sighed. "This whole thing

has been upsetting. And confusing, too. I don't understand why you pretended to be the injured party that morning after we made love. You seemed shocked to find out who I was."

"Are we back to that again?"

She shook her head. "Ben, please, just tell me the truth, then I won't ask again. But I need to know this. Did you or did you not know who I was at Cassidy Place and play me, seduce me, to get back at my father?"

"Of course I didn't."

It hit him then that she'd believed her father, because his taunt kicked into her insecurities. *Paul said I don't know men, don't know how to please them... I'm not woman enough....*

Damn Mackenzie. Damn Erickson.

She swallowed hard and continued. "Then you made love to me because you were attracted to me?"

"Because I was attracted to you, and I liked you." Hell, he'd been half in love with her.

"Really?"

He couldn't help it. She looked so fragile. So breakable. And he hated to see her questioning her femininity. He brushed his knuckles down her cheek. "Really. I told you Paul was an idiot. Your father misled you again, Emily. Intentionally, I'd guess."

"No, he didn't. He was just—"

"Don't defend him to me!" He hated her siding with

Mackenzie. Abruptly he stood. "I won't talk about him anymore," he said staring down at her. She was cradling her stomach again. "I don't want you to work for him. You can work at Cassidy Industries. With me. And," he added because he was so pissed off at the man, "I'd prefer you didn't even see him."

She drew in a deep breath. "I'll work for you, Ben, for the time being, at least. But I'll see my father. I won't back down on that."

Her words were brave, but she seemed frail sitting there, cuddling the child who slept inside her. "All right, see him. Just not at the house where I'll be living."

"Fair enough."

Taking her hand, he drew her up and they headed for the door. Nothing was going as it was supposed to. At first he'd really believed she'd been in cahoots with her father. Now he wasn't so sure. But in the long run, it didn't make any difference. She was Lammon Mackenzie's daughter and she'd always choose him first, over Ben. Her defense of the man tonight bore that out. So, Ben could never trust her. And he'd never give her his heart, as he had that night in her bed. If he did that, and she betrayed him for Mackenzie, he'd never survive. All around, it was a hell of a mess.

AS SHE OPENED THE FRONT DOOR, Emily felt the exhaustion settle over her like a shroud, so heavy she sagged with it. "I have some spare keys and another garage-door opener for you," she told Ben as he followed her inside, carrying some of his belongings.

He'd been quiet on the way home. But his attitude had seemed to soften after they'd talked in the ladies' room, and they'd eaten dinner in as relaxed an atmosphere as could be expected given the situation. "I'll need them for tomorrow."

She wanted to know what she was to do at Cassidy Industries come Monday morning, but she was afraid asking would only lead to conflict again, and she wasn't up to another round with him. But there *was* something she needed to know—imminently.

He stood surveying the great room. Before she could question him, however, he said, "It looks bigger than I remembered." There wasn't rancor in his voice, but wistfulness.

She didn't respond.

He cleared his throat. "Where's Lady?"

"Out in the back. I have a pretty good size heated porch and a fenced-in yard, with a dog run." She pressed a hand to her stomach. "I put in a doggy door after I got pregnant."

His gaze dropped to her belly. Suddenly she wished he'd touch her—anywhere, really, but there especially. The baby must have been in tune with her thoughts, because he kicked her hard.

Ben's eyes widened. "What was that?"

"The baby." She cocked her head. "Do you want to feel him?"

He looked so torn, she longed to go to him and comfort him. Tell him everything was going to be all right. Silly thought.

Finally he said, "No thanks," and changed the subject. "Did you give away all the puppies?"

"Except for Jack."

"Jack?"

She grinned. "As in Jack and Jill."

He gave her a weak smile.

Gesturing to the suitcases, she asked the question that had been on her mind since he'd told her he was moving into her house. "Where are you going to put those, Ben?"

As if he realized he was still holding his things, he set the suitcase down and laid the hanging bag on the staircase railing. "In the spare room."

Stupid, stupid, stupid for her to be disappointed.

He crossed to her, then, tilted her chin and looked into her eyes. His had gotten a hard gleam in them, again, but he touched her gently. "What did you think I'd say, Emily? Your room?"

"Truthfully, I have no idea what you're thinking. Or what you're going to do next."

Waiting a heartbeat, he asked, "If I'd said your room, would you have let me?"

Don't do it, protect yourself.

On the other hand, somebody had to be honest in this relationship. And Emily had never been one to dissemble. Besides, what did she have to gain by pretending she felt differently? She wasn't ashamed or even embarrassed by her feelings for Ben. "Yes," she said bravely. "I would have agreed."

He drew in a deep breath. "Why?"

She gripped his wrist. "For the same reason I slept with you six months ago. I know you still don't believe my feelings for you were real, that I cared about you then. But those are the facts, Ben, no matter how much you deny them."

Dropping his hand, he stepped back. "I can't trust you, Emily."

"So you said."

"But I'll try to be nicer. I'll try to reduce this godawful tension between us. I hated making you sick back at the restaurant. Don't mention your father to me anymore, and I won't bring up what's between us. We'll try to peacefully coexist."

She wanted more than that, but let it go. "Then the spare room's upstairs to the left, down the hall from mine. It has its own bathroom."

He nodded. "You look exhausted."

"I'm dead on my feet. I don't usually stay up this late, even on a Saturday."

"Go on upstairs. I'll get the rest of my things inside, then I can find my way to my room."

"All right." She turned away, but called over her shoulder, "Good night, Ben."

As she climbed the steps, she thought, *Some wedding night*. She glanced past the banister and found him staring up at her. His features were inscrutable.

BEN CAME OUT OF THE BATHROOM and looked through the door of the spare room, which was still ajar. The crack under Emily's door sent a beacon of light down the hall, telling him she was still up. He wondered if she was sick again. It had been a half hour since they'd arrived home.

Damn, she said she cared about him, would sleep with him again. His body, abstinent since that last fateful encounter that had brought him here to this spare room, responded to the knowledge, hardened at the thought. He remembered the silky feel of her skin, the scent and taste of her, how she closed around him.

He swore. He'd never sleep feeling like this. Might as well unpack. As he did, he argued with himself. No good would come of taking what she offered. Still, it was their wedding night. But she'd been ill. Carefully, he hung up his clothing, stored his things in the closet and headed for the dresser, feeling his control slip inch by inch. He wanted to go to her....

His control snapped abruptly into place when he saw the framed photo of her and Mackenzie on the dresser. They were smiling broadly, their heads tilted toward each other. Ben felt a surge of hatred so strong it shocked him. But it also sobered him. This man was important in her life, and best Ben remember that.

He finished unpacking, slipped on cotton pj bottoms in deference to her, switched off the light and turned to the bed. Again, he glanced toward his door. Her light was still on. The red numbers on the clock told him they'd been home an hour.

Ignore it. Ignore her, and her siren's invitation.

When he was still tossing and turning thirty minutes later over that damn light, he threw off the sheet and headed for her room.

At the door, he knocked softly. "Emily? Are you all right?"

No answer. What if something happened to her? He turned the handle and the door opened.

She was lying on the side of the bed with the covers beneath her turned down. His mouth went dry. One shoe was on her foot, the other had fallen to the floor. She had her top off, thrown on the bed, but she still wore the skirt. Her upper body was covered with a silk slip, lacy across her breasts. They swelled over the bodice. She was bigger than six months ago. In the dim light, her skin glowed with her pregnancy.

What had happened here? He checked the room. The bathroom light was off, the bed turned down, the blinds shut. She must have sat down while undressing, lain back to rest and fallen asleep. God, was she that tired and worn out?

Why not, asshole? She'd had a horrible day, a horrible few weeks. He waited, deciding what to do. Oh,
hell. Bending over, he removed her other shoe, her
skirt. And was astounded by how her stomach bulged
under the tight slip—with his child. She nestled into the
pillow on her side, her hands by her head, her knees
slightly drawn up. Knees, he saw, covered with panty-
hose.

Leave it.

But they'd be uncomfortable to sleep in.

Don't do it.

Sitting on the edge of the bed, he slid his hands
under the slip to the elastic band of the hose. Slowly,
so as not to awaken her, he drew down the stockings.
The slip inched up as he pulled them off. She stirred
but settled back into a deep sleep. When he was done,
he couldn't take his eyes off her stomach. After a long
moment, he lifted the slip up to her chest. What he saw
stopped his breath.

Her skin was stretched mercilessly over his child.
She was so big, he was shocked that her body could accommodate a baby. She wore red lace bikini underwear
that just barely covered what it was supposed to.

But that didn't intrigue him as much as her belly. He
just stared at it. Then it moved. Her whole stomach! Oh
Lord, it was like a wave coursed through her abdomen.
For a minute he didn't grasp what had happened, then
he realized the baby had turned over. He chuckled out

loud, ridiculously smitten by the simple movement. Now, he couldn't resist the temptation. He placed his hand on her stomach. Man, it was hard. He waited. Nothing. He lowered his head and kissed the bulge. "Come on, buddy. This is me, Daddy. Kick for me." Still nothing. "Please."

Then he felt it. A good, strong kick into his hand. Worthy of a soccer player. A football player. A pro wrestler. He felt a sudden swell of love for this baby. His son. He'd never known the meaning of the word *miracle* before.

"Ben?"

He snatched his hand back as if he'd been caught doing something illicit, and quickly tugged down Emily's slip. She smiled sleepily at him, took his hand and placed it back on her belly. "I'm glad," she mumbled, turned her face into the pillow and closed her eyes.

He let out a deep breath. He gave the baby one more quick pat, stood and covered them both with a blanket. Hopefully, Emily wouldn't remember what had happened here tonight.

But in his heart, he knew *he'd* go to his grave remembering the first time he felt his child move in her body.

Maybe that was why he bent down and brushed his lips over Emily's forehead. As he left the room, he refused to admit the kiss meant anything else. He did vow, though, to be better with her, more careful. That baby was real, and was his, and he'd die before he hurt his son.

CHAPTER SEVEN

EMILY WAS WELL RESTED WHEN she and Ben rode to Cassidy Industries the following Monday morning in his Jag. She'd gotten more than enough sleep and the remainder of their weekend had been without incident. She glanced over at his face, now set in stern lines. "Anxious?" she asked him.

"Somewhat. It's been a long time since I've seen these people."

"They'll be so glad to have you back. When I worked in the building a few days a week, I overheard them talking about how they missed you. What a wonderful boss you were."

He opened his mouth to say something, but seemed to think better of it. Emily guessed the comment was a nasty one about her father, and she appreciated his effort to quell any negative remarks. They'd made a truce on Saturday night, and he'd kept his part of the bargain. He'd been unflaggingly polite Sunday, if distant.

She sighed. "Trey fell madly in love with Jack yesterday, didn't he?" They'd given Lady's last pup to Ben's friend when he'd helped Ben move in.

"He seemed to."

"I hope he doesn't miss Lady too much."

"Jack's more than ready to be away from his mama."

"Ben, I know the story behind your father from what you did at Cassidy Place. What happened to your mother?"

"She died when I was two. That's when my father hit the bottle."

"You said he was in and out of your life?"

"Yes. I'd live with foster parents for a while, then he'd come back and get me. Finally, the state had enough, and they wouldn't let me go with him anymore. Thanks to some good foster care, I grew up healthy enough. He died when I was fourteen."

"From what?"

"Malnutrition."

"I'm sorry." She thought for a minute. "Oh, now I see the connection with starting the soup kitchen in his memory."

He shot her an easy glance. "Yeah, pretty sentimental I guess. What about your mother?"

Emily sighed. "She left when I was five. Apparently she told my dad she didn't want to be a wife to him or a mother to me anymore."

Ben was silent for a moment. "Did you ever try to find her?"

"No." She moved her hand to her stomach. "Now, more than ever I wish she was in my life. I'd like support for this baby."

"Support?"

"Yeah, somebody to advise me. Reassure me. Go to childbirth classes with me."

This time, the silence lasted longer. "Well, I don't know enough to advise or reassure you—" here he cleared his throat "—but I'll go to the classes with you."

"Oh, Ben." She got teary. "I was going to ask Jordan."

He stiffened. "Go ahead then."

"No, no, I'd rather have you. I'm…touched."

His interest in the baby surprised her. She'd awakened when he'd come into her room Saturday night. She knew he'd felt the baby kick. On Sunday when she'd asked him about it, he'd shrugged it off.

They entered the parking lot and pulled into the spot marked President. Ben switched off the motor and stared at the big green building. Since it housed the manufacturing plant as well as the offices of Cassidy Industries, it wasn't terribly impressive, but Ben was looking at the place as if *it* were his child. She noticed somebody had taken down the Rockford Instruments sign and put back up Cassidy Industries.

"You going to be all right?" she asked.

"It's somewhat overwhelming."

"I bet."

He got out of the car and circled around to her side. She managed to open the door, swing her feet to the ground, but she couldn't stand. "What's wrong?" he asked.

"I, um, the car is so low, it's hard to get out."

He grabbed her hand and gently tugged her up. She winced.

"Are you in pain?"

"My back. The pressure there is uncomfortable and movements like that hurt."

"Why didn't you say something before?"

"Because I don't like to make a fuss. Besides it's my own fault I've gained so much weight."

He scanned her. She was wearing a demure navy-blue suit. "You look fine to me. What did the doctor say?"

"The same thing."

"When's your next appointment?"

"In a week."

He hesitated, then said, "I'm coming with you."

"I'd like that." She turned to the building. "Let's go in."

"I guess."

They approached the guard station. An older black man glanced up from the magazine he was reading. His weathered face wreathed with smiles. "Ben! Good to see you again. We missed you."

Emily knew an announcement had been sent out at the end of last week informing the entire staff that Ben was taking over the business again.

"Hasn't been the same without you. You know that other guy never even said hello. Unfriendly SOB."

Emily blushed. She hadn't thought about enduring negative comments about her father or being the object of people's dislike.

But when the guard recognized her, his demeanor changed. "Sorry, ma'am. Didn't know that was you." His tone said he was anything but sorry.

"Good to see you, Cecil." Ben took Emily's arm and steered her away.

They went inside, up the stairs—the factory was on the first floor—and found the administration area. The president's office was at the end of the long hallway. For a moment, Ben just stood staring down the corridor. Emily waited beside him.

"It smells the same," he said wistfully.

"Does it?"

"Hmm." He started down the hall. At the first office, he stopped. Dan, the comptroller, lounged back in a chair with his feet up on the desk and his notebook computer in his lap. "Drinking coffee and playing on the Net, I see. I'll have to report you to the new president."

Dan dropped his feet to the floor and hurried over to shake Ben's hand. "Oh, wow, am I glad to see you."

"Hello, Dan."

Emily had had to work with the comptroller on occasion. She'd tried to be nice to him, but he'd resented her and all their interactions had been strained. The frown on his face as he looked at her was testimony to how he felt. "Ms. Mackenzie."

Ben seemed startled, and then he scowled. His pique appeared to be directed at her.

Dan stepped back. "Will she be working here, Ben?"

"Yes."

"Why?"

"She'll help with the transition."

"I don't get it."

"Nothing complicated about it. She'll work for me directly. Is the staff meeting all set for ten?"

"Yeah."

"I'll explain my plans then."

They continued down the hall. At each office, Ben stopped and staff welcomed him warmly. Janice, in Human Resources, bolted out of her chair and hugged him. So did the secretaries. One had tears in her eyes.

And, though they didn't show outright animosity about her being here, like Dan had, no one spoke to Emily.

If Ben noticed, he didn't say anything. Did he know this would happen? Did he want her to work here as some kind of punishment for what her father had done? The notion made her ill.

At his office, he stopped abruptly. The assistant her father had appointed as acting president had used the space. At that time, it had been stripped of all Ben's things. Over his shoulder, Emily could see they'd been replaced.

She studied the Willie Mays montage on the left wall, a print of the exterior of Cassidy Place on another. There were a few framed photos and a poster of a Caribbean beach.

He cleared his throat and turned to the secretaries, who were just outside his office. "Wh-who did this?"

"I did." Betty, his executive assistant, stepped forward. "Your stuff was all in storage. We found some files from the takeover, too." When he said no more, she added, "I hope it's all right that we redecorated for you."

"It's wonderful." He thanked them and gave them a brilliant smile. Then he said to Emily, "There's a small office off mine. You can have it for now."

The secretaries exchanged confused looks.

"Go on inside and get settled. I'll let you know what you'll be doing at the staff meeting."

"Can I get you coffee, Ben?"

"I can get my own coffee, Betty. For now, I'd just like a few minutes alone."

Ben stepped in his office and closed the door.

Emily walked down to the next doorway. She didn't look at the women who stood guard by their leader's office. She didn't have to. She knew she'd see dislike and distrust on their faces. She didn't deserve it—she'd been nice to everybody when she'd worked here—but her father had earned both those sentiments. He'd been anything but kind. As she entered her office, she wondered how long she'd be paying for her father's sins.

"WELL, I GUESS THAT'S IT. Thanks for the warm welcome, and it's good to be back." Ben stood, signaling the end of the staff meeting.

"Are you coming to the cafeteria now?" Janice asked. "We've got a little luncheon planned."

"Sure, I'll be right down." He glanced at Emily, whose face was practically bloodless. "Ms. Mackenzie," he said with emphasis on her last name, "would you wait a minute?"

She nodded and crossed to the window while everybody else filed out. Ben knew she felt bad; he knew things had been unpleasant for her this morning. He could have stopped it all, hell he'd planned to after the guard's cold shoulder, but when Dan had called her by her maiden name, Ben had realized she'd been using it here. And that she'd purposely used Erickson at the soup kitchen. Why? Maybe she was lying after all and knew all along who he was and hid her identity. Still, he hated to see her suffer. When the others had gone, he said, "You're upset."

She stared out the window to the parking lot below.

"Mostly I just feel bad. They see me as a representative of my father. He stole the company from their obviously beloved founder and fired a lot of people. And he wasn't very nice to those who were left."

"Were you?"

She turned, her face flushed. "Of course I was."

He'd known the answer to that. He'd watched her for a year with guests at Cassidy Place. She didn't seem to have a mean bone in her body. If she had indeed tricked him, it wasn't out of malice, but out of love and loyalty to Daddy. Once again that infuriated him.

"You go by Mackenzie."

"What?"

"Dan called you Ms. Mackenzie. Why did you use that name here, and Erickson at the soup kitchen, if you weren't trying to trick me?"

Anger sparked in her eyes. He preferred that over having her feel bad. "My father wanted me to use Mackenzie in the business."

"Why didn't you use it at Cassidy Place?"

"Because I didn't want the people *there* to know I was part of the organization that tried to close them down."

Sounded reasonable.

"You don't believe me."

"I'm not sure. But we've decided not to go there, remember?"

I'll try to be nicer... Don't mention your father to

*me anymore, and I won't bring up what's between us.
We'll try to peacefully coexist.*

"Yes, I remember."

"Fine. Let's go to lunch, shall we?"

She shook her head and placed her hand on the baby.
"I'll bow out, if you don't mind. My stomach's queasy."

"Then you need to eat. Besides, it'll be worse for
you if you hide in your office."

Her pretty eyes narrowed on him. "Are you sure you
don't just want to see them treat me like a leper?"

He *was* sure of that. He was taking no pleasure in
watching his staff treat her as if she weren't there. "No.
I think it's best for you."

Reluctantly, she headed to the cafeteria with him.
There was no executive dining hall. Ben had routinely
eaten with the factory workers. He wanted his administration to bump elbows with the employees, too.

Absently, he noted the offices they passed were
empty and, when they reached the first floor, the factory seemed quiet. Still, he was shocked when he
reached the doorway of the cafeteria and found the entire workforce of Cassidy Industries inside, on their
feet, smiling. They clapped when they saw him. He was
so stunned, he grabbed onto Emily's arm. Gently, she
squeezed his hand. "Oh, Ben, this is so sweet," she
whispered, leaning close to his ear to be heard.

He stood frozen.

When the applause finally died down, Jim Macy, the

foreman of the plant, spoke into a microphone. "Come on in, Ben. We're glad to see you."

At Emily's slight nudge, he entered the room. It was too small for everybody to eat together; people were now standing wall-to-wall. Behind them hung a banner. It read *Welcome Back, Ben.*

Jim spoke again. "We wanted to give you a proper welcome today. We're all getting back to work in a few minutes, but before that, we've got some people who especially wanna say, 'It's good to see you.'"

He handed the mike to a worker whose husband had died of cancer three years ago. She was a big woman and sassy as hell. "I sure you missed you, boss. I'll never forget how you gave me those last three weeks off with pay before my Harry died. At least I could give him a proper send-off." She passed the mike.

"Me, too, Ben. So glad to see you. Dolores isn't the only one you gave time off to for family illness. When my mother died, you let me have a week with pay."

Macy gestured to the crowd. Several among them shouted out, "I got four days when my daughter was sick... Two days when...."

Ben shook his head as he listened. His heart was full in a way it hadn't been for a long time. Though he was embarrassed, he kept smiling through all the comments.

From the people he'd visited in the hospital when they'd been sick...from the employees who'd suffered a death in the family and Ben had gone to their funerals...from the man whose house burned down and Ben had had the HR department organize a fund-raiser and donations. He himself had bought kitchen appliances for the guy. The accolades went on a long time.

The foreman handed the mike to him at the end of the remarks. "Well, that's quite a welcome. I don't know what to say except thank you and it's really good to be back. This place has always been like my family and I appreciate your good wishes." He glanced to the tables. "Let's have some of those desserts over there before you get back to work."

The employees began milling around and coming up to Ben for a hug or a handshake. It was heartwarming...except that he saw what was happening to Emily. People shot her angry looks, murmuring things he could hear, and so could she. It didn't seem right that Ben should feel so much affection from the group while Emily was the object of their contempt. He believed her when she said she'd done nothing to earn this treatment—except for being the offspring of Mackenzie. So, when the party was ready to break up, he went back to the podium. "Could I have everybody's attention for a minute, before you leave?" he said into the mike.

He nodded to his wife. "Emily, could you come up here?"

Pure, undiluted fear crossed her face. Hell, what did

she think he was going to do? Embarrass her further? Her expression said, *Please don't,* as she reached him.

He took her hand and squeezed it, saying only to her, "Easy now," and faced the crowd. "I realize you all know who this is. And there are hard feelings among you toward her. But you don't know the whole story behind what happened—" hell, neither did he "—and I'm sure Emily was always kind to you."

His staff's sheepish looks and exchanged glances told him that was true.

"In any case, I'd like you to take it easy on her. And—" here he smiled "—accept her, because last Saturday, she became my wife." He slid an arm around her shoulders and she leaned into him. He patted her stomach. "This is my son she's carrying."

The shocked expressions on the faces of his employees were accompanied by absolute silence. Ben broke it by saying, "You can go back to work now. And thanks again for the welcome."

People filed out.

Ben stood by as they left, spoke to each person, but kept Emily close to his side. When the place had emptied out, except for those whose shift it was to eat, he nodded to the table set up for him and his staff. "So, are you hungry now?"

She stared at him with gratitude and something else. "Yes, I am." She touched his arm. "Thank you, Ben."

"You're welcome." He leaned over. "Despite what's

between us, you didn't deserve that." Then he pulled back. "Besides, it isn't good for the baby."

He thought he saw disappointment flicker over her lovely features. Hell, what did she want? A declaration of love or something? *That* wasn't going to happen. Though he didn't intend to let anybody be mean to her, he still didn't trust her.

And never would.

THE RED DIAL ON THE CLOCK clicked 1:00 a.m. Swearing, Mac slipped out of bed, leaving Tami, a woman younger than his daughter, asleep on his king-size mattress. He'd had insomnia since last week. It wasn't the loss of the company that bothered him. That happened all the time in business. Some strategies didn't pan out, though after two years without repercussions, he'd believed he was home free from his…maneuvers to get the company. No, Mac's sleeplessness was caused by the fact that Cassidy was the father of Emily's child. Mac had tried like hell to get her to reveal the paternity four months ago when she'd told him she was going to have a baby. She'd refused—she could be a pit bull under that marshmallow exterior—and she'd been so happy about finally being pregnant, Mac had decided he could live without knowing. He'd thought she'd probably gotten together with Paul; it happened all the time in divorces. But no, Cassidy had seduced her to get back at Mac. Someday, he'd make the guy pay for using his only child.

Mac made his way to his first-floor den, scrounged the Marlboros out of his desk and lit up. It was a dirty habit he'd kicked more than once. He sat in his plush leather chair and watched the smoke curl into the darkness. *Please darling, quit. I hate to think of you endangering your health like this. I want to grow old with you.* Well, Anna had reneged on her part of the bargain, so why should he have kept his?

Emily had gotten him to quit once, too. He clenched his fist at the thought of his precious daughter married to Cassidy. How did the man know that Mac loved her more than anything else in the world? So much so she would probably have been able to keep him from using…spurious means to get Cassidy Industries. If she'd been home. If she'd known.

And while she'd been gone, he'd done his thing. The thing that he was good at. He'd been a lousy husband, a mediocre father, but he was at the top of his game as a businessman. Sure, he'd exerted his influence over Rockford Gas & Electric. Hell, it was the way things were done. If somebody cried fraud every time a guy used his connections to get a bid or a contract, the courts would be full. Logic told Mac that Cassidy wouldn't go that far with his threat, and the case probably would have been thrown out since there was no hard and fast proof that he'd bought the condo and car for his buddy Al. Mac certainly could have withstood the blow to his reputation—he was the most feared, and respected, businessman in the community. He was a shark and everybody knew it. People were afraid of getting eaten up by the big fish, so they didn't mess with him.

No, he thought, stubbing out the smoke, it wasn't either of those two things that had him up tonight. It was what *else* Cassidy might uncover if he and his hotshot lawyer kept digging that had made Mac acquiesce so fast. Not only could Mac be charged criminally, but Emily would find out what he'd done and that, Mac thought, wouldn't do at all.

CHAPTER EIGHT

EMILY WAS THE SALAD GIRL tonight at the soup kitchen. She filled and refilled the bowls on each of the twenty tables, and pitched in when the servers needed a plate fetched or a place set. Since she'd arrived, the workers had been abuzz with talk of Benedict Cassidy resuming the helm of Cassidy Industries and what effect it might have on the operation. Emily had shared nothing with them about Ben—not who he was, not her connection to him.

"Here you go, Franny," she said to the small guest with the red hair and sad eyes. "Eat as much as you can, it'll be good for the baby."

Franny smiled. "How you feeling, Miss Emily?"

"Terrific." Physically, anyway. "You?"

"Tired."

Emily gave the woman's shoulder a squeeze then took the empty salad bowl back to the kitchen and set it on the counter. "I need more, Christine," she told the woman who mixed the greens.

Christine chatted as she added cheesy dressing to the

lettuce. When she finished, she looked up and frowned. "Where's the cart?"

"It's out on the floor."

"You're not carrying this big bowl, girl." She peered over the rim of her glasses into the room. "Howard," she called out, "take this to the floor for Emily, would you?"

Howard beamed. "Of course." He came over. "How's the baby?"

"Getting big."

Ever since they'd found out she was pregnant, people at the soup kitchen had been fawning over her. She allowed the pampering and appreciated the sentiments, even though coddling wasn't necessary. Emily was in good shape from dancing and could easily lift an aluminum bowl full of salad.

Back on the floor, she refilled the smaller containers on the tables until Alice told her to get off her feet.

"I'm fine, Alice."

"For a bit."

"Keep me company?"

They took stools at the side counter. Alice scanned the area. "It's just not the same, is it?"

"What?"

"Without Ben around."

"No, it's not."

"I miss him."

"I do, too." She truly missed having *that* Ben in her life. As reticent as he'd been here, he was even more cold and remote at home. And when he'd been at the soup kitchen, he hadn't looked at her as if she'd betrayed him.

"Wonder what happened to him." Alice folded some napkins while they talked. "That pretty Hanson woman asks me about him all the time."

Emily shrugged. "Maybe he fell on better times."

"*You* don't seem too concerned. Especially since there was a soft spot for him in your heart."

Emily longed to tell Alice the truth. At first, she'd been embarrassed by what had happened between her and Ben, so she hadn't said anything. Then when she'd found out she was pregnant, she was at a loss what to do. Last week, she'd asked Ben when he planned to tell people here who he was. He'd said he'd deal with Cassidy Place and she should stay out of it. So she'd taken off her week-old wedding band before she'd arrived tonight, but kept it on a chain around her neck. Close to her heart. She sighed, wondering if she and Ben would ever have a real marriage.

"What is it, Emily?"

"Um...I was just thinking about my job." Well, he was part of her job.

"You don't talk much about it. You work for your father, don't you?"

"I did. I just got new position. I don't know anyone there, and it's lonely."

Alice laughed. "Don't fret. You'll have everybody

in the office eating out of your hand in no time." She pointed out a guest holding up an empty salad bowl. "Looks like you're needed. Want me to do it?"

"No, I'll go."

As she refilled more bowls, Emily thought about Alice's reassurances—and how wrong the woman was. Emily would never fit in at Cassidy Industries. Everyone was polite to her; but no one sat with her at lunch, no one asked about the baby, no one really talked to her. And she missed her father, too. She'd had a quick lunch with him once, and been over to his house for a few hours on an evening when Ben was out. Combined with Ben's absence from home most nights, and his detachment when he was there, Emily was lonelier than she'd ever been in her life.

After the soup kitchen, she headed for dance class. The exercise felt good, though she could no longer do some of the jumps. "Hey, Em," Jordan said after class. "I watched you after I finally arrived. Your balance all right?"

"No, it's off." She wiped her face with a towel. "I'm going to have to slow down here, I think."

"Maybe you should quit."

"I can't, Jordan. It's the only thing I have left besides the baby. And I get to see you here."

"Not after this week." At Emily's puzzled expression, she said, "I've got the studio space. I can practice there until I open."

"Oh, I forgot."

Emily had lost track of when Jordan would take possession. Or maybe she just didn't want to know because she wished so much she were part of the venture and it hurt to see Jordan proceed without her.

"It's not too late to come in on it with me, Em. You said you don't have much work to do at Cassidy Industries."

"Ben wants me there."

"Yeah, well I don't care one bit about what Ben wants." Jordan slipped into sweats and other shoes as she talked. "Those two are a pair."

"Who?"

"Cassidy and his lawyer."

Emily wiped her brow and then brushed out her hair. "Trey seemed nice to me."

"Well, in case you didn't notice, we were at odds. When he took me home after that mockery of a wedding, we had a real row."

"I'm sorry you had to go through all that."

Jordan smiled. "It's okay. It was kind of fun tangling with him."

God, she missed Jordan. "Want to come over for a drink?"

"Won't Mr. I'm-in-Charge be there? I'm not his favorite person."

She glanced at the clock. "It's only nine. He rarely comes in before ten."

Jordan cocked her head. "Emily, why are you letting him dictate everything? You said you care about him, and wanted to marry him, but I don't really get it. How can you even *like* him?"

"He's been hurt, Jordan. Betrayed and tricked. And he's wary."

"You're trying to win him over?"

"Maybe. All I know is that I do care about him. I wouldn't have slept with him if I didn't." She smiled sadly. "Now how about that drink?"

When they arrived at her house, Lady was waiting in the kitchen and jumped up on Emily. "Hey, girl, how are you?" She tugged the dog's collar. "I'm going to put her on the porch so she can go outside."

"I'll get the wine," Jordan said. "Oh, I forgot, what are you having?"

"There's sparkling grape juice in there." She rubbed her stomach. "We like it."

Later, in the great room, with Lady sleeping on the floor, Emily had relaxed back into the pillows, her feet on the table, sipping the juice, as she listened to Jordan talk about the dance studio, when she heard Ben at the front door. She glanced at her watch. He was earlier than usual.

"Hi, Ben," she said as he came to the doorway.

"Hi." He glanced from her to her friend. "Jordan."

"Ben."

His eyes focused on Jordan's merlot and the bottle

of wine she'd brought in from the kitchen. "What the hell do you think you're doing?"

"Excuse me?"

He strode to Emily and snatched the glass out of her hand. Some spilled on her dance skirt. "It's bad enough you're still taking dance classes. Now you're drinking wine? Don't you care what happens to the baby?"

Her eyes widened. "Of course I do. That," she said nodding to the glass, "is grape juice." She brushed at her skirt. "And the doctor said I can dance a while longer. I know when to quit."

For a moment he stared at her. Then he turned and stalked out of the room.

BEN SHUT THE DOOR to his bedroom, leaned against it and closed his eyes. He was such a jerk. He'd accused Emily of something she hadn't even done. And he was afraid he knew why.

As he headed for the shower, he admitted to himself what was happening in their relationship. He was beginning to feel things for her again, intensely, so he'd been trying to distance himself. At work he'd given her assignments that wouldn't include him. At night, he'd exhaust himself at the gym, maybe have dinner with Trey, and come home late, hoping she was in bed. He'd thought avoiding her would make him worry less about her and the baby. Instead, he worried more. But he had to stay away from her. Every time she did something nice for him, every time she was kind to him....

Shedding his clothes and turning the water to cold, he stepped into the stall, braced his hands on the tile and ordered himself not to think about her. But he couldn't help it—he wished she were under the spray with him. He thought about her like that, about sex, or the lack of it, way too much. Being in such close proximity made him nearly desperate to have her. Smelling her perfume in the hall, seeing the lotion in the downstairs bathroom and remembering the taste of it on her skin, the glimpses he caught of her still-shapely legs....

Maybe he should go to someone else. He and Emily hadn't discussed fidelity, though he was pretty sure she wouldn't feel like sleeping with another guy when she was six months pregnant. Still, he could have sex with another woman. Mallory had called him three times, and he'd finally agreed to see her next week.

Who was he kidding? He knew he wouldn't sleep with Mallory. The thought of being with another woman left him as cold as the water in the shower. He didn't want Mallory or any other woman in his bed. He wanted his wife. A wife who, just a few days ago, had said she wanted him there, too. That made him crazy.

He toweled off and dressed in sweats. Out the window, he could see that Jordan's car was still there. She was probably consoling Emily, advising her to get as far away from Ben as she could. What if Emily listened to her?

That possibility drove him from the bedroom to the first floor. Sure enough, he found Emily with her head resting on her arms on the back of the couch, and Jordan smoothing her hair. Emily looked incredibly sad. He heard her friend say, "Maybe it's time to rethink staying with him, honey."

Because Ben was afraid she was going to do just that, he made his presence known. He raked a hand through his wet hair and addressed Emily. "I'm sorry I overreacted about the wine. I should have known better than to think you'd do something to hurt the baby." Then to Jordan he added, "I know you don't like me. Hell, I wouldn't like me if I were her best friend. I've been trying to make this easier on Emily since our wedding, but I messed up tonight. I apologize to you, too." He looked at his wife. "Once again, I'll try to be better."

Emily said, "Ben...."

Jordan lifted her chin. "Apology accepted. Just do it right from now on."

Ben bit back a grin at the motherly warning. He was absurdly glad Emily had such a staunch advocate in her life.

Jordan stood. "I'll be going." She found her shoes, leaned over and kissed Emily on the cheek. "I'll see you soon." As she passed Ben, she glowered at him. "Remember what you said, Cassidy."

"I will."

And then they were alone.

He leaned against the doorjamb. "I am sorry."

"I know." Her expression was serene. "You've had a tough week, with everything that's happened. Your stress level has to have skyrocketed."

"I have. But it's no excuse for yelling at *you.*"

She smiled and patted the cushion beside her. "Come sit." She nodded to the bottle on the coffee table. "Want some wine? I'll get you a glass."

He stared at the ruby liquid, remembering when alcohol had been his sole source of comfort. God, he never wanted to be that kind of man again. "I, um, don't drink, Emily."

"I didn't know that. Why?"

Leaning back into the couch, he stared straight ahead. "Because when I lost my company, I lost *myself* in alcohol for almost a year."

"Oh, Ben." She touched his hand. "I never knew."

He didn't look at her. "Once I realized I'd become just like my father, I sobered up. I haven't had a drink since." He glanced at her. "I started going to Cassidy Place because it was the one tangible thing left that was testimony to the good I'd accomplished. It helped keep me sober."

"I admire your strength. Not everybody can bite that particular bullet."

"That's obvious with all those people who come to the soup kitchen."

She smiled again. "They miss you there."

His head snapped toward her. "You don't still volunteer, do you?"

"Of course I do. Why?"

"You shouldn't be on your feet after working all day."

She just stared at him.

He ducked his head. "I guess I'm overreacting again."

Rubbing her belly, she said, "In another month or so, I'll quit the soup kitchen and dancing, too."

"All right. As you said, you know what's best for you."

"Thank you for acknowledging that."

She was something else. Forgiving. Sweet. Sensible, too.

It made him want her more. Sitting here in the great room, talking intimately about his past, wasn't helping his need to distance her, either. "I'll clean up in here. Why don't you go on to bed?"

She gestured to the table. "You don't have to take care of our mess."

"I want to. It'll make me feel better after behaving like an ass."

"All right." She stood. "This will work out. There are bound to be rough spots. We'll find a way to live together."

He looked at her stomach. "We will. For him."

"Maybe for us, too." She kissed his cheek. "Think about that." And then she was gone.

"HERE'S THE REST OF THE FILES on the takeover. These deal with your patent." Betty dropped several more folders on his desk. They'd been kept in storage with his things, accidentally Ben guessed, and he'd been elated when they found them. "Can I ask you a question?"

He smiled at her. She'd worked for him for years and mothered him. "Of course."

"Why are you doing this?" She nodded to the files. "It's all water under the dam, isn't it?"

Leaning back, he shook his head. "Not quite. I want to know exactly what we did wrong so that we can preclude another takeover."

"Makes sense." She crossed her arms. "He played dirty, didn't he?"

"I can't divulge that, Betty."

"You don't have to. It's all over the company that he used fraudulent means to get Cassidy Industries." Glancing to the small office that shared a door with his, she added, "And people believe she helped him."

"She didn't help him. She was having some personal problems and wasn't working for him then. Actually she was out of the country most of the time."

Betty sighed. "Be careful, Ben. You know the adage, 'Fool me once....' Ms. Mackenzie could be more trouble. Too bad you got...in this situation."

"Don't bad-mouth her, please. You don't know everything."

"Do you?"

"What do you mean?"

"Right now she's having lunch with her father."

Damn it. "How do you know that?"

"I overheard her on the phone with good old Daddy."

He didn't respond. They'd agreed that she could see Mackenzie, but he hated the thought of her with the man. Just when he thought he'd overcome the suspicion, she spent time with her father, and it returned.

Since Monday night after her dance class, and the fool he'd made of himself, they'd gotten along well. He'd come home for dinner a couple of nights, and they'd watched some TV like normal people. Though he didn't let himself touch her, he felt more at ease and closer to her.

Not good, he guessed.

As soon as Betty left, Dan stuck his head in. "Want to have lunch before we meet today?"

"Sounds good. I'm free." He rose and left the office, wondering where his wife was eating.

He got back to the files about two. Ben didn't know precisely what he was looking for, except that he did want to make sure he knew all that Mackenzie had done to get the company away from him. Carefully, he read every detail of every page in the patent folders. The only thing that distracted him was the open door to Emily's office; she wasn't back yet. What were she and her father talking about? Was Mackenzie plotting something with her? More likely he was trying to get her away from Ben. If not physically, emotionally. Hell, Ben hated the thought of that.

As he studied the patent information, he remembered the breakthrough he'd had with the fuel-cell technology, remembered the zing he'd gotten when he'd realized he'd created something unique in the field. Usually, a new product was either in the development stage or completed before the patent came through, which was what had happened in this case. So, when Mackenzie had swindled him out of the company, he'd gotten the patent when it had been finally awarded. Ben wondered when that had been. At the time he'd left, the patent had been still pending.

Something had always bothered him about this whole thing, and now, with a clear head not muddled by the loss of his company, he spent a full hour going over the file.

Two things caught his eye. First, the patent had been awarded to Cassidy Industries one week after Mackenzie had taken over.

Second was something Mackenzie had added to the file—a list of people's names. Ben checked the header. Employees of U.S. Patent Office. Four names were circled. He found the date—the list had been made right after Mackenzie had become an investor.

Ben's heartbeat raced.

He'd called the patent office several times. At first

he'd heard, "Yes, Mr. Cassidy. Your patent shouldn't take too long. Easily within six months." On a second call: "No, everything's fine. Just the usual delays." Three, four and five calls later, Ben had had Trey take over. Apparently there'd been a patent dispute over a similar product, so Ben's application had been delayed.

Hmm. Ben had researched patents before he'd sent in his application. There had been none on record for this kind of product. Trey had hounded the patent office to get the names of who'd submitted a similar request, but was told that would remain confidential until the patent was awarded. It didn't sound at all odd at the time; they'd put their faith in the government representative. Now he went on the Net again and clicked into the U.S. government patent Web site to search for patents filed, given and denied. He spent a half hour, looking for one like his.

It wasn't there. Son of a bitch. Someone in the patent office had lied. Why would that be? *Hell,* he told himself, *take a wild guess.*

EMILY HURRIED DOWN THE HALL to her office, later than she'd wanted to get back. Though she was doing so little at Cassidy Industries, no one would miss her.

Her dad had been in a bad mood. He'd criticized her about her marriage, about her working here and about spending time with Ben. Trying to placate him hadn't worked. So finally she'd confronted it head-on.

I care about him, Dad. A lot.

I don't believe that.

I wouldn't have married him if I didn't. I wouldn't have slept with him six months ago if I hadn't.

She smiled, thinking how her dad had blushed. Sex was not something he felt comfortable discussing with her. Though to give him credit, when she'd been a teenager, he'd had "the talk" with her about her period and about sex. He'd truly been a good father in many ways.

Ben's door was closed, so she entered her office from the hallway. The adjoining door was open, though. From there, she studied him. Bent over some papers, he worked furiously making notes. His computer was on and occasionally he glanced toward it. Today he wore a beautiful heather-gray suit and striped tie. She knew what lay under those clothes—muscles and hard planes—and drew in a deep breath, remembering.

He must have heard it because his head came up quickly. For a moment, he looked glad to see her.

"Hi."

"Hello, Emily." He glanced at his watch. "Long lunch."

She cocked her head.

He leaned back in his chair. "How's Daddy?"

Ah, so he knew. Well, she had no intention of hiding her visits with her father. "As well as can be expected."

"You must have had a lot to talk about."

"He did." As she came into the room, she noticed he closed the folder he was working on and minimized the computer screen. "Are you upset that I was gone so long?"

"As a boss, I might be."

"You know very well I don't have enough to do here. I've been meaning to talk to you about that."

"Don't you? I'll have to remedy that so you don't waste your workday off with your father."

She shook her head. Three steps forward, two back. "Well, if you're going to ream me out, do it now since I'll be leaving again in an hour."

"What for?"

"A doctor's appointment at four."

He frowned. She loved his face. His brows were dark and thick. His mouth firm. And his jaw was so angular. He called up the calendar on his computer. "There's no appointment on here."

"Really? I told Betty to put it down for today." She smiled. "It's a prenatal appointment."

He rose from the desk and crossed to open his door. "Betty, could you come in here?"

Betty entered, smiling. When she saw Emily, her smile died.

"Did Emily tell you to put an appointment on my calendar for this week?"

The older woman reddened. Emily had heard stories about her attachment to Ben.

"I—"

Emily interrupted. "Look, maybe I was wrong. I gave Betty a few dates, and I might have missed this one."

Betty looked to Emily, then to Ben, and didn't say more.

Ben's gaze narrowed. "All right, you can go back to work." When she left, he faced Emily. "What's going on?"

"Nothing, she probably missed this date."

"I can deal with my own staff, Emily. You don't have to protect them from me."

"Of course I don't." She squeezed his arm. "It's going to take her a while to accept me. I'm working on her."

He stared at her a long time. "All right." He glanced at his watch. "I have something I want to finish up, but we'll leave in plenty of time."

Emily went back to her office, but didn't close the door to his. She opened her e-mail, glad to see Janice had sent her something to do. She downloaded the attachment and became entrenched with the benefits program. God, it felt good to work again. Almost normal.

She heard the click of Ben's keys on the computer. Heard his cell phone ring. A pause. "Hello, Mallory." Another pause. A very male chuckle.

Mallory. Who was Mallory?

Emily wasn't going to find out, though, because just then, the door between their offices closed.

"WELL, IT'S NICE to finally meet you." Joan Davidson, the ob-gyn, assessed Ben shrewdly when he entered the exam room with Emily. A nurse hovered in the background.

Emily and Ben had chatted on the way over about what would happen during the appointment—usually just a tummy check without a pelvic exam at six months. He seemed excited about the whole experience, so much so, he missed the underlying criticism in Joan's tone. The doctor hadn't been happy that the baby's father wasn't in the picture all these months.

Neither was Emily. She'd wanted Ben at these visits every time, and now he was! She vowed to be happy with what she had. Keeping the status quo was one of the reasons she didn't bring up this Mallory person who'd called Ben earlier.

"It's nice to meet you too, Dr. Davidson." Ben's smile was genuine. "I wish I'd been here from the start."

Joan glanced at Emily. "Well, let's see what's going on with the little guy today. Does he have a name yet?"

She smiled. "No. I'm going to let Ben name him."

Shock suffused Ben's face, soon replaced by a look so profound it warmed her. "No kidding?"

"No kidding."

"Scoot down on the table." Emily stretched out and Joan raised her shirt. Ben's eyes focused on her stomach. She wished he'd hold her hand, touch her, but he just stood over her. A bit awestruck, she guessed.

Joan felt her abdomen. She cocked her head, felt some more. "Hmm." She took out the Doppler probe.

"What's that?" Ben asked.

"A device to hear the baby's heartbeat."

She placed the probe on Emily's stomach. After a few adjustments they heard a steady, impossibly fast thump, thump, thump, thump.

"Oh, wow!" Ben's eyes were huge. So was his grin. "The heartbeat's so fast."

"*That's* normal." Joan continued to examine her.

"Is something wrong?" Emily asked.

"Not wrong exactly. You've just gotten really big in a month."

Emily blushed. "I gained seven pounds."

"Well, you could use that. I didn't like your weight loss initially."

"Weight loss?" Ben asked.

"Yes, Emily was run down when she first came to me." She gave him another displeased look. "And stressed. I'm glad to see she's happier these days." She checked Emily's chart. "In any case, I think we'll do another sonogram. The baby's bigger than expected at this point."

Without thinking, Emily reached for Ben's hand.

He took it and held hers tightly. "Is...is that a problem?" she asked.

"Only if he gets too big for you to deliver vaginally. Or if he comes early."

Myriad emotions crossed Ben's face. "Could there be confusion about the due date?"

Joan's eyes narrowed on him; she was getting odd vibes. Then she turned her attention to the chart. "No, we did a sonogram in the first trimester, and the due date is January 10. We estimate the date of conception to be mid-April." Joan pulled down Emily's shirt. "Okay, sit up, Emily. Here's what we do. You'll go next door for the test." The doctor nodded to the nurse. "Patty, take Emily over. Make her comfortable. I'll do the procedure myself." She glanced at Ben. "You wait here, until she's ready."

Ben knew when the door closed behind Emily and the nurse that he was in for a grilling. In some way, he was glad, as with Jordan, that Emily had a doctor who went the extra mile.

"Mr. Cassidy, I don't know what's going on here, Emily never would tell me. But I want some assurances that the initial stress she was under isn't going to return. It seems to me things are strained between you two. It's mostly your business, but becomes mine when it affects the baby."

Ben folded his arms across his chest. "This has been complicated. I just found out she was pregnant. We

were married as soon as we had the DNA tests done."
At her questioning look, he said, "I wanted to make
sure this was my baby."

He didn't expect the doctor's laughter. "You honestly think Emily would lie about it?"

"No, actually, I don't." He didn't know how true that
was until he said it. "I just needed to know for sure."

"You want him to be yours, don't you?"

"Of course I do." He felt a swell of pride and posses-
siveness so strong it shocked him. "I want my son."

"Good. I hope you value Emily as much. She's the
kindest, most honest, unselfish person I've ever met."

He just stared at her.

"Now here's the deal. It's your responsibility to
make sure the end of this pregnancy is as easy as possible for her."

"Well, she insists on working, taking dance and
volunteering."

"I don't mean physically, though we'll talk today
about curtailing a bit of that. I mean emotionally." She
leaned back against the counter. "You're aware that the
psychological state of the mother affects the well-being
of the baby, aren't you?"

"Yes."

"Then let's keep both of them happy."

"I'll do my best, Dr. Davidson."

She headed for the door but called out over her
shoulder, "And sex is okay until I say so."

Hell, he didn't need to hear that.

The ultrasound room was cold. Emily lay on a table, stretched out again. There was a monitor with some sort of instrument attached to it at her head, a technician standing by.

Dr. Davidson explained the procedure as she slipped on new gloves. "A sonogram is noninvasive, Ben. It directs sound waves to the fetus. It's harmless and uses no radiation. On the screen you'll be able to see your son." Lifting Emily's shirt, the doctor squeezed gel on her very rounded stomach. Emily squealed, and Ben grabbed for her hand.

"What is it?" he asked.

She chuckled. "The gel's cold. I'm okay." But she didn't let go of his hand, which made him happy.

"This is a transducer. It'll give us a picture of this little guy."

Slowly the doctor ran the probe over Emily's belly. "Look, Ben."

He stared at the monitor. At first it seemed like a snowy TV screen. Then he saw movement. A shape began to crystallize. It took him a few moments to make out the form. A head. A butt. Something beat at a clip. "This is the heart." It seemed like the doctor was speaking from a distance. "This is the head." She chuckled. "And this is his very definite penis."

Ben watched the screen.

He swallowed hard, gripping Emily's hand.

When moisture clouded his eyes, he tried to look away but he couldn't. This was his son. His child. A baby created by him and the woman who lay before him. He was so humbled by it, so in awe, he couldn't speak.

"He's big," Dr. Davidson finally said.

That brought him to reality. "Wh—" He cleared his throat. "What does that mean?"

"That we'll have to keep good tabs on Emily. She's small in the pelvic area, and if he grows too much, we'll have to do a C-section."

Alarmed, Ben said, "That's serious, isn't it?"

"Any major surgery is serious. But the procedure is less dangerous than it was even five years ago. You still get to be there, Dad, and the recuperation doesn't take as long as it used to."

"Oh."

Emily squeezed his hand. "Ben, it's all right. Nothing's going to go wrong with me or the baby."

"The other thing is he could come early. But he's developing fine, so I'm not buying trouble at this point."

Ben couldn't stop staring at Emily as the doctor cleaned off her stomach and helped her sit. She was radiant, beautiful. And in that instant, Ben was very afraid he was falling in love with her.

On their way to the car, holding hands, pictures of the sonogram tucked into Emily's purse, she suddenly asked, "What is it, Ben?"

He loosened his tight grip on her hand. "Nothing. I'm a bit shell-shocked is all."

He was shell-shocked, all right. Ben had been hit by the realization that if he pursued what he suspected to be true about Mackenzie's actions concerning the patent, that he wouldn't only be destroying Emily's father, but his little boy's grandfather.

CHAPTER NINE

THE WEEK HAD BEEN such absolute torture for Ben, he'd agreed to dinner with Mallory. Primarily because he was afraid to spend this Friday night alone with his own wife. She'd gotten to him. Plain and simple. And totally unacceptable.

Ben took the picture of the sonogram out of his desk and stared at it like a sap. He and Emily had gone to dinner that night to celebrate. Emily had been so tickled he'd taken her out, he was ashamed of not having done it since the wedding.

Her reaction to a simple supper out showed he'd been neglectful and though she never complained, seeing her so happy made him wish he were the man he'd been before Mackenzie had come into his life. That man would have spoiled her, cherished her, done anything in his power to put a smile on her face. Ben was beginning to hate Mackenzie more for making him so cold-hearted than for taking over Cassidy Industries.

Ben had been further knocked off balance this week

by Dr. Davidson's comment about sex. "Don't even think about *that*," he told himself in the bathroom mirror of his office, where he was changing, "or you'll go crazy." Adjusting his tie, he switched off the light and crossed to his desk. He stopped and stared at the folders he'd been working on.

Maybe if he hadn't gotten wind of the possible patent irregularities, he wouldn't be trying so hard to distance Emily. But he'd hired Trey's private investigator to check into the names circled on the list, and he hoped to get information soon that could very well put Mackenzie in jail. How could Ben let himself make love to Emily and plan a future with her when he was aggressively pursuing information to put her father behind bars?

The intercom buzzed and Betty's voice broke into his wandering thoughts. "Ben, Mallory Kemp is here to see you."

"Be right there." Time to face the music and let Mallory know he was off the market. He strode to the door and opened it. His first glimpse was of Betty, who gave him a disapproving look. Hell, she didn't even like Emily, though he knew his wife had been patient with her snubs and had even asked Betty's advice about pregnancy concerns. Damn, it seemed like everybody was getting sucked in by his wife.

Mallory was right behind Betty. "Hello, darling."

"Mallory, you look wonderful." And she did. She

was tall, model-thin and wore a classic black-and-white suit. Her hair was shorter than the last time he'd seen her. It was thick and glossy and as black as night. Had he really, once, found that slick look attractive?

"Come on in. I'm just finishing up." He said to Betty, "You can leave any time."

Betty scowled. "I've got a few things to clean up on my desk." She added pointedly, "Emily gone for the night?"

"Yes, she's meeting her *father* for dinner."

"Who's Emily?" Mallory asked as they went into his office. He thought about leaving the door ajar. Mallory could be naughty anywhere, anytime when she wanted something. And he was pretty sure she wanted *him*. She, however, closed it, cocooning them in what now seemed a claustrophobic space.

He strode to the sideboard and poured her a drink. The stinging smell of scotch no longer tempted him. Handing her the glass, he leaned against the edge of his desk and stretched out his legs. "There's something you need to know and I wanted to break the news to you in private." He drew in a breath. "I married Emily Mackenzie two weeks ago."

Her pretty face flushed. Her big blue eyes widened and she frowned. "Married? You…wait, did you say Mackenzie?"

"Yes."

"As in Lammon Mackenzie's daughter?"

"Uh-huh. And there's something else. She's pregnant with my child."

"Ah, I see." She set down her drink. Before he could stop her, she moved to stand between his spread legs. He was forced to widen his stance.

"Poor Benedict. Always the good guy. You got her pregnant and felt you had to marry her, despite the fact that she's related to your worst enemy. Or maybe because of that." Placing her hands on his shoulders, she leaned into him. Her perfume was cloying. He wanted to shrink from her touch. "Someday, I'd like to hear the whole story. But right now, just tell me, how long is this marriage of convenience going to last? Until the kid's born?"

The kid. Jeez. He remembered the living, breathing, heart-pounding miracle he'd seen in the sonogram just a week ago today. "I'm not sure."

"Well, none of this means we can't pick up where we left off."

His hands went to her waist to set her away. "Wait, I—"

Both he and Mallory heard a gasp and looked up. His wife stood in the connecting doorway of their offices, her hands splayed protectively over her stomach.

The expression on her face told Ben he'd just made a very big mistake.

EMILY STARED AT THE COOL, sophisticated woman who'd been fondling her husband. Their position was so intimate, so sexy, it silenced her. She couldn't believe Ben was having an affair.

Where the hell do you think he's been all those nights he was out?

Oh, God. What a fool she'd been.

She swallowed back the emotion crowding her throat. She'd be damned if she'd cry in front of them. "Well, I guess I won't worry that you don't have anything to do tonight."

His face blanked, and the cold, remote Ben reappeared. "I thought you were having dinner with your father."

Is that why he was doing this? "I am. I came back to get the picture of... Never mind." She summoned her most scathing look. "Perhaps it's just as well I returned. Otherwise, I wouldn't know I'd married a liar and a cheat." Turning abruptly, she hurried out of her office.

And bumped right into Betty in the corridor.

Betty steadied her. "Are you all right?"

She couldn't deal with the secretary's gloating.

She glanced toward Ben's closed door, shook her head and stumbled down the hall to the ladies' room. Once inside, she braced her back against the wall and covered her face with her hands. Damn it. Damn it. Damn it. She'd been so sure she and Ben had turned a corner after they'd seen the sonogram. Ben hadn't even seemed particularly upset about her dinner with her father tonight, which she'd dreaded because of his constant criticism of Ben and had only agreed to because he was leaving town for a few weeks on business.

Dropping her hands, she forced herself to breathe normally. Well, so much for hope. For optimism. For believing things could work out for her and Ben. "Time to get strong, baby," she said aloud. "Looks like we're going to have to take care of each other without help from your daddy." She threw water on her face and was drying off with a paper towel when the door opened.

It was Betty.

Emily stared at her in the glass. "Please don't gloat, Betty. I'm trying like hell to keep it together."

Tipping her head, Ben's secretary asked, "Did that bother you?"

"Of course it bothered me. I walk in and catch some other woman with her hands all over my husband, and you ask me if it *bothered* me?"

The older woman folded her arms across her chest. "I had the impression that this wasn't a love match."

"You know it wasn't. For him, at least." She assessed her face in the mirror.

Great. Her skin was blotchy now, her hair a mess. She was fat, too. In contrast, the lovely Mallory had sleek hair and an even sleeker body. Which was wrapped around Ben.

Coming to stand behind Emily, Betty shocked her

by placing her hands on her shoulders. It was a motherly gesture. "You really do care about him, don't you?"

She turned around. "I love him."

A smile split Betty's face. "Then I suggest you fight for him."

Emily shook her head. "I'm tired of fighting."

"I don't think it'll take much effort." She nodded to the door again. "He wasn't a happy man when he just left."

"Well," Emily said somberly, "that makes two of us."

"Don't give up on him."

Betty's words stayed with Emily as she left Cassidy Industries.

As she endured an endless meal with her father.

As she woke up from the nap she took on the couch waiting for Ben to come home.

By the time he did, at 11:00 p.m., she was spitting mad.

A LIGHT WAS ON in the great room when Ben entered the house through the garage. What a night. His whole plan had backfired. Oh, he'd distanced Emily by going out with Mallory. Damn it, he could still see the wounded look on her face when she'd found them together. But her grit had surfaced. She hadn't dissolved in front of them. She'd told him off but good.

He'd thought of going after her, but had decided

against it when he'd realized Emily finding him with Mallory was a blessing in disguise. It would erect a wall between them that would be unbreachable. If the idea had caused a sinking sensation in his chest, he'd ignored it.

He'd explained to Mallory that he wasn't looking for a fling with another woman. She'd insisted they go to dinner anyway. Throughout the meal, all he could think about was Emily.

Did she get sick tonight? He hoped not.

Here's the deal. It's your responsibility to make sure the end of this pregnancy is as easy as possible for her. He was doing a hell of a job.

The downstairs was empty. He checked the porch to see if Lady was all right. She was sleeping soundly. As he doused the lights and climbed the steps, he prayed Emily was asleep, too. His emotions were in a wild tangle, and he was aroused as hell! Not from Mallory, though she'd given it the old college try and kissed him good-night. But from wanting his wife.

Her door was closed and it was dark under the bottom crack. Good. He made his way to the spare room, sick of the seesaw, sick of wanting her, sick of sleeping alone. He switched on a light—and stopped abruptly.

Emily was standing by the window, bathed in moonlight. Her hair was fluffy and full around her face. She wore the peach robe she'd had on the morning after they'd made love. Though her belly protruded, and she looked more like a Madonna than a siren, his body hardened at the sight of her.

He had no idea what to expect.

"You bastard!"

Well, that was clear. He stayed where he was, waiting.

"How dare you go to another woman?"

"I didn't exactly—"

"You're married, in case you've forgotten. It's bad enough you won't wear my ring—" she held up her left hand, splayed, palm in "—but I've got yours on. And in my book that means no other women."

"I—"

"Particularly—" her voice rose as she cut him off again "—your ex-girlfriend."

"Ex-fiancée," he said. "We were engaged."

That piece of news made her even more angry. She took several steps toward him. He could see fury coloring her cheeks, sparking in her eyes. He hadn't anticipated this. He thought she might pout or be hurt, but this righteousness, this outrage...all it did was make him want her even more.

"*Ex* is the operative word here, *Benedict*." She stepped even nearer, only inches away, studied his face. Then her gaze focused on his collar and her composure slipped. "Oh, God."

"What?"

"You have lipstick on your shirt." She looked into

his eyes. He thought she was going to cry. Instead, she slapped him across the cheek and started for the door.

He got his wits back in time to catch her by the arm. "Not so fast."

Turned away from him, she shook her head, sending all that glorious hair flying. "Let me go."

"No. Not until we have this out." He tugged her around.

She stared at him, her expression full of sexy indignation.

"What did you expect from this relationship, Emily? Fidelity?"

Her eyes widened. "Of course I did."

"It's a marriage of convenience. You know that as well as I do."

"Did you have sex with her?"

"No."

Her gaze dropped to his shirt.

"She kissed me good-night."

"Oh, great. Just great."

"Emily, what do you *want* from me?"

She lifted her chin again. "What I've always wanted from you."

He closed his eyes. He didn't know if he should get down on his knees in thanks, or turn tail and run.

"Look at me, Ben." He did. "I won't allow you to go to another woman. You only have two choices here. Either you stay celibate—"

"Em—"

"No." She held up her palm. "Let me finish. This is hard enough as it is, but I'm going to say what's in my heart, even if you won't. Your second choice is to sleep with me. If you'd give me a chance, I'm sure I can satisfy you again." She bit her lip, her righteous stance eclipsed by that show of vulnerability. "I did when we made the baby, didn't I?"

His control snapped. He'd wanted her too long, had come to like her, as well. And he couldn't stand to hear the insecurity creep back into her voice, see the lack of confidence in her face again. He dragged her to him, locked his hand at her neck and kissed her hair. "You have no idea how much you satisfied me that night, sweetheart." He cradled her to his chest, and the tender gesture was in such contrast to the storm of desire raging inside of him, it unbalanced him. "How much I want you right now. Have wanted you every single day since then."

She drew back. "Then make love to me. It's best for us, I *know* it is."

He cupped her cheeks in his palms. "I don't want to hurt you."

"You mean physically? Because of the baby?"

"No. Emily, we've been getting along better. Sharing the joy of having a child together. But I still don't trust you."

"That I'll betray you somehow to my father?"

"It used to be that," he admitted starkly. "But now

I'm afraid that if push came to shove, you'd choose him over me."

"I—"

He put his fingers over her mouth, silencing her. "Don't deny it. I wouldn't believe you anyway. But I want you to know why I've got to stay detached. Why I can't be around you too much. Why we shouldn't make love."

Instead of stepping away, she moved in closer. "Then let's just have sex."

"What?"

"I want you. More than I wanted you last time."

"Emily, no. That wouldn't work."

"Of course it would. You need sex. And God knows I do."

"Emily!"

She bumped her hips against his. "I can tell you're aroused. You didn't sleep with Mallory. This is for me." There was that siren's smile again. He was fascinated by the layers of her. He'd come home expecting hurt and recriminations. Instead he'd gotten indignation…and a proposition. She kissed his neck. "Pregnant women have a strong libido, Ben," she whispered against his skin. "Something to do with hormones."

"I heard that," he said, his lips already in her hair. She smelled so good. Looked great. Felt fantastic.

"I understand the conditions. I won't ask any more

from you right now than companionship and sex. What do you say?"

His strength, his suspicions, evaporated in the face of her daunting honesty. And hell, he was only human. "I say yes, Emily." His arms encircled her. "A definite, definite yes."

"AH, BEN, YES, RIGHT THERE."

"I don't want to hurt you."

Only the moonlight was witness to their intimacy in bed. She felt his breath whisper over her bare skin.

"Ah—I'm going to…I…" She came into his hand then, in an orgasm that seemed as if it would last forever.

Afterward, she hid her face against his chest, breathed him in. "I'm sorry, I wanted to wait for you."

"We've waited long enough." He brushed his lips over her mouth. "Come again."

"Ben…."

He took the decision from her, sliding his hand back down her body. She arched into his touch, drank from his mouth, and let him take her over the soft, sensual edge once again.

ONCE AGAIN, BEN LAY in Emily's house—this time in the spare bed—holding her naked body against his while she slept in his arms. He'd planned never to be with her again like this, but he hadn't been able to stop it.

The baby kicked. Because Emily's stomach was wedged against his, he actually felt it! After the initial surprise, he wondered if his son was chiding him or welcoming him? "Hey, little, guy," he whispered softly, so as not to wake Emily. "You okay?"

He felt a lighter kick this time.

He chuckled, charmed by the silent—probably imagined—communication. "Good." He moved in closer and felt the baby turn over. "I hope this was the right thing to do for all of us."

Nothing, as if the baby was thinking. Then a different stroke, like the punch of a tiny fist. Was it a yes or no?

He cuddled them both closer. "I won't hurt you," he promised. "You or Mommy." He kissed Emily's hair. "And I'll never abandon you, little guy." The thought, though, of abandoning his son's mother caused a groundswell of sadness in him.

The baby gave several small jabs into his stomach.

"I might have to leave her." How could he not at some point? After tonight, they'd only get closer. He couldn't let himself fall in love with her. He couldn't. Even now, if—when—she picked her father over him, Ben would be devastated.

"I love you already," he said again to his child.

Just not her, he thought, cuddling Emily closer. I don't love her. *Please, God, don't let me love her.*

He sighed heavily and his eyes began to close. The

last thing he felt before he drifted off was one more gentle kick from inside Emily.

"Good night to you, too, buddy."

CHAPTER TEN

BEHIND LOCKED DOORS, FEELING like an idiot, Ben slid a book out of his desk drawer and opened it. He was reading up on Italian names today. Hmm. *Angelo* meant angel. Nah, he didn't want his son to be an angel. A little mischief was good in a boy. *Carlo* meant manly. Too macho for Ben's taste. *Donatello* stood for gift. Nice thought, but he didn't want to name his child after one of the old Ninja Turtles. *Giovanni* meant gift from God. And it was Italian for *John.* Ben remembered something and flipped to Scottish names. *Ian* was a form of *John*—and also meant gift from God. But it was more modern. Calling up a file on his computer, Ben place *Ian* at the top of the list he'd labeled "My Son" and chuckled. Hell, he had it bad for this baby.

And for the baby's mother, which was no laughing matter. Ben didn't want to feel as much as he did for Emily. But ever since last Friday, when they'd made love, he'd been even more smitten by her and by his child. So much so he'd told her he'd come home tomorrow night for Halloween and help her give out the caramel apples she'd made for the trick-or-treaters.

He had no business doing something so domestic.

She'd gotten to him in other ways, too....

I dropped your shirts off at the laundry... Please come home for dinner, I made you fried chicken... No, I'm not the least bit tired. I told you pregnant women want more sex. Come to bed with me....

She'd had a few crying jags—typical, he'd read, for women in her condition—and even that charmed him. He had no idea what had set her off any of those times. He'd tried to ignore her, or leave her alone in her room, but he couldn't. Each time, he'd ended up holding her and telling her that her hormones were wacky and she'd be fine in a few minutes. She always was. Outwardly, Ben might be maintaining the distance he'd said he would, but inwardly he was going under for the third time.

The intercom on his desk buzzed and Betty's voice came through. "Ben, there's a Luke Harrington here to see you."

Luke Harrington. The private investigator he'd hired to look into the delay of his patent two years ago. Betty showed the man in. A bulldozer of a guy, Harrington greeted him and dropped down in a chair across from the desk. As his image projected, he pulled no punches. "The four names on that list you found in the folder were all U.S. patent employees the year you filed for yours." He read from his notes, "The first two worked in low-level jobs and had no opportunity to influence your application. However, the second two were in a position to stall it. One still lives in DC and works at the same job. I'm flying down there tomorrow. The other's in Florida. I'll go there next, if I have to."

Ben leaned back in his chair. "What will you do? Just ask them if they took bribes?"

"Not exactly. I'll interview the first guy. See what he's made of. I've got background checks in the works on the two of them already. The Florida guy retired and bought a house down there just a year ago."

"Right timing, but not unusual for older people to save for their retirement."

Harrington frowned as he glanced at his notes again. "He's forty-six."

"Ah, the plot thickens."

"Sure does." The P.I. stood. "Be back in touch." He'd just stepped out the door as Emily came up flush with it. "Oops, sorry ma'am," he said, steadying her.

"No problem. I'm a bit clumsy these days." She entered Ben's office and smiled at him. "Hi."

He loved how her eyes lit up when they first focused on him. As if there wasn't anybody else she'd rather see. He was very afraid his did the same when she walked into a room.

Not good. Their reaction to each other bore too much resemblance to a couple in love. He glanced after

Harrington. No, that couldn't happen. Ben had to keep this relationship in line while he nailed her father.

"Ben, are you all right?" She tracked his gaze. "Who was that man? He seems to have upset you."

"No, it was good news." His smile was perfunctory. "How was your lunch with Jordan?"

"Great." Despite the comment, she seemed sad. "The dance studio is beautiful. And she already has a waiting list for five- and six-year-olds when the place opens officially in January." There was something odd in the way she always talked about Jordan's dance business. He made a mental note to find out why. "Oh, well," she said and glanced at her office. "Is there anything for me to do this afternoon?"

"Why don't you go home and rest?"

"No! I want to work. This inactivity is driving me crazy. Last week you said you'd get me more to do."

"I'm afraid you've distracted me lately."

Her eyes widened. Neither had mentioned their physical relationship at work.

"In any case, I'll talk to Janice right now. Get you something to keep your brain busy."

She sighed.

He studied his wife. "Emily, I'm getting mixed messages here. Do you or do you not want more work—"

Her cell phone rang. She fished it out of her purse and checked the caller ID. "I have to get this."

Rising, she crossed through Ben's office into her

own. He went back to his desk and tried not to eavesdrop on her conversation. When he heard, "Dad, hi," he shook his head. When he heard, "What are you doing in DC?" Ben let out a quiet whistle.

Hmm. So Mackenzie was in Washington. The plot did indeed thicken. A lot. He glanced at the baby-name book. Talk about gifts from God. Ben had just gotten a whopper.

HIS UNCLE, WHO'D ROUTINELY beat the crap out of him, had taught Lammon some valuable lessons. One, muscle got you what you wanted. Two, taking advantage of the weak was excusable if you got what you were after. And three, if you wanted something done right, do it yourself. Mac approached the meeting down in Foggy Bottom with the last adage uppermost in his mind. He'd done the original deal himself, and he was personally going to make sure the details stayed buried. With a pocket full of persuasion, he intended to get what he wanted today.

Antler's Bar and Grill sported a hunting motif. Mac had hunted until he'd met Anna. *Oh, dear, Lammon, it's like killing Bambi's mother. How can you do it?* He hadn't all the time they'd been married. As soon as she'd left him, he'd bought a cabin in an outlying area of Rockford and had gone there to hunt. Not that he'd enjoyed it. Eventually, he'd sold it off and bought a cottage on Catasaga Lake, which Emily particularly liked.

When his eyes adjusted to the dim light of the bar, Mac saw a snip of a man sitting in the corner. He still had horn-rimmed glasses and dressed like someone out of the fifties. This would be a piece of cake. "Curtis."

The guy looked up at him through Coke bottle lenses. "Mr. Mackenzie." He sipped what appeared to be water.

Mac sat down and ordered a martini. He had his strategy planned, like any mover and shaker worth his salt. From his suit coat, he drew out an envelope. He pushed it across the table.

"What's this?"

"Read it."

Curtis shook out the contents. He held a sheaf of papers up to the light. "What's USC 201?"

"It's a statute passed by the government in 1999."

The man read the documents. "Oh, no."

"What did you think, Curtis? Only the briber broke the law?"

"I wasn't thinking clearly then, or I wouldn't have accepted it."

"Spare me." Mac's martini arrived and he sipped it. "Two years in jail. You wouldn't last a day."

Mac wasn't sure he would, either, but he didn't plan to put it to the test. He'd keep these bozos quiet however he had to accomplish it.

Curtis looked like he was going to puke. He thrust back the papers. "What do you want?"

"Just for you to keep your mouth shut. You don't tell anybody, we'll both be fine."

"Who would there be to tell?"

"Nobody." He hoped. The documented proof had been destroyed as soon as he'd taken over the company; nobody else had been in on the deal. Still, Cassidy was crafty. And the guy hated Mac. "Just wanted to make sure we're on the same page."

Curtis stood abruptly. "I think I'm gonna be sick."

"Remember what I said. Take your stuff. I don't want to see you again."

The jerk grabbed his briefcase and hurried away.

"One down," Mac said, taking another sip of his martini. "One to go."

Oh, darling, what's happened to you? Anna's words. He'd been tempted to beg his wife to stay and promise her he'd change. But he'd been on his knees enough in his childhood. If she wanted to leave, he'd thought at the time, let her.

He'd had no idea she'd take so much of him with her.

AT 4:00 P.M., Emily switched off her reading lamp and crossed to the doorway to Ben's office. Head bent, he was studying spreadsheets. For a moment, she indulged in the sight of him. She hoped her son inherited those mile-wide shoulders and long, lean bones. And she was getting partial to gray-suede eyes, especially when they warmed. He was so handsome he took her breath away. And when she let herself think about them in bed together, she got downright hot. They'd had great sex, but no matter what he said, they'd made love, too. She'd felt it in every gentle touch and whispered word in her bedroom.

She cleared her throat. "Ben?"

He looked up. "Going home?"

"Not yet."

He frowned, concerned. "Where are you headed?"

"Cassidy Place."

Absently, he reached up and massaged his shoulder. "I see."

"Does your neck hurt?"

"I must have wrenched it working out this morning."

Smiling, she closed the distance between them. Before he could stop her, she began to massage his neck. His white shirt felt starchy and stretched taut over his muscles. Tending to him was a wifely duty, and filled her heart with love. "You're tense."

"Long day."

She wanted to say, *Come home, let me take care of you.* But she'd been careful not to overstep her bounds. He allowed the ministration for a few minutes, then covered her hand with his. "That's enough. Thanks." He rubbed his fingers over hers, stopped and tilted his head to the side. "Where's your wedding ring?" He sounded irritated, and a bit hurt.

She leaned against the edge of his desk. From inside the neck of her long white blouse, she pulled out a chain. "Right here."

His eyes narrowed on the jewelry. "You don't wear it anymore?"

"Of course I do. But I can't leave it on at Cassidy Place. No one knows I'm married."

"What do they think?"

She shrugged. "I guess that I got knocked up by some guy and he wouldn't marry me."

He rested his hand on her stomach. "A blasphemous term for creating this little gift, wouldn't you say?"

"I would."

"Are you sure you should drive over there tonight? It's windy out, and dark already."

"Ben, I love volunteering there."

"You shouldn't be on your feet."

"I won't be. I got milk duty last week, where I can sit on a stool most of the time."

"Oh. Well, good." He watched her, rubbing her belly, without realizing he was doing it. "You always liked being on the floor. Do you miss it?"

"Not so much since my favorite guest isn't there anymore."

He shook his head. She loved the little smile that broached his lips when he didn't even know it. "I can't believe you were attracted to me. As I was then."

She frowned. "That's a stupid thing to say. Of course

I was attracted to you. Very. You were kind and sensitive to others, always making people feel better. Especially Helena."

"She still coming?"

"Yes." Emily sniffed. "She asks Alice about you all the time."

"Hmm. Maybe I should go back and see her."

Emily's eyes narrowed on him.

"Just kidding. But you know what? I've been thinking about telling the people at Cassidy Place who I am, that we're married." He took her hand. "Then you wouldn't have to hide your ring. Tonight might be a good time to do it." His look was little boyish. "I always loved the Halloween celebrations at Cassidy Place."

"Oh, Ben, it would mean a lot if you'd come with me."

Glancing down at his suit, he frowned. "Can you wait till I change? I've got some jeans in the bathroom."

"I can wait. Forever if I have to."

For a moment, he stared at her. He knew exactly what she meant, even though he didn't believe it yet. Then he stood. "Well, it won't take that long. Be out in a bit." He strode to the lav.

Emily watched him, caressing her stomach. "We *hope* it doesn't take that long, don't we little one?"

A small quick kick made her smile.

THE INSIDE OF CASSIDY PLACE had been decorated like a haunted house. Ben remembered vividly when he'd purchased the black vinyl sheets that covered the walls, the cauldrons and witches made out of papier-mâché. Huge white sheets floated from the ceiling like flying ghosts. And each table was decorated in black and orange with pumpkins as centerpieces. They were early and the patrons hadn't arrived, so Ben could just absorb the transformation. It felt like home no matter how it looked.

"Whose idea was this originally?" Emily asked him.

"Mine. I thought a little fun might go a long way to perk up everybody's spirits." He smiled. "And I liked watching the kids in the play area over there."

"You did so much with this place."

"I wanted to do more. There was a train at this Christmas shop on Ridge Road. I wanted to buy it and set it up around the perimeter, but it cost too much. I spent the money on necessities for the guests instead."

"You have a lot invested here."

"I know. It meant everything when my company…" He trailed off when he saw her glance away. He'd stopped talking about her father because his negative comments, even his tone, made her sad. When exactly had it become his mission in life to keep her happy?

His back to the kitchen door, he heard, "Emily, girl, you here again tonight? That baby—" Alice's reproaches ended abruptly when Ben turned around.

"My goodness! Ben."

He stared at her.

"Where've you been in the past six months, boy?"

"A lot's happened to me."

She studied his designer jeans and Nautica sweat-shirt. "Good things, by the looks of you."

Glancing at Emily, he said, "I guess you could say some wonderful things have happened." He crossed to the older woman and gave her a hug. When he stepped back, he felt somewhat sheepish. "Alice, I don't know how to tell you this any other way than to come right out with it. I'm Benedict Cassidy."

It took her a minute. "Oh, my, well. I had no idea."

"Because I didn't want you to. When I lost my company, I...went downhill. After I pulled my life together somewhat, I came here to remind myself that something I'd done, something good, had lasted."

"I'm so glad. I heard you got your business back from that bastard."

Again, Emily averted her head. Ben hadn't imagined this. How long had she been subjected to these kinds of comments at his soup kitchen? "There's more. Emily and I are married. It's my son she's carrying."

The older woman chuckled. "Well, that doesn't sur-prise me as much as who you are."

"It will, though, when you find out who *she* is. Her name is Emily Mackenzie."

He saw Alice's brow furrow. "Mackenzie? As in Lammon Mackenzie?"

"He's my father, Alice."

Before the older woman could react, Ben said, "But don't hold that against her. She's nothing like him."

"Of course she's not. Emily, it just seems bizarre that you came to work here after what he did to us."

Emily sighed. "I came here to work *because* of what my father did."

"No matter. Just so everything turned out all right." When Emily bit her lip, Alice said, "It did, didn't it?"

Ben slipped an arm around Emily's waist. "Yes, of course. Now, put me to work, and find something my wife can do so she can sit."

"Ah, a man after my own heart."

"Mine, too," Emily whispered.

Ben tried to ignore her comment. Still, it warmed him. So did the sight of her hand at her stomach. His ring on her finger.

EMILY SMILED OVER at Ben as they rode home in his car—a big SUV she could get in and out of easily. Hers was in the locked lot at Cassidy Industries. When they'd left for the soup kitchen, he'd told her they'd ride to work together in the morning. The lights from the street illuminated his face, free of the lines of distress and disapproval. His relaxed expression made him look younger.

"Let's volunteer on Thanksgiving Day at Cassidy Place," he said casually. "I'd like to be a part of that celebration, too."

When she didn't respond, he continued, "Then we can go to Trey's. He always has this elaborate buffet at his place for his friends. I haven't gone in two years, but it's fun."

She shifted on the seat.

"The baby okay?"

"Yes. It's not that."

"What?"

"Ben, about the holidays. I've got to spend time with my father."

"Ah. Of course. Your father. I'd forgotten."

Oh, God, it was just what she wanted...him to forget what was between them.

She covered his hand on the gear shift. "I want to be with you on the holidays, too."

"Then be with me. Just me," he added meaningfully.

"I can't abandon my father on the holidays. I'm all he has."

There was a long, stony silence in the car.

"I don't know what to do, Ben. How to handle this."

"It's simple," he said coldly. "Choose to work at Cassidy Place on Thanksgiving Day. Choose to be with me."

I'm afraid I'll come to care for you and then when push comes to shove, you'll choose him over me.

"Ben, please, don't ask me to make that choice."

He pulled the car into the driveway, then the garage.

"Forget it. We're not going to rehash everything again."
He ran a hand though his hair. "What was I thinking?"

"You were thinking that things could be better between us. Work out long term. So was I."

The overhead light cast them in shadows. "Well, if
I was even remotely thinking that, then I was wrong.
Your father will always come between us like this.
Everything will seem fine, seem *normal,* then your
choices will ambush us."

"What do you want from me, Ben? To cut my father
out of my life."

"It doesn't seem to matter what I want. You already
said you'd never do that. Even if it would give us a
chance at a future together." He reached for the door
handle. "Let's go. Getting a chill isn't good for the
baby."

Damn it! She hated this seesaw. But she had no idea
how to get off it.

*Don't have anything more to do with your father. You
can have Ben and the happy family you've always
wanted if you'd do that.*

The thought broke Emily's heart. No woman should
have to make that choice.

CHAPTER ELEVEN

SHAKING OFF THE REMNANTS OF THE cold November rain, Ben bumped into Jordan Turk in the foyer of Cassidy Industries. Emily's friend eyed him warily. "Hello, Ben."

He wondered if Emily had told her that the past week between them had been strained. That they'd argued about where she'd spend Thanksgiving. That he'd been angry when she'd resisted doing what he'd wanted. And that he'd managed to distance himself after the incident out of pure self-protection.

"Jordan. Come to see Emily?"

"Yes." She held up a folder. "She's helping me figure out the budget for my studio. Don't worry, she doesn't have much to do here, so I didn't take her away from anything."

"I'm not worried. Seeing you makes her happy."

Jordan shook her head. "I just don't get you. Sometimes, you seem to have her best interest at heart, and sometimes, you're a bastard to her."

"Most of the time, I do have her best interests at heart. I want her to be happy."

Snorting, Jordan leaned against the railing of the staircase. "Then why the hell didn't you let her pursue her dream? You finally got her out of her father's clutches, then you turn around and imprison her like he did."

"I have no idea what you're talking about."

"Are you for real?"

Cold swirled around their feet as two of his employees came in through the door behind them. Ben said, "Look, do you have a few minutes? I want to talk about this with you."

"Yeah, I have a few. Have you got a cafeteria? I'd love some coffee."

A half hour later, Ben was frowning as he made his way to the second floor. He stopped at human resources, then headed for his office. Damn her, why hadn't she told him about her dream to own a dance studio?

Oh, yeah, Cassidy, you invite confidences. She's probably afraid you'll jump on her for wanting to leave Cassidy Industries like you did about good old Daddy and the holidays.

Still, she should have told him. Even after what had happened on Halloween at the soup kitchen, they'd made love, and had talked in the darkness. There had been plenty of opportunity.

Reaching his office, he checked his messages and saw there was one from Luke Harrington. Before he called the guy back, he closed the connecting door to Emily's office, which was empty.

"Harrington," the gruff voice on the other end of the phone answered.

"Cassidy, here."

"I'm on my way to Florida. The meeting in D.C. was interesting—the guy who works in the patent office was so nervous I thought he was gonna pee his pants. It's hard to believe that little twerp would have the guts to take a bribe. But his colleagues gave me a few leads I'm following up. And his background check reveals a sick mother with no insurance, whose bills miraculously got paid."

Hell. Ben knew the penalty for bribery wasn't confined to the one who paid the money. He didn't want the sad sack to be punished, too.

"He's pathetic really."

"So you're going check out the other one?"

"Yeah." Background noise. "That's my flight. I'll call you when I know more."

They disconnected. Ben sat back in his chair and wondered how many people's lives he'd have to destroy to get revenge on Mackenzie. He was angry at all of them, but this guy at the patent office had needed the money. Mackenzie had taken advantage of him.

Ben forced himself to settle down to work. An hour later, Janice knocked at his door and came into the office. "Here it is." She handed him a paper, her expression disapproving.

"What's wrong?"

She sank into a chair. "Why are you doing this?"

"I've got my reasons." He studied her. "I thought nobody at Cassidy Industries liked Emily."

Janice rolled her eyes. "How can you not like her? She was nice even when we snubbed her. She goes out of her way to talk to everybody. She's so good with people. That's probably why she's in HR. In the month she's been here, she's won us over, I guess." Janice waited a beat. "Has she won you over, Ben? It's obvious she's crazy about you."

"Of course she has. She's my wife."

Janice shook her head and nodded to the form. "Do you want me here when you do this?"

"No, thanks."

"Fine." Janice left the office just as Emily came by. "Hey, Emily. Cute top."

Today she wore navy slacks and a matching oversize shirt, embroidered with pink flowers on the collar and sleeves. "Thanks. He's really getting big. I just keep getting fatter."

And more beautiful, Ben thought.

When Janice left, Emily approached his doorway. "You're back. How did the meeting go?"

"Good." He glanced at the paper on his desk. "Come in a second, and close the door."

Once she was seated, he handed her the form Janice had prepared. She smiled at him before she looked at it. As she read the contents, the color drained from her face and she bit her lip. "I see." Her eyes were full of hurt. "Well, I could have done a better job here if you'd given me anything worthwhile to do."

Watching her, he steepled his hands. "I'm aware of that. You've done a fine job at Cassidy Industries."

"Then why are you firing me?"

"Letting you go."

"Why?" Now her eyes sparked with rebellion. "If it's to stay home until I have the baby, I told you I'll go crazy with nothing to do."

Rising, he came around the desk. He leaned against the edge and stretched out his legs. "I'm not letting you go so you can stay home. I bumped into Jordan on the way in today. We had coffee."

"And?"

"She reamed me out—again. This time for keeping you from your dream of going in on the dance studio with her."

"Oh." Emily glanced away. "She shouldn't have told you about that."

"She said your father had talked you out of pursuing that dream. He wanted you with him at Mackenzie Enterprises."

In truth, Jordan had let slip that Mackenzie had also rushed Emily into marriage with a man he thought suitable. Jordan had said she wouldn't be surprised if he'd driven Emily's mother away, too.

"Jordan also told me you thought that staying at

Mackenzie Enterprises would keep your father in line, at least personnel-wise."

"Yes. That sentence was self-imposed. I felt I had to stay connected to his business to help protect the people in the companies he took over." She faced him squarely. "I could have stopped him from doing that at Cassidy Industries if I was here at the time."

His whole body tensed. "This isn't ground we should be covering."

"You brought it up."

"My mistake. I won't again." Nor would he ask her decision about spending Thanksgiving with him. "Why didn't you tell me what you'd rather be doing?"

Now anger flashed across her face. "You haven't exactly asked me, ever, what I want in all this." She swept the room with her hand.

"True. I haven't." He nodded to the form she held. "Now I'm asking. Is this what you want? To leave here and own a dance studio with Jordan?"

"For the past ten years, I've only wanted two things. A baby. And a dance studio."

He straightened. "Well, you can have the studio now, if you want. I'll give you the money to buy in if you need it."

Her chin dropped and she stared down at the paper.

"Emily? Did you hear me?"

Not looking at him, she nodded.

"Em?"

He could see her swallow hard; her knuckles were white as she held the paper. Kneeling in front of her, he tilted her chin to find eyes filled with unshed tears.

"Aw, sweetheart."

"I don't know what to say. I never really expected to get all the things I wanted in life."

He kissed her fingers. "You should have everything you want, Emily." And suddenly, he wished like hell she wanted him as much as the studio and the baby. He hadn't given her much impetus to feel that way, though.

She wiped her cheeks as he started to stand. Grasping his hand, she kept him where he was. "I love you, Ben."

Thunder clapped in his heart. "I—"

She put her fingers on his mouth. "Shh. It's not because of this—" she held up the paper "—or the baby. I've loved you for a long time. I was just afraid to tell you."

He choked back the emotion clogging his throat. "I—"

"No, don't say anything. I only wanted you to know how I felt." She kissed his cheek. "Thank you so much for this."

His own voice hoarse, he said, "I'm glad you have what you want now." He stood, drawing her up with him.

As she was leaving, she stopped at her office door. "What about you, Ben? Do you have what you want now?"

"Of course, I've got the baby and Cassidy Industries."
And soon, I'll have my revenge against Mackenzie.
Would Emily still love him after he put her father in jail?

EMILY SCANNED the small restaurant, enjoying the cozy interior with its wood walls and fireplace. "Thanks for taking me out to dinner. I love Rooney's."

"We're celebrating." Ben placed a hand on her stomach. "This little guy and a new business."

She felt lit from within. "I talked to Jordan late in the afternoon. She was ecstatic."

"Maybe she won't throw invisible daggers at me anymore."

"Maybe." Reaching across the table, she covered his hand with hers. They rarely touched outside of bed. And she'd given him space since their argument last week, mostly because she was at a loss over what to do about the holidays. She didn't want to choose between him or her father on Thanksgiving Day, or any day.

And she hadn't meant to tell him she loved him today. The words had popped out when he'd encouraged her to go in on the dance studio with Jordan. Not that she regretted telling him. She did love him, and what did it matter if he knew?

Just as he unclasped their hands and pressed his to her stomach, a shadow loomed over them. Emily was shocked to see Paul standing at their table. He was still classically handsome, not that his looks held appeal for her anymore. On his arm was a stunning young woman with dark hair and a model's body. "Emily, hello."

"Hello, Paul."

Ben linked his hand with Emily's again on top the table.

"Paul, this is Ben Cassidy, my husband."

"I, um, heard you got married." He smirked and nodded to her stomach. "Now I see why."

She could feel Ben stiffen.

"And this is?" Emily asked.

"Marissa Carson. Mar, my ex-wife, Emily. And her *husband*."

Ben watched him with hooded eyes, then stood and shook Paul's hand. Instead of sitting back down, he placed a hand on Emily's shoulder. "Emily told me all about you, Erickson." He brushed a palm down her hair. "Aren't you going to congratulate us on the baby? We're having a boy and naming him Ian."

We are? Emily thought.

"Ian?" Paul's face was blank.

"Yes, it means gift from God. We're both thrilled about this little guy."

The snide expression vanished from Paul's face. He nudged his date's back. "Nice to see you both," he said as they left.

Ben sat back down. "He's an ass."

"He wanted a baby. He's unhappy I got what he wanted."

"After how he treated you, I don't have much sympathy for him." Ben zeroed in on her. "Jordan said you almost backed out of the wedding, but your father convinced you not to." He knit his brows together. "Hell, I'm not surprised. They're cut from the same cloth."

"Please, Ben, don't spoil tonight."

"All right."

She glanced across the restaurant to see Paul staring at them from another table. Ben followed her gaze. Bending over, he brushed his lips across hers. "Let's really make him jealous. Show him just how wrong he was about you."

"Sure." She smiled, but her heart was heavy. She didn't give a whit about Paul's reaction, though she truly appreciated Ben's gesture.

Damn it. She wanted the affection to be real, not for show.

I LOVE YOU.

Ben couldn't get those words out of his head since Emily had uttered them, hours ago. All through dinner, all the way home, he let them fill his heart. And so, at ten that night, he found himself poised at the entrance to her bedroom. She was sitting in bed, dressed in some silky pink thing with cute little sleeves capping her upper arms. She'd gained weight in her stomach but not too much elsewhere. "Aren't you tired?"

Glancing up from the book, she shook her head. "No. You?"

"Don't seem to be. What are you reading?"

"Come and see." She patted the mattress.

He dropped down on the edge of the bed and looked at the book. *Starting Your Own Business.* "Where'd you get this?"

"I've had it for a while."

He studied her face. "I hope this makes you happy." He shrugged. "You've had a rough year."

"It's looking up," she said. "Ben, the name you picked out for the baby is very meaningful."

He put his hand on her stomach. "Is he sleeping?"

"I think so." She rolled her eyes. "He'll wake up as soon as I try to go to sleep."

She was so beautiful, sitting there in the light, her hair down, her face flushed. "God, you're lovely."

"I'm glad you think so."

He picked up her hand and brought it to his lips. "I want you, Emily." At least they could communicate here, in this bedroom. At least nothing was between them when they came together in this bed.

She smiled and placed his hand on her breast. "Let's make love, then."

He didn't correct her. He didn't say it was just sex between them. After what she'd told him today—that she loved him—he couldn't diminish her feelings with a crude remark.

A little while later, after he'd aroused her, and himself in the process, to the point where neither of them could think straight, he entered her gently.

"Tell me again," he whispered achingly.

"I love you, Ben. I *love* you…."

THREE DAYS LATER, Ben found himself in Luke Harrington's office. It was up three flights of steps and had a glass window in the door. Inside, the filing cabinets and furniture were all a muted gray, reminding him of an old black-and-white P.I. movie. "Good morning," Ben said when Harrington didn't look up.

The man raised his head. Without preamble he said, "We hit pay dirt."

"Is that why you wanted to see me here?"

"Yeah. More privacy. Have a seat."

Ben took the chair nearest his desk. Harrington pushed a file toward him. "It's all there."

Ben opened the folder. First were reports on Josh Curtis, the nerdy patent guy from DC. As Harrington had recounted, income statements indicated a windfall, which the guy had used to pay his mother's medical bills. Damn it. "I wish Curtis had spent the money on booze and whores."

Harrington grunted.

Ben read further. The second guy, Frank L. Emerson, was living in Florida in a home he'd bought six

KATHRYN SHAY
201

months after Mackenzie had taken over Cassidy Industries. "At least this guy spent it on himself."

"He didn't, really."

"What?"

"Read on."

Two children. One born with spina bifida.

"He brought the boy down there because it's easier
for the kid to be in the warm weather in a wheelchair.
And because there's a center in Orlando for help with
this kind of disease."

"He's using the money on that?"

"Yep. Mackenzie picked his guys wisely."

"This isn't exactly proof, even if I did want to impli-
cate the other two."

"Look at the rest of the stuff."

Ben leafed through the file until he found pictures.
One was of Mackenzie and Curtis at a bar in D.C.

"How did you get this?"

"Damnedest piece of luck. I talked to a couple of co-
workers about Mackenzie. Showed them his photo.
They said he'd been spotted at a bar where they all hung
out. The place has a surveillance camera because
they've been ripped off several times. I got stills made
out of them."

Ben looked down again.

A second photo was of Emerson and Mackenzie at
a restaurant in Florida. "Another surveillance camera?"

"Nope. Live. Mackenzie got down there just before

I did. I followed them. What we have here is Mackenzie covering his tracks. With these photos, the background checks, the unexplained income of the two guys
and the timing of the patent, I'd say you got enough to
send the bastard away for a couple of years."

And two others in the process.

Who were anything but innocent.

Still, would Ben really be able to destroy them, and
maybe Emily, to get Mackenzie?

CHAPTER TWELVE

"THIS IS THE MAIN DANCE AREA, but there are two other large rooms through there." Emily smiled like a kid at Christmas. Mac could picture her then, all those years ago, in little red-footed pajamas, thinking he was a hero. So much had changed.

"Interesting." He leaned against a barre. "Lots of mirrors. Nice wood. When do you open?"

"After the holidays." She cradled her stomach. "I won't be doing much teaching for a while, but I can run the business side, even from home if I have to."

Folding his arms over his chest, he stared at her. "Why are you doing this? Did Cassidy finally get tired of you?"

His daughter's face clouded. God, he hated the idea of that man making her unhappy. "I don't think so." She shook her head. "And don't pretend you didn't know I wanted this. I first told you when I graduated from college. You always convinced me to stay at Mackenzie Enterprises."

"I thought a business like this was just some pipe dream. I didn't know you meant it."

"No, Dad, like always, you thought you knew what was best for me. And you wanted me to work for you."

"Is that so bad?"

"Maybe not. In any case, it's in the past."

"So how did this come about? Last I heard, Cassidy bullied you into working for him."

"Jordan told Ben I've always wanted to own a studio, so he encouraged me to become a partner with her."

"He's got to have an ulterior motive for this."

"Stop, Dad. I mean it. I won't listen to you bad-mouth Ben." She veered down a corridor. "Come on, I'll show you my office."

He followed her, hating the fact that Cassidy had given Emily something Mac had kept from her. But he meant what he'd said; he'd never truly thought she was serious about a dance studio. And she was right—he wanted her with him. For Cassidy's part, Mac knew the guy hadn't let her go out of the goodness of his heart. The upside, however, was that Emily was no longer working for the bastard.

In her office, he sat and she leaned against her desk, bridging her hands on her stomach. She wore dark brown pants and a top that stretched across the baby. It was hard to believe she was pregnant. He remembered when Anna had been carrying *her*....

Lammon, come feel her... It's a miracle... I love you so much....

Mac wondered if Emily was as elated as her mother

had been when they'd found out about the pregnancy—
after trying to conceive for a long time. Anna had reli-
giously recorded her whole nine-month experience,
along with the birth. Had she taken that journal with
her?

"Dad, what is it? You look like you've seen a ghost."

"I was thinking about when you were born."

"Tell me about it."

"You were so beautiful. I was afraid to hold you. You
were tiny, with sprouts of red hair. Your mother...."

He trailed off.

"You can talk about her."

"No. No, I can't."

She assessed him with a shrewd gaze. "All right.
Then, tell me what you think of this place."

"I think it's a solid business venture. Nice location.
How are the enrollment numbers?"

She fished out her logs and they moved to a small
table in the corner to study them.

"Which classes will you teach?"

"Ballet, primarily, though not until well after Ian's
born."

Mac stilled in the act of perusing their business plan.
"You're having a boy? And he has a name?"

"Yes." Again she grinned ear to ear.

"Why didn't you tell me that?"

"You didn't seem inclined to talk about the baby."
When he said nothing, she added, "And you've been

out of town a lot this last month when we decided on a name. Where have you been, anyway?"

Covering my ass. "I'm thinking about acquiring a new company. I've been scouting out potential businesses."

"Anything in particular?"

He dragged his mind away from the fact that he was going to have a grandson. "A small company in Florida, but they make a good product." After he finished giving her the details, he sat back in his chair. "Emily, I'm going to ask you something and I want the truth."

"Go ahead."

"How long are you going to continue this farce of a marriage?"

"It's not a farce."

"Of course it is."

She grasped his hand, and he knew she was going to tell him something he didn't want to hear. "Dad, this marriage may have started out wrong. But I'm in love with Ben. I want a life with him and our child. I told you all this before."

"I'll never accept that."

"You have no choice."

"Of course I do!" he said, louder, more forcefully than he intended, causing Emily to jolt back.

Sighing, he drew her close again so their heads were touching. "I'm sorry, Emmy…."

"Am I interrupting something?"

They both looked up to see Cassidy standing in the doorway. He was holding a bouquet of red roses. Wearing the expression of an unhappy man.

Ah, now that was nice to see.

BEN HATED THE SIGHT of Emily with her father, their heads bent, talking softly. He hadn't seen them together since that day in Mackenzie's office when Ben had taken back his company. And, of course, Thanksgiving plans were still in question. Damn it, she had to choose! A voice inside him warned he was being irrational and unfair, but he ignored it. His common sense fled at the mere idea of Mackenzie.

Emily stood and crossed to Ben. "I'm so glad you came to visit." She nodded at the flowers. "For me?"

"Yes. For the studio's opening." He couldn't take his eyes off Mackenzie, who stood, too, and jammed his hands in the pockets of his suit.

Emily whispered, "Please try to be nice."

Okay, so he'd try. He knew he had to get some perspective on her relationship with her father. For his son, if nothing else. "I can see you're busy. I'll come back later."

Mackenzie smirked. "Good idea. Emily and I need to finalize our plans for tomorrow." The man crossed to his daughter and put his hand on her shoulder, effectively tugging her away from Ben. "What are you going to do to occupy yourself this Thanksgiving, Cassidy?"

His gaze flew to Emily's. She said, "Ben, I—" Then she faced her father. "Dad, I'm planning to work at Cassidy Place with Ben until mid-afternoon. Then you and I can have dinner."

"Nonsense." He clasped her harder. "You have to cook. We'll spend the day together at my house, like we always do."

Ben was infuriated by Mackenzie's taunt. "No! She'll be with me, all day—we'll start a new tradition." He looked at his wife. "Push just came to shove, sweetheart," he said, hating what he became when he was around Mackenzie, but unable to control himself. "What'll it be, Emily?"

The tableau wasn't lost on Ben. His wife stood between him and her father. Her shoulders slumped and her face white.

"Please, both of you, don't do this."

Mackenzie frowned. "What's there to do? It's all settled. We'll celebrate the holidays like we always have."

Ben's expression was harsh. "She just told you things have changed."

"The hell they have." Mackenzie swore vilely.

"I want you to leave my wife's place of business."

"I'll stay at my *daughter's* place of business as long as I want. Who the hell do you think you—"

"Stop it!" Emily yelled. "Both of you." They turned to her. "I can't stand this anymore. This push-pull. You two have to declare a truce."

"When hell freezes over," Mackenzie spat out.

"At least we agree on one thing," Ben put in.

Ben caught the tilt of Emily's jaw and the tautness of her features that signaled an inner strength he usually admired. "Then fight without me. Beat each other to a pulp if you want, but I won't be part of this tug-of-war any longer."

With that, she strode out.

Both men stared at after her.

"Satisfied?" Mackenzie finally asked him.

Ben detested the man. And suddenly he wanted nothing more than to wipe that smirk off Mackenzie's face. "No, not yet. But I will be as soon as I file my report with the authorities."

"What the hell are you talking about?"

"I know about the patent."

Ben gave Mackenzie credit for his poker face. "I have no idea what you're talking about."

"Of course you do. I have proof, too, that'll put you in jail for two years and fine you enough that even your monster of a conglomerate will feel the bump."

Mackenzie's hands fisted at his sides. "You really are pathetic, you know that? You can't make your wife do what you want, so you fabricate this ruse about bribery." He shook his head. "I feel sorry for you, Cassidy. Now, I'm going to see if my daughter's all right." He brushed past Ben on his way out.

"Mackenzie?"

"What?" He didn't turn around.

"I didn't mention bribery."

Mac stood still for a moment, then swore as he left the office.

Ben stared after him. He'd won this round, but it was another hollow victory. Even though he was about to get his final revenge, hadn't Emily, in the end, chosen her father over him? And ultimately, wasn't that Ben's worst fear?

"I'VE HAD IT. I am done with this feud between them." Emily paced Jordan's office.

Sitting with her feet propped up on her desk, sipping a bottle of water, Jordan shrugged. "If I were you, I'd pick Ben."

"Jordan, this isn't helping."

"Your father is not a good man, honey. I know that hurts you when I say it, but it's the truth. He doesn't have your best interests at heart. On the other hand, I think Ben does."

"Just because he encouraged me go in on the studio with you...."

Jordan swung her feet from the desk. "It isn't only that. It's the way he talks about you. Looks at you. He's a man in love."

Emily forced back tears. "He's never said that to me. I've told him how I feel about him, but not once has he given me any reason to think he has more than affection for me because I'm carrying his baby." She sighed. "And he's still so furious with my father. If he did love me, he'd find a way to make peace and compromise about the holidays."

"Maybe he should be able to do that." Jordan dropped her feet to the floor. "Speaking of holidays, I want to tell you something."

Emily stopped pacing. Her friend's face lost the hard edge it took on whenever they talked about Emily's father. "What?"

"I'm going to Trey's tomorrow for Thanksgiving."

"You're kidding me."

"No, we've seen each other quite a few times."

"Seen each other, as in socially? As in male-female stuff?"

"Uh-huh."

"I'm dumbfounded. You don't even like him."

"Now I do. He pissed me off at first, but basically he's a nice guy."

"I don't know what to say."

"Say you'll come to Trey's for Thanksgiving."

Emily sank onto a chair and caressed her belly. Little Ian was kicking up a storm. "Jordan, I can't abandon my father. He loves me."

"Yes, but he's selfish and controlling. You just don't see it."

"I hate this."

Jordan sat back. "Then we'll stop talking about it

after I say one more thing. Mallory Kemp's going to be there tomorrow. She's in Trey's circle of friends. And she wants Ben."

"Ben is taken."

"If I were you, I wouldn't let him go there alone tomorrow."

Damn it. "I'm sick of this whole thing. Of both of them manipulating me. If Ben's going to be tempted to stray because I'm not around to watch him, or because he's mad at my father, then so be it." She felt her anger intensify. "And if my father insists on goading Ben, there'll be consequences to pay for that, too."

"Wow! Who are you and what have you done with my friend Emily?"

"Your friend Emily's had it up to here." She made a chopping motion with her hand near her chin. "To hell with both of them."

"I'D LIKE EVERYBODY TO BOW their heads before we go out to the dining hall and serve. This is a special occasion, so we'll pray today." Alice smiled at the twenty or so volunteers. "Ben, would you like to do the honors?"

Ben sucked in a breath. "Me, why?"

"Because we wouldn't be here if it wasn't for you. And I think I can vouch for everybody in saying we're thankful for all you've given us."

The group applauded. Ben was warmed by it, which

was a good thing, since he felt like a first-class jerk today. "All right." He bowed his head. "Thank you, Lord, for bringing us here together to help others. Let us always remember how fortunate we are and be kind to those who aren't as lucky as we've been. Keep us, as well as our guests, in your good graces. Amen."

When the prayer ended, a flurry of activity ensued. Ben was assigned the job of coffee server, so he headed out to the floor, heeding his prayer and thinking about how fortunate he was this year, on this day. Last Thanksgiving, he'd come to the soup kitchen as a guest. Now, everything had changed.

Alice joined him at the coffee cart. "Emily loves working here on the holidays. I'm sorry she couldn't make it today."

"Me, too."

The older woman had no idea how sorry he was. Emily had slept in her own room last night and was gone when he'd woken up this morning from a restless sleep. He'd dreamed about her father. Emily would never forgive him for putting Mackenzie in jail. It was the worst catch-22 he'd ever been in.

"Ben, oh, my goodness, is that you?"

Ben turned to find Helena standing before him. Such a lovely woman in such downtrodden circumstances. "Helena, hi."

She scanned his designer clothing. "You've had some good luck."

"Yes, I have. How are you?"

She coughed. "Fine."

"You don't sound fine. Are you ill?"

"Yes and no." She rolled her eyes. "I'm pregnant."

"Ah."

"It's hell being alone and expecting a baby." She looked around. "Where's Emily? She's pregnant, too."

"I'm not sure where she is today." But he knew she wasn't alone. Apparently Mackenzie's pressure had worked. Emily must've gone over to her father's to cook. Still, he'd held out hope she'd show up here. The statement made by her absence was loud and clear.

Pouring coffee, talking with each of the guests helped him forget about himself for a while and lightened his heart. These people were a poignant reminder of how much he had to be grateful for—the return of his company, good friends like Trey, a baby on the way. Ben spoke with Hugo and helped the refugee family get their kids settled. As he bused some left-behind dishes, he was astounded by how much good fortune he'd had returned to him—but still he wasn't happy.

His cell phone buzzed and he stepped to the alcove where Lady had had her puppies. *Please let it be her,* he prayed as he clicked on.

It was Trey. He asked Ben to stop and get ice before he headed over there.

Ben returned to the floor determined to enjoy the bright orange-and-yellow decor, the turkey centerpieces, the walls he himself had helped paint just a few short months ago. The night he and Emily had made their baby.

"Your gift bags are going over well." This from Janice, who stopped to talk now that the steady stream of guests had dwindled. Several of his employees were here today, and not only for the comp time he'd reinstated.

"You orchestrated it." Ben had suggested hats, gloves and scarves be given out after Emily had pointed out the need for them.

"Yeah, boss, but you paid."

He tried to smile.

"Where's Emily?" Janice asked.

"Dinner with her father."

"Ouch, that must hurt."

"Yes, she missed out on all of this."

Serving and cleanup took the better part of the day. At three, Ben left to go to Trey's. He stopped home to change, hoping Emily would be there, or there'd be a note. He'd found neither.

The party was in full swing when he arrived. And Trey's condo was packed. "Hello, Benedict," Mallory said through a sweep of hair she let fall into her eyes. She looked sophisticated in brown suede.

"Mallory."

She glanced behind him. "No wifey?"

"No."

"Come on, then," she said. "You can get me a drink."

He allowed Mallory to lead him to the bar, where he opted for a club soda. She tried to entertain him with stories of people he'd known a lifetime ago. Within a half hour, he was bored out of his mind and glad when Trey came up and pulled him away.

Over his friend's shoulder, on the other side of the room, Ben caught sight of Jordan. "What the hell is she doing here?"

Trey rocked back on his heels. "Oh, well, we're, um, seeing each other."

"You and Jordan? She hates your guts."

"Seems as if everybody's acting out of character."

Ben shook his head.

"On the other hand, *you* look like you've lost your best friend, buddy."

"Nah, you're right here."

"You just can't get past it can you?"

"What?"

"Your feud with Mackenzie. Even if it costs you Emily."

"Odd comment from my lawyer."

"Wise comment from your friend."

He didn't want to fight with Trey. "Go tend to your guests," Ben said.

Ben spent the rest of the afternoon and evening wandering around the condo talking to people he had no desire to see, eating turkey he had no appetite for, and checking his cell-phone messages every hour. Finally he begged off about eight. He was hoping Emily would be back from her father's house by now.

He had his hand on the doorknob when Jordan caught up with him. "Hold on a second, Cassidy."

Taking a deep breath, he faced Emily's best friend. "All right, let me have it." He deserved her contempt, her anger; she'd glowered at him all day and apparently was going in for the kill now.

But he never expected the blow she delivered. "Emily's gone, you know."

"Gone?" His wife was gone? "She left me?"

"Well, not just you. Everybody."

"What do you mean?"

"After what you and her father pulled on her yesterday, she left town this morning."

"She isn't with her father?"

"No, and don't you dare gloat. You didn't win. Neither did he. But Emily's the biggest loser. Thanks to both of you, she spent today by herself."

He grasped her arm. "Tell me where she is."

"Not on your life. She needs time away from both of you."

"Well, hell."

"Think about what you did to drive her away, Cassidy. It'll give you something to do until she comes back." Then Jordan added pointedly, "If she comes back."

Ben swore all the way home. When he pulled into the garage, it was empty. He hurried up to her room, just in case. She wasn't there, either, but he found a note on her bed that he must have missed earlier. Damn. It was addressed to him and said only, "I'm going away for a while. I hope you have a nice Thanksgiving." Disgusted, he tried her cell and heard, "This is Emily. Leave a message."

"Emily, it's Ben. Where are you? Call me, I'm worried about you."

He prowled the house. In an hour he tried her again. "Emily, please, call me back. I need to talk to you."

By midnight, he'd phoned twice more. Still no response from her.

Okay, so Jordan knew where Emily was. That she was all right. Damn it, though, she shouldn't be alone while she was pregnant. And the doctor had said the baby could come early. Still, she had two more months left, and she'd never go anywhere that help wasn't immediately available. She'd probably be sad, though. She loved holidays, loved working at Cassidy Place during them. And he'd deprived her of all that today. How the *hell* had Ben let things get to this point?

Those thoughts kept him tossing and turning most of the night. But he waited until six to pick up the phone to call Jordan. This time he was prepared to beg.

CHAPTER THIRTEEN

EMILY LOVED THE COTTAGE on Catasaga Lake. It was a beautiful A-frame, sided with cedar. Yards of glass, skylights and high ceilings brought the outdoors inside. At six o'clock on Friday night, she'd built a fire in the fieldstone fireplace with wood left inside the back door. Sitting in front of the blaze, with a cup of hot chocolate, and Lady asleep by her feet, she stared at the boxes she'd found in one of the bedroom closets this morning while looking for winter clothes. There were several cartons, all labeled Emily—Baby.

She hadn't opened them because she didn't recognize the handwriting on the cardboard and was afraid it was her mother's. So much was happening in her life, Emily didn't know if she could handle whatever was in these boxes. After all, her mother had abandoned her. And right now, Emily was feeling left out in the cold by her father and her husband. "It's just us again, little guy," she said to the baby.

Still, her gaze kept straying to the boxes.

Hell. Setting down the cocoa, she got up on her

knees and tugged open the flaps on one carton. Tissue paper. She pulled it away. A scent of sachet wafted up to her. Inside were dresses of all sizes and colors. She took out the first. It was pink gingham and had EMILY stitched across the front. She put her hand on her belly. "You probably don't like girlie things, do you, sweetie?"

Ian kicked a strong objection.

She grinned and pulled out a blue velvet dress with a bonnet to match. She'd seen pictures of herself as a child, of course, but none wearing these pretty things. She wondered why. Each outfit was more exquisite than the one before. Off-white lace. Pastels and bold greens and reds. There was a knit geranium coat with a beret. And last, at the bottom, she found her christening gown. "Oh, baby, look, you can wear this one."

A burst of kicks. She laughed. "No, your daddy probably won't let you wear it, either."

Then she remembered. And stopped laughing. She intended to stay all weekend and think things through.

Her situation was untenable. She couldn't tolerate being caught in the middle anymore. As she clutched her own baby things, she admitted some truths to herself. She was very afraid she was going to have to give up on Ben. Not because of her father, but because Ben didn't feel about her the way Emily felt about him. And it was beginning to hurt too much to be with him.

The thought of leaving him caused real pain, so she banished it and turned her attention back to the boxes.

The next carton was filled with books. "Oh, look, sweetie!" *Lady and the Tramp*. She sat back on her heels. "What was I thinking?" she asked her unborn child. "That we could really make a go of it? That we'd have a happy ending like these two?" She opened the book.

"For my darling Emily. May you always see the worth in people who are different from you. Love, Mama." Mama? Is that what she'd called her mother? She couldn't remember.

She frowned and pulled out the other books. *Goodnight Moon*'s inscription was "Always follow your heart. You'll sleep well then."

For *Aesop's Fables*: "There's much in life to learn, baby girl. Learn it and live by it."

They were all such lovely sentiments. Written by a mother Emily couldn't even remember. Tears clouded her eyes and she closed the book she was holding. How could a woman leave her child? How could a woman write these wonderful things to her little girl and be the kind of person who simply no longer wanted to be a wife or mother?

Emily was about to stuff the books back in their box when she saw something at the bottom—a leatherbound book embossed with "A Mother's Journal." Just as she pulled it out, there was a knock at the door.

Emily jumped at the sound and Lady began to bark furiously. Only Jordan knew she was here, and she'd promised not to tell anyone else. Slowly, she rose, placed the precious book back in the box and made her way to the door, with Lady at her heels.

She was shocked to find her husband on the porch. Shocked and not at all pleased. "Go away," she called through the window.

Lady, however, had other ideas. She scratched at the wood. Her dog had gotten used to having a man around.

A man, who, under the halogen lamp, looked incredibly handsome in tight jeans with a red thermal shirt peeking out beneath a bomber jacket. "I'm not leaving, Emily. Let me in."

"I'm going to kill Jordan."

"Don't. I begged." He rubbed his arms up and down. "It's freezing out here. Let me in."

"No. I'm mad at you."

"I know. I'm sorry."

"It's not enough."

He put his hand on the glass. "Look, if I can't convince you in ten minutes that you should have let me in, I'll leave. I promise."

She stared at the door.

He said simply, "Please, we have to talk. Let me in, love."

HE SAW EMILY SHAKE HER HEAD and turn away, dragging Lady by the collar into the other room. Well, hell, he hadn't expected this. He'd been on an emotional roller coaster for two days, unable to reconcile his feelings for her and his desire to destroy her father. In the end, he'd simply come to the lake to beg her to help him find some sort of peace.

He sank down on the steps. There was no way he was leaving, not after he'd finally dragged her whereabouts out of Jordan. It had taken him all day, and some fancy two-steps, but he did it.

Shivering in his bomber jacket, he stared at the lake. It was late November and the water wasn't frozen, but it looked cold. Like he was—inside and out. Damn it, he wasn't letting her cut him from her life. He was prepared to do anything he had to in order to make things up to her. He got up and pounded on the door until she opened it.

"You'll get sick sitting out there in the cold," Emily said, standing in the entrance. "Go home."

Ben could see the puffs of air coming from his mouth. "I'm not leaving here until we've talked. You don't think, for one minute, I'm going to let you go, do you?"

She cradled her stomach. Her outfit—a baby-pink sweatsuit and pink slippers—was at odds with the way she tossed back her hair and pierced him with her gaze. "I've decided a few things. I'm done letting you or my father or anyone run my life. I'm making my own decisions now."

"All right." He rubbed his hands together and blew on them. "Can I please come in?"

She stepped aside. Warmth encompassed him when he crossed the threshold. He turned and found her leaning against the door, watching him. "Can we go by the fire?"

Her eyes narrowed, then she nodded. He followed her inside. His brief glance took in the fire, stuffed couches, lots of glass and boxes. Shrugging out of his coat, he dropped next to her on the couch. "I have a lot to say."

"Go ahead, then."

How to start? Now that he was here, words wouldn't come. Reaching into his pocket, he drew out a pouch and handed it to her.

"What is it?"

"Look inside."

With delicate fingers she untied the ribbon and shook out the contents into her other palm. Frowning, she picked up the man-size wedding ring. "What does this mean, Ben?"

He held out his hand. "I want to wear it. I want to really be married."

She sighed. "It's not enough."

He brushed his knuckles down her cheek. "Then maybe this is. I love you."

Her face drained of color. Tears clouded her eyes.

"Please don't cry. I've never said those words to a woman in my whole life."

"I've waited so long to hear that…" Her eyes widened. "Really? Never? Not even to Mallory."

"I didn't love Mallory."

Emily began to cry in earnest.

"I'm sorry…" He kissed her wet cheeks. "Please don't feel bad. I love you and I promise we'll work this out."

She let him cradle her neck before drawing back. "How Ben? How will we work this out?"

"Well, I hadn't gotten that far yet. I'm going to need some help from you to figure it out. All I know is what I feel and that I'm willing to do anything to make this work."

"You can't wave a magic wand and make everything go away, no matter how much you want to. You resent my father so much. And I need him in my life." She glanced at the boxes for some reason. "I already lost my mother."

"I know, sweetheart."

"He hates you, too. How can this ever be settled?"

"We'll find a way. I promise. We'll talk about it, make some decisions, get some help if we need to."

"Ben, I—"

"Shh. We'll stay here this weekend and hash it all out." He could tell she was torn. "Please, Emily, I love you. I'm here baring my soul, making a commitment because I don't want to live without you."

"Oh, God, I want to believe that."

"Take the risk. Give me a chance."

She bit her lip. It seemed like an eternity before she said, "All right."

His eyes stung. Because he hadn't really believed she'd agree. All along, he hadn't believed she loved him. She took his hand and slid the wedding band onto his finger. It looked right there; she raised it to her lips and kissed it.

Then he tugged her onto his lap and sat back, holding her. He smoothed down her hair. As she curled in closer, the baby kicked hard enough for Ben to feel it. The fire crackled as darkness settled over the lake.

Ben really had a lot to be thankful for this Thanksgiving season.

THEY LAY IN A MOUND of blankets and pillows, blissfully satisfied. Emily yawned and nestled into him. Nothing had been settled, yet everything seemed right. Making love tonight had transcended every other time because Ben was ready to commit to their relationship. And to making some kind of peace with her father.

His breathing evened out and she saw his eyes close. "Tired?"

He kissed her hair. "I hardly slept last night."

"How did you get Jordan to tell you where I was?"

"I showed her this." He lifted his hand and the fire caught on the gold reflected there. "She was at Trey's— all night I might add—and he helped convince her."

Emily chuckled, then quickly sobered. "How are we going to deal with this, Ben?"

"*This* being your father?"

"Yes."

"I'm not sure. I don't think I can forgive him for what he's done, Emily. But I don't like what I've become."

"You are the same man you used to be." She laid a hand over his heart. "In here. If you'll just let go of your resentment."

"All I can do is try. But I can't say something I don't feel just to make you happy." He kissed her on the head. "I wish I could. But it wouldn't be true." He thought for a minute. "I can tolerate your relationship with him, but I need to know some things."

She came up on her elbows so she was lying over him, her hair grazing his chest. "What?"

"It's so lame."

"Tell me."

"I need to know you'll stay with me. You won't kick me out of your life because of him. I realize that sounds stupid and childish, but that's the bottom line for me. If I can be sure of that, I think I can live with him in your life."

"Ben, I love you. I want a future with you. I'll never abandon you. I promise."

He let out a heavy breath. "Then I'll work on some kind of acceptance of your father." He kissed her head. "I shouldn't have insisted you not see him yesterday."

"He shouldn't have taunted you."

"I'll be better."

"I'll make sure he is, too." Her gaze turned dark. "But there's something else. I've been thinking about this for a long time."

"What?"

"I don't want you to intentionally try to hurt him."

Had Mackenzie told her about his threat with the patent? "What do you mean?"

"Ben, I know my father has done some unethical things—like stalling your contracts with Rockford Gas & Electric. I want your promise you won't go after him."

"I signed the waiver that I wouldn't prosecute him for stalling the contracts."

"I know. But I suspect that's not the worst thing he's done. I want your promise that if he did other unethical things—anywhere—that you won't try to prove his guilt."

"Do you realize what you're asking? He'll go on to cheat and defraud other people, other companies, like he did me."

"No, I won't let him. He listened to me all these years about saving people's jobs. He'll listen to me on this."

"You don't work for him anymore. How are you going to stop him in the future?"

"I'm not sure. I'll find a way, though. Please." She eased back and took his hand and pressed it into her belly. "For us. Promise me you won't pursue any kind of revenge."

Could he do that? Forget about the patent charges? The man Ben swore he wanted to be again would let it go. To that end, he said, "I promise."

She lay back against the pillows. "Let's take a nap now. Then I'll fix you dinner."

As Emily dozed in his arms, Ben prayed he hadn't just made a promise he couldn't keep.

BEN AWOKE TO UNFAMILIAR SOUNDS. Reaching for Emily, he found she wasn't next to him. He sat up and in the firelight saw her sitting in a rocker with a book in her hand. Sobbing. Somewhere in the cottage, a clock chimed eight times.

"Emily, sweetheart, what…."

Still, she cried.

Whipping on his jeans, he went to her. She'd switched on a small light and wrapped herself in a soft-weave lap blanket, but still she shivered. He knelt before her and took her ice-cold hands in his. The book in her lap was some kind of journal. "What is it, love?"

Tears coursed down her lovely cheeks. "My mother's journal."

He waited. Ben knew the abandonment of her mother when she was five had wedged inside her like shrapnel, unable to be removed, bothering her at the oddest times.

"From when she was pregnant with me."

"What does it say?"

"I—" She glanced down at the book as if to make sure it was real. "Nothing I expected."

"Can I read some of it?"

She just stared at him.

"Or you can read it to me."

She picked up the book. "The first entry is September 1971. 'I had the most wonderful news today. I'm pregnant. Lammon and I have been trying to conceive and I can't believe it's happened. I'm sure she's a girl. I'm going to give her my mother's name. Welcome to my body, my life, little Emily.'" She looked at Ben. "I didn't know I was named after her mother. All my grandparents were dead before I was born."

He was now sitting on the floor with his back to couch. "It's a beautiful name. It suits you."

She smiled weakly.

"Read me more."

"'I wish my stomach would grow. I want to see proof of you, baby girl. Lammon is so excited. He brought home your first doll. It's Raggedy Ann.'" Emily wiped away tears. "I remember that doll. I loved her."

Ben stifled his response. This was killing him, but he guessed she needed the catharsis to put the issue of her mother to rest.

She read more…a recounting of the gradual stages of her mother's pregnancy. The first time the baby moved… "'I felt you, love, a fluttering like butterflies flapping their wings.'" The first kick… "'A dainty jab. Your daddy got tears in his eyes.'" The first time she hiccuped, turned over in the womb.

"This is how I felt, too," Emily whispered as if to herself. "Almost the same at every phase."

He waited patiently.

"That's as far as I got. Right up until seven months, where I am now." She bit her lip. "Oh, Ben, it's like she's here, talking to me."

"You said you wanted her advice, her support. Maybe this is the gift she left you."

"I know." She hugged the journal to her heart. "I can't believe I found this. My father didn't keep any of her things. I always wished I had a scarf or bracelet— something that belonged to her."

He cocked his head. "Emily, you speak as if she's dead."

"She was, really, to us. Dad treated her that way when she left."

"*Why* did he say she left?"

"I told you she didn't want to be a wife or mother anymore."

For her sake, because he loved her, Ben bit back a nasty retort about what hell it must have been to be Mackenzie's wife. "I'm sorry."

She stared at the journal a long time. "This doesn't make sense."

Of course it didn't.

"How could she write this, how could she feel so blessed to be pregnant and then not want me anymore?"

"I can't answer that, love."

She sat back in the rocker and watched the fire. "I feel so bad."

"I know. Maybe you shouldn't read any more tonight."

She smiled over at him. "Maybe. I said I'd cook for you."

"Why don't I cook while you rest?"

"That sounds good." He stood, drew her up and walked her over to the couch. When he got her settled, her eyes closed.

With more willpower than he'd believed he possessed, he didn't voice his suspicions to Emily. Instead, he forced himself to act calmly. When he was sure she was asleep, he picked up the journal and read the rest of it. After he finished, he was positive something wasn't right here, that Mackenzie's story about her mother was not the truth, at least not all of it. Ben strode to the kitchen and whipped out his cell phone.

His private investigator answered on the first ring. "Harrington."

"Luke, it's Ben Cassidy. I have another job if you can take it."

"Just finished something else, so I can."

"I want you to find a woman named Anna Mackenzie." He flipped to the front of the book. "Anna McGee Mackenzie. She lived in Rockford until about thirty years ago."

"This woman any relation to Lammon Mackenzie?"

"Hmm. His ex-wife."

"What are we looking for?"

"Where she is now." He glanced toward the living room. "And why she left her husband and daughter."

"I could guess why she left that bastard."

"But not the child," Ben said.

He gave Luke the sketchy details Emily had told him, and then hung up.

Promise me you won't do anything to hurt my father.

At that point, Ben had thought he was promising not to use the patent information against Mackenzie. Was Ben betraying her trust by searching for her mother?

The hell he was. Emily had a right to know what had driven her mother—totally enamored with her unborn child—from their lives.

And God help them, Ben believed it was something despicable Mackenzie had done. If that was fact, it would put a whole new spin on Ben's duty to his wife and unborn child.

CHAPTER FOURTEEN

EMILY ENTERED BEN'S OFFICE with Janice and Betty and stopped short. Her husband was hunkered down at his computer and he looked as if the sky were about to fall. His tie was askew, his jacket off, his shirtsleeves rolled up. When he glanced up, his expression was panicky.

"What's wrong?" Emily asked. Since they'd come back from the cabin, everything between them had been idyllic. She didn't want that to change.

"Okay," he said as if he were unaware of the others' presence. "I've done all the research. Stork Smart, Birth Works, the Bradley Method and Lamaze seem to be the most popular childbirth methods. I've made up a spreadsheet, and listed the times and dates of the classes, the pros and cons of the programs. Then I did an ancillary study and printed out testimonials. It seems most women prefer—"

"Ben, stop." Emily winked at the other women. "I've got everything arranged. I'm going with this new Chinese philosophy on childbirth, and a midwife will deliver our baby at home in the bathtub."

"What?" He threw back his chair. "That's not safe. We need to have all the modern…" He trailed off as he realized all three of them were laughing. "You're making fun of me."

Emily circled around his desk and kissed him on the cheek. "Since you've gone off the deep end about this last phase of my pregnancy, it's hard not to tease you."

He placed a hand on her stomach. "I just don't want anything to happen to him. Or you."

"That's our cue to leave." Janice chuckled. "We just wanted to double check the date of the shower with you."

"Shower?" Ben asked.

"Hmm, for little Ian. Everybody here wants to be part of the celebration. It's equal opportunity, so the guys will come, too. Next Thursday."

"Oh, sure, fine." He shrugged as if they were speaking a foreign language and he was struggling to understand it. "I can't keep up with everything."

Emily straightened his tie. "I can, so don't worry."

His staff said their goodbyes and left. Emily tugged Ben onto the couch. "Ben, childbirth is a natural process. I'm going to be fine."

"So much can go wrong."

"Nothing will."

He shook his head. "I'm a basket case. I read all that stuff on childbirth education classes and it scared the shit out of me."

"We're going to the Lamaze classes. Four three-hour sessions. They start this Wednesday. It's a little late, but with everything that's happened, I didn't sign up in time to get us in sooner. I had Betty add the dates to your calendar."

"Lamaze! No, that's all natural. You have to suffer through labor with no drugs, and I don't believe for a minute that the breathing helps."

She laughed. She couldn't help it. "Breathing techniques are just one of their methods of coping. Movement and positioning, back massage, even hydrotherapy are all elements of natural childbirth."

"You can't have drugs if the pain gets too bad."

"I can have an epidural if I need it." At his blank look, she said, "That's a spinal block. Granted, the Lamaze people don't recommend it because the anesthesia makes it difficult to respond to the contractions, but it's not ruled out if the pain is too much. Joan Davidson said I can have the block if necessary."

"Hell—the thought of you being in that much pain…."

She warmed at his concern, and at the love he'd shown in a thousand different ways since Thanksgiving. "Ben, women have been giving birth since Eve. It's a natural process that I'm sure I can handle." She frowned, remembering the journal. "I just wish my mother were here. I can't stop thinking about her."

Ben slid his arm around her. "Wasn't there a record about the delivery?"

"Yes. She was going to have natural childbirth, too. But there were complications. She had to have a C-section. My dad was out of town."

No surprise there.

"My mother had a backup coach. Her name was Millie something." Emily had made a decision to ask her father point blank about the discrepancy between the story he'd told her and what Emily had found in the journal. But he'd been out of town since the day after Thanksgiving and she didn't want to get into all of that on the phone. For one thing, she wanted to see his face when she confronted him. "Anyway, I want to try Lamaze."

Ben drew in a breath. "If you think it's best." His look was sheepish. "I'm supposed to be reassuring you."

"You'll have plenty of opportunity." She raised her hand to his hair, enjoying the freedom of touching him openly. "Do you have any idea how much all your interest, your worry means to me?"

"I love you. Of course I'm interested. Worried."

"Ben." Betty stood in the doorway. "Mrs. Smith from the soup kitchen is here to see you."

"Oh, fine." Emily had come to Cassidy Industries for this meeting about the Christmas activities at the soup kitchen. "Send her in."

Alice whistled when she entered Ben's office. "Wow. This is impressive." She eyed Ben's expensive suit. Gestured to the cherrywood desk and furniture, and to the backdrop of windows. "Sometimes I still can't believe who you are."

Emily kissed her cheek. "Hi, Alice."

"You've really popped out. You sure you got two more months to go?"

"That's what the doctor says. Come sit."

After Ben poured Alice some coffee, he brought a legal pad to the table. "Let's start with what you did last year and what we might feasibly add."

Alice's expression was nostalgic. "You were there, you know."

"I helped put up the tree." He smiled at Emily. "You wore this green velour dress that made your eyes sparkle like the lights on the Christmas tree. I couldn't take my eyes off you."

"I wish I'd known. I scolded myself a thousand times over for noticing how good you looked in those black jeans."

They laughed. Then Alice got down to business. "First off, the dinner will be ham with all the trimmings. Second, we'll do the same gift program."

"Are churches providing the presents again?".

"Yes. They'll be wrapped and labeled Adult Male, Child Under Three, etc."

Emily grinned. "Will Howard play Santa again?"

"Couldn't keep him away."

They talked about bus tokens, a coveted commodity, and some activities for the children. Ben looked thoughtful. "I'd like to add something this year."

"What?"

"Boots. At Thanksgiving, the guests appreciated the hats and gloves so much, I thought Cassidy Industries could purchase boots in all sizes to distribute."

"Oh, Ben," Emily said. "That's a great idea."

"We have a lot to be grateful for this Christmas, honey. I want to make everybody's holiday the better."

When they were just about done, Betty came to the doorway again. "Ben, Luke Harrington's on the phone. He said he needs to talk to you ASAP."

"We're done here, right?"

They all rose. Emily turned to Alice. "I'll walk you out." She glanced back at Ben as they left. "Are you all right? You're scowling."

"I'm fine. See you in a minute." He closed the door behind them.

Outside his office, Emily wondered at Ben's shift in mood. And who Luke Harrington was.

"I FOUND HER."

Ben sank into his chair. "That was fast."

"She goes by Anna McGee now. She owns a book-store on Fourth and Twenty-third. Lives in the Village alone."

"Great."

"You want me to go down? See what the story is?"

Ben stared at the picture of Emily he now displayed on his desk. "No, I'll do that. All I needed was her location. Send over what you have."

"You got it." The man paused. "Do you want the patent files along with it?"

"Yes."

"You gonna use the information?"

He thought about his promise to Emily that he wouldn't intentionally hurt her father. "I'm not sure. Some of it might depend on what I find out about Ms. McGee."

"It's your dollar."

"And well worth it."

Harrington hung up and Ben rubbed a hand over his face. Emily didn't need this kind of upheaval at such a late stage in her pregnancy. The appearance of her long-lost mother was bound to be upsetting. But Ben felt compelled to find out the real story. He pulled out his PDA and studied his calendar. He could get away at the end of next week—after the shower and the first childbirth class. Damn, he hated leaving Emily alone now. But New York was only an hour's flight. He'd go down and back in one day. Depending on what he found, he'd make a decision about what to tell his wife about her mother. And, then, he'd decide what to do with the incriminating patent information.

He had a bad feeling about all this. A bad feeling that Mackenzie had not been telling Emily the truth. Damn the man. Did his machinations never end?

MAC LIKED MIAMI'S WARM WEATHER, particularly at this time of year. As he booted up his laptop in his Crown Plaza suite, he decided he'd go out to the beach when he finished his meeting. You'd never know it was the beginning of December when you were in Florida.

He hated December. It was the month Anna had left him. He called up the stats on Southern Instrumentation and Commodities. He needed a company to buy, and this one was so vulnerable, he could get it away from the family owners for a song. He had to have something to occupy his mind or he'd go crazy.

How the hell had Cassidy found out about the patent? Mac had given instructions to destroy the files and computer records. His acting president had assured Mac he'd taken care of it. Damn, he should have disposed of them himself. What if Cassidy used the information against him? He'd been thinking about how to derail any plans the man might have. Trying to steal back the files wouldn't work—Cassidy would have copies. Appealing to his good nature wouldn't cut it. Worse came to worst, Mac would have to get Emily to stop her husband. If Ben loved her back, then Emily would have sway over him. How could Cassidy put his wife's father in jail?

Then there'd been Thanksgiving.

When he'd gotten the message from Emily that she'd be spending the holiday alone, Mac had been livid. He'd driven over to her house but she hadn't been there. He'd called her cell, but she hadn't answered. He'd been reduced to phoning Jordan Turk, who had not been kind.

He'd sworn to someday get even with the woman for treating him badly. He'd ended up spending the day with his date and had never been more miserable. Ever since Cassidy had come into their lives, Mac had not been happy.

You'll always be unhappy, Lammon, until you change your ways. Anna had been sitting in a hospital bed, looking so fragile, he almost couldn't stand it.

I'll change, please, come home.

I can't. I'm not well. Emily and I will be leaving as soon as I can make the arrangements.

He'd lost it then. He'd thrown such a fit, the security people had had to drag him out of the hospital. His last image of Anna was in bed, crying, as he'd shouted, *You can go. I can't stop that, but I sure as hell can stop you from taking my daughter.*

And he'd done it. By some of the most vicious means he'd ever employed. Sometimes, during the night, he'd wake up in a cold sweat over it.

Damn, why was he going down that old road? Because it was December? Son of a bitch. It didn't matter. Nothing about Anna mattered anymore. Forcefully, he shoved her out of his mind and turned back to the company he was about to acquire. He wondered what he'd have to do to get it. He'd need a good strategy, which he brainstormed for almost an hour on the computer. Poised for the kill, he felt a lot better.

And, this time, if he had to do anything that skirted the law, he'd be sure to destroy the evidence himself.

THE UNDERSHIRT WAS the tiniest piece of clothing Emily had ever seen. It was hard to believe it would fit her baby. For some reason, the sight of the small shirt brought tears to her eyes.

"What's wrong?" Ben asked. He sat beside her, surrounded by presents and staff.

"The clothes make it all seem so real." She leaned into Ben and whispered, "I never thought I would have a baby, I guess."

His grin was a mile wide. But there was something else in his eyes. Some kind of worry. Maybe put there by the childbirth class last night where they'd shown a video of the actual birth of a baby. Ben had turned green and had had to leave the room. "We'll have more babies, too," he said smiling. "Maybe a little girl next time."

She chuckled as she opened the next gift. "It's a mobile. To hang over Ian's bed." She grinned at Betty. The tiny stuffed animals on the end of six strings were replicas of Lady and Tramp and their babies. "How did you know?"

"I saw mobiles with storybook characters on the Net and asked Ben if you had a favorite."

Emily cried her way through footed sleepers, overalls and shirts, a walker, and a swing and car-seat combo. By the time they were finished, she was exhausted.

Scanning the room, she couldn't believe all these people had done this for her baby. "I don't know what to say," she told them. "I'm so glad to share this with you."

After they had some cake, they gathered the presents and packed the SUV. As they were about to leave, Betty grabbed Ben. "Here's your electronic ticket information. The plane leaves at seven."

Emily turned to Ben. "What plane?"

"I'm flying to New York tomorrow. Business."

"Oh, I didn't know."

"I hate going out of town this close to the due date."

"It's not that close. I've got six weeks left."

"I won't leave town again until after the baby's born. This is unavoidable."

"I understand."

On the drive home, Emily hoped she'd get a chance to see her father when Ben was gone. He'd be back from his trip tomorrow. She'd talked to him on the phone, but conversation was stilted and her dad had been distant. He always acted that way when he was displeased.

Once they arrived home, Ben said, "Want to rest before dinner?"

"Yes. Come sit in front of the tree with me."

They'd cut down a twelve-foot tree and decorated it

with homemade ornaments. The lights sparkled in the dim room. With Lady at her feet, Emily leaned into her husband. "It's hard to believe next year at this time, we'll have a baby."

"Yeah. He'll probably be crawling over to the tree to pull the ornaments off."

"I feel so lucky this Christmas."

He kissed her head. "Me, too."

She sighed.

"What is it?"

"I don't know. Just a feeling I guess. I've never been this happy in my life. I'm worried something will go wrong."

She felt his body stiffen and he pulled away.

"Ben, what is it?"

"Nothing we should be discussing."

"Are you thinking about my father?"

"No, not really. Are you?"

"Some. He's still angry at me for leaving on Thanksgiving."

"You've talked to him."

"Yes." She told him where he was.

"Did you ask him about the journals?"

"No, I don't want to do it on the phone. It's too important."

"What's he doing in Florida?"

"He's buying another company."

"The poor employees."

She stretched out her legs. "Let's change the subject. It's spoiling my mood."

He kissed her hair. "This will perk you up." He reached beside the couch and produced a gift bag.

"What is it?"

"Your last shower present."

"From…?"

"Your dog."

She tore off the paper. Enclosed was a huge illustrated storybook and a DVD of *Lady and the Tramp.* "Ben, this is beautiful." She shook her head. "Thank you so much for getting it for me, for being there for me."

"I love you, Emily. And nothing's going to change that, or ruin it, or interfere with it."

"Of course it isn't." She cocked her head. "Is something going on I don't know about?"

"No. Nothing. I'm just spooked, I guess. This is almost too good to be true." He opened the book. "Come on, I'll read you the story until you fall asleep."

Emily laid her head on his shoulder. His husky voice lulled her. She felt safe and secure in his arms, in his love, and in the belief that he'd keep his promises to her.

CHAPTER FIFTEEN

DECEMBER BROUGHT ICY RAIN to New York City, causing Ben to duck under an awning across the street from Lady's Bookstore. The brick exterior of the store, which specialized in children's literature, sported big windows filled with huge displays. On either end of the sign was a cutout of Lady and the Tramp. He suspected that what he found here wouldn't be good news for Emily.

After the weekend at the lake, Ben had decided to give Emily the folder on the fuel-cell patent. His reasoning was simple: he'd promised not to pursue any kind of revenge on Mackenzie, and he couldn't hurt Emily by putting her father in jail. He'd also had a vague notion that perhaps she could use the information as a weapon to keep her father in line. But in the end, what Ben might find out today kept him from turning over the folder. Best to find out exactly what he was dealing with.

He crossed the busy road, dodging slippery patches and ignoring the honking of horns. He opened the door to the shop. *Please don't let Emily's mother be the monster Mackenzie made her out to be.*

Inside it was warm and, as Ben unbuttoned his leather coat, he studied the layout and design. Each wall was painted a different primary color, sporting huge posters of books like *The Polar Express, Where the Wild Things Are* and *The Berenstain Bears and the Bad Dream.* Stacks were child-height and easily accessible to the smallest toddler. An adult coffee bar and children's snack areas, along with spaces to sit and play, were scattered throughout the store. It was obvious both kids and parents were welcome here.

Noise off to the side attracted him, so he made his way through the aisles. In a corner, he found several children, sitting on the floor, enthralled by a storyteller.

Who was Emily's mother.

Ben sucked in a breath at the rare opportunity to see what his wife would look like in twenty or so years. Anna McGee was a beautiful woman, even now at almost sixty. She wore her graying hair in a stylish bob and, slender like Emily, she had his wife's smile. From this distance, he couldn't see her eyes, but her face was remarkably unlined. Her voice was as soft as summer rain, again just like her daughter's.

"'What do you mean I can't eat the corn?' the little pig asked." She scrunched her face like the story character might. "The father replied, 'You didn't plant the corn, you didn't harvest it, so you can't eat it.'"

The children cheered in agreement. Ben was mesmerized by the woman reading and watched her until she finished the story. Then she looked up. And he saw Emily's eyes. Anna smiled at him. "If you're here to pick up one of the children, we're not quite done yet."

"No," he said hoarsely. "I'd like to talk to you."

"Fine, I'll be done in a bit. There's a coffee bar up front."

Ben nodded and left the story area, his mind buzzing. He needed to find out some information quickly and didn't have time for Anna McGee to dissemble.

She approached the coffee bar ten minutes later. An assistant had taken the kids to a back playroom. Smoothing down the peach sweater she wore with black pants, she gave him a questioning smile. "I'm sorry to keep you waiting. Is there something I can do for you?"

Up close, Ben studied her fine features, so much like Emily's it broke his heart. "I hope so. You are Anna Mackenzie, aren't you?"

The woman's porcelain skin paled. "I'm Anna McGee."

"Let me rephrase. Were you Anna Mackenzie?"

"A lifetime ago." She wrapped her arms around her waist in a protective gesture Emily often affected. "Who are you that you know my married name?"

Ben slid his hand into the breast pocket of his coat. Pulling out a picture of Emily that he'd taken last week, he gave it to her mother. And watched the woman closely. He knew her reaction would be truthful even if her words weren't.

When she looked at the picture, Anna burst into tears.

Thank God, Ben thought and assisted her to a chair. Anna let him help her sit down and after a moment, she met his gaze. "Who *are* you?"

"Your daughter's husband. You recognized her?"

"Of course. She looks so much like I did at that age." Reverently, as if viewing an ancient artifact, Anna touched the image in the photo, outlining Emily's hair, shoulders and rounded stomach. "She...she's having a baby?"

"Yes."

"Her first?"

He nodded.

"When?"

"Six weeks."

More tears. "How did you find me?"

"A private investigator."

"Why, after all these years?"

He dropped down next to her and scrambled for a good place to begin. "Emily's pregnancy has made her wonder more about you. Then she found a journal you kept when you were pregnant with her. The woman who wrote those words doesn't fit with the story Mackenzie told her about her mother, so I decided to find out the truth."

Anna shook her head. "Why? If she thinks I'm dead, isn't it better for her to go on believing that?"

Damn it. He was afraid of something like this. "Emily doesn't think you're dead. She thinks you abandoned her when she was five."

"What?"

"Mackenzie told her you left because you didn't want to be a wife or mother anymore."

"Oh, Lord, no." She dropped the picture in her lap and buried her head in her hands.

Ben waited for her to gain control again. "I suspected something was amiss, but not this, Anna. Do you want to tell me what happened? Then we can decide what's best for Emily."

She had her daughter's grit. Even though she was devastated, she sat up and wiped her cheeks. Her voice was steady when she spoke, despite the sadness in her eyes. "I married Lammon when I was twenty. I fell madly in love with him. He wasn't the man then that he became years later." Grasping the picture, she stood and began to pace. "I don't know what changed him. He'd had a horrid childhood—his parents died when he was five and he was raised by an uncle. The man was sadistic. Lammon was beaten by him." Again, tears came to her eyes. After all Mackenzie had done to her, she could still feel sorry for him. "The change in him as an adult was gradual. I think it was the lure of control, a control he'd never had as a child. I couldn't get pregnant right away, and he became more and more involved in the business. By the time I did conceive, he'd been seduced by power. By the time I admitted to myself that he was doing things he shouldn't—unethical business—Emily was four. I couldn't tolerate it any longer and asked for a divorce."

Ben watched her.

"He was enraged. He threatened me."

"Did he blackmail you with something from your past?"

"No, there *was* nothing from my past. I had a very ordinary life until I met him. What broke me was the fact that a man I loved so much turned on me so completely. I...I didn't handle it very well. I was weak, and it cost me my daughter."

"How, Anna?"

"I became agitated, unable to sleep. I took antianxiety drugs for a while, but eventually stopped."

"Why?"

"That's another story. In any case, I ended up in the hospital from exhaustion and worry. After a few weeks, Lammon made arrangements for me to go to a private hospital. I didn't realize he'd use that against me. By this time, he was very powerful, had made more than his first million. He used my stay in the sanitarium— about three months—to get Emily. His team of lawyers convinced a judge I was an unfit mother. Thirty years ago this was easier to do than it would be today. I fought it as well as I could, given my circumstances, but in the end, he got custody. When I followed through on my plan to leave him, he was bitter and hurt, I think, that I'd really do it. When I left, he warned me never to come back."

Something didn't fit. "How could you leave her with that monster? I can't ever imagine deserting my child, let alone handing her over to someone like Lammon Mackenzie."

"I was physically and mentally depleted. Once I recovered, and I got my wits back, I called him and told him I wanted joint custody of Emily. He said he'd already told her I was d-dead…" she started to cry again "…and if I came back into her life, I'd scar her irrevocably."

Though he shouldn't be, after all he knew about the man, Ben was once again amazed that Mackenzie could be so treacherous. "Still, you gave up on your child. I don't understand it."

Anna swallowed hard and looked at him with bruised eyes. "Of course you don't, because I left out one important piece."

"What?"

"I was pregnant again, but I kept it from Lammon. That was why I stopped the antianxiety medicine. My doctor was a woman and never liked my husband, so she agreed to conceal the pregnancy from him. I was afraid he'd take that child, too, if he knew. So when I discovered he'd told Emily I was dead, I decided to stay here in New York and keep my own secrets."

"Are you saying Emily has a sibling?"

"Yes. A brother. His name is Dylan." She shook back her hair. "And I told *him* his father was dead, Ben. Maybe I'm not any better than Lammon."

Ben drew in a heavy breath. "This is an incredible story."

"What are you going to do with the information?"

"I don't know." He nodded to the picture Anna held. "Emily's in the last stages of her pregnancy. I'm not sure it's the best time for her to find this out about a father she loves despite the despicable things he's done." He shook his head. "However, since she found your journal, she's wanted you in her life now, while she's pregnant. Maybe it's time to tell her the real story."

"It's hard to know what's best for her."

"I'd like to kill that bastard of a father of hers."

"He had a good heart once. And this situation isn't entirely his fault."

She was so like Emily.

"Don't defend—"

Ben's cell phone rang. He fished it out of his pocket and checked the caller ID. "It's Emily. I have to take this."

Anna's hand fluttered to her throat.

He watched her as he clicked on. "Hi, love."

"Ben, thank God I caught you. My water just broke, and Jordan's taking me to the hospital...." Her voice caught. "Oh, Ben, the baby's coming today and he's six weeks early. The doctor says he'll be all right, but please, come home."

His heart stuttered but he kept his voice even. "I'll be there in a few hours. The doctor's right. She estimated he weighed over six pounds at our last visit, and he's fully formed. He might be little, but he'll be fine. I'll catch the next plane out."

After he clicked off, he turned to Anna. "I've got to go. You're about to become a grandmother."

Anna stood abruptly. "I'm coming with you." When he opened his mouth to protest, she said, "Please Ben, don't deny me this. I won't see Emily. I just want to be out in the waiting room for the delivery. Then I'll leave town again without her knowing I was there, if you think that's best. I promise." Again he hesitated. "I missed so much of her life. If I can have this tiny piece, give it to me. Please."

"Get your things. We'll talk on the plane."

EMILY HAD HELD ON WELL ENOUGH through the ordeal that had begun once she'd gotten out of bed this morning and her water had broken. Ben had already left for New York, so she'd called the doctor, then Jordan. She'd phoned Ben as she'd packed a bag. Jordan had arrived, driven her to the hospital and taken her through the admission process. Now, hooked up to a fetal monitor, with Jordan seated across the room, flipping through a magazine, Emily forced herself to hang on while she waited for her husband to arrive. All the while, she silently talked to the baby. *Don't worry, sweetie, we'll be fine. I won't let anything happen to you. And we're going to see each other today. Hang on, little one.*

Ben flew through the birthing room's door three hours after she'd called him.

And Emily burst into tears.

"Oh, honey." He rushed to her bedside. "Are you…is everything…?"

"I'm fine," she mumbled through the tears and hiccups. She buried her face in his chest and inhaled the clean, strong scent of him, which clung to the cold leather of his coat. "I just wanted you here."

He sat on the side of the bed, his big solid form comforting. From across the room, Jordan said, "I'll wait outside," and left.

Ben held her close. "Shh. It's okay. I'm here."

"I…it *is* okay. At least Joan says it is." She drew away, groping for control.

His gray eyes filled with worry, he brushed back her hair. "What happened?"

"I woke up after you left and my water broke. When we got here, Joan said the baby will have to come today."

Just then a contraction hit. She'd been having them for a few hours and they were getting stronger. "Oh…" Pain shot through her stomach.

Ben's face turned white, but he held her hand, coaxed her through it.

"They're not too bad yet. Tolerable. But it's been three hours, and I haven't made much progress. I think the doctor might have to do a cesarean. Oh, Ben, I didn't want that."

He looked at her sternly. "Of course you want that. If it's best for the baby, and for you, you definitely do want that."

"My sentiments exactly." Joan Davidson strode through the door and picked up Emily's chart. "Hi, Ben. You're going to be a daddy today."

He glanced at the clock. It was early afternoon. "I guess."

After examining Emily, Joan gave her the news. "You're not making enough progress. And the sonogram shows the baby is big."

"Even six weeks early?"

"Yes. Given his size and the fact that you're not any further in dilation or effacement, it's my opinion that you should have a cesarean."

"Whatever's best for us," she said, grasping Ben's hand tightly.

Ben ran a knuckle down her cheek. "We'll see Ian in just a bit, sweetheart." He looked at the doctor. "I can stay with her, right?"

"Yes." She nodded to a set of doors at the far end of the room. "We'll take her there, into the delivery room. You'll have to leave while we prep her, then you can go back there with her. She'll be hooked up to a lot of things, so don't worry about that when you see her."

"Like what?"

"This fetal monitor. A catheter. An IV." She recorded something else on the chart. "And you'll be draped, Emily, so Ben doesn't have to worry about fainting."

He drew in a breath. "I won't faint."

Joan laughed. "It's common procedure. You'll both be fine."

"What about anesthesia?"

"She'll have a spinal. That way she'll be awake, and can see the little guy after he comes out. But we'll need to spend some time finishing up with Emily. Meanwhile, if everything goes well, you can stay with the baby, Dad."

"If everything goes well?" Emily said, frightened.

"It will," Ben assured her.

"No reason to think it won't. Let's not buy trouble." Joan stepped back. "I'll go get things started. When they come in to prep, Ben, you have to leave."

When the doctor left, Ben smiled at Emily. "I know this isn't what you planned, but we'll get through it." He rested a hand on her stomach. "All three of us."

"As long as I have you." She gripped his arm, struck by a huge bolt of pain. She moaned her way through it. "Wow."

His face was stricken. They sat there for few minutes until a nurse entered the room. Ben stood to leave. "I'll be in as soon as they let me."

Her hand on his arm, Emily held him back. "Ben... my father's in Florida. Somebody has to call him. Will you do it?"

He gave her the phoniest smile she'd ever seen. She'd never loved him more. "Of course."

She told him her dad's cell-phone number.

"I'll be right back."

Another contraction hit and the nurse shooed him out.

Emily made it through the pain, through the prep and prayed everything would be all right. Now that Ben was with her, she believed it would be.

BEN FOUND EMILY'S MOTHER in the waiting room. Jordan, hovering in the background, frowned as she listened. "Emily's doing well. But the contractions aren't progressing like they should be. And the baby's big. Her doctor was afraid of this all along. She's going to have a cesarean."

"Oh." Anna raised her chin. "She'll be fine. I had a cesarean, Ben, when I delivered Emily, right here in this hospital. She and the baby will be just fine."

"I wish you could go tell her that. I know you can't, the shock would be too much for her to handle. But damn it, she needs her mother now."

From across the room, Jordan gasped. "Her *mother?*"
She straightened, pushed off from the wall and came toward them.

Anna turned.

Ben introduced the two women.

Jordan's gaze hardened. "You left her when she was
five. Do you have any idea how much she's mourned
the loss of you?"

"Jordan, it isn't Anna's fault."

Thoughtful, Emily's friend cocked her head. "Don't
tell me, this is good old Dad's handiwork."

Ben nodded.

Emily's best friend swore like a sailor.

"Let's not lay blame now." Anna shook her head.
"We need to decide what to do from here."

Jordan smiled. "Emily's just like you."

"What will happen now, Ben?" Anna asked.

"As soon as she's prepped I'm going back in. I can
be there for the delivery."

"Good. She'll need you."

"She wants me to call Mackenzie."

"I'll do it," Jordan told him.

"No, I will." He turned to Anna. "He's in Florida, so
he won't get back here for a while. You can stay until
then, or you can face him if you want, Anna. Emily will
have to be told about you, but we'll deal with all that
later."

"I understand."

He whipped out his cell. As both women watched, he punched in Mackenzie's number.

"Mackenzie here," Ben heard after the second ring.

"Mackenzie, this is Ben Cassidy. Emily's gone into labor and is in the hospital. They'll be doing a C-section in a few minutes."

"What the hell? It's two months early." Ben didn't want to be moved by the alarm in Mackenzie's voice.

"Six weeks. But they did tests. The baby's plenty big. That's part of the problem. The doctor assures us they'll both be fine."

"I'll catch the next plane out."

"I'm sure Emily will appreciate that."

Mackenzie hung up.

"You're welcome," Ben said dryly into the dead phone line. When he looked up, he saw Trey in the doorway. Well, he'd need his best friend here. This whole damn thing was turning out to be very complicated.

EMILY GRIPPED BEN'S HAND. She was experiencing no pain, but her heart beat fast. The drape prevented her from seeing the doctor, and she and Ben were in a cocoon of sorts. "I can't believe this is going to happen now," she whispered.

His smile was reassuring. "I know, me too."

"They said five minutes to get the baby out, right?"

"Yes," she heard from the other end of the table. "And here he is."

Emily didn't hear a cry. Oh, no. "Is he okay?"

"See for yourself." The drape lowered and Joan put a squirming little bundle on Emily's stomach. Oh my God. This was her baby! He was very long, very red, and the most beautiful thing she'd ever seen. Her tears overflowed as she cradled him. He stared up with big eyes, a stubborn chin and still he didn't cry. "Oh, my. Oh, Ben, look."

Her husband's voice was husky. "I see." Sniffing, he grasped the baby's hand. "Hi, little guy."

Emily brushed Ian's red cheek. "Hello, sweetie. Aren't you beautiful?"

Ben couldn't take his eyes off the baby. "I can't believe it. He's gorgeous. And big."

Joan smiled. "Almost seven pounds. I guess he was ready to come out."

The nurse circled around to the head of the bed. "There's more to do for you, Emily. I'll take the baby and clean him up. Dad, you can come with me."

Ben followed the nurse to the side of the room. As Joan worked on Emily, Ben talked to her. "Wait till you see, honey… He's really long… Twenty-two inches… His eyes are gray just like mine." He kept up the commentary, and finally, after the doctor finished, returned to her with little Ian wrapped in a soft white blanket wearing a blue cap.

She looked over and saw tears in her husband's eyes. "Ben…" She reached out for his hand. He took hers and held it tightly. "It's a miracle, isn't it?"

"Yes. *Our* miracle. I love you so much." Leaning over, he kissed the baby's head. "And you, buddy."

"I love you too, Ben." She smiled down at her son. "And you too, Ian."

IT BOTHERED BEN that Trey and Jordan were able to see Emily soon after the birth and her mother wasn't. So, when they'd finished up with Emily, and she'd gotten to feed the baby, he asked the nurse to take Ian to the neonatal center for a few hours. Then he found Anna in the cafeteria where she'd told him she'd be. She looked so lonely, sitting at a table by herself, sipping coffee, staring blankly off into space. "Anna?"

She looked up with sad eyes. "Ben. Are they doing well?"

"Come see for yourself." He held out his hand.

"I can't show myself to Emily now."

"I know. But you can see your grandson. Emily's sleeping, but the baby's in the nursery."

Now *she* started crying. "I'd love that."

"Then let's go!"

They talked about the delivery, Emily's recovery and the baby all the way to the nursery. Once there, they stood in front of the glass. The crib two over was marked Ian Cassidy. "There he is."

As they watched, the baby stretched and kicked at the blanket. "Oh, Ben, he's beautiful. Just beautiful."

Ben tugged at her arm. "Come on back. I checked. You can hold him."

"I can?" She looked like she'd won the lottery. "Oh, dear." More tears. He flung his arm around her shoulders, feeling like *he* could climb Mount Everest. "Come on, Grandma."

They both suited up in blue gowns and the baby was brought to them in a tiny anteroom with a couple of chairs. Seated in a rocker, Anna held out her arms; the nurse placed Ian in his grandmother's embrace. "Well, now, hello there. My, aren't you handsome?" She crooned to him, unfolded the blanket a bit, and his hand stuck out. Placing her pinky inside it, she watched as he reflexively grasped it. "You're going to be a strong one, aren't you? Just like your daddy."

When she began to sing, Ben crossed to the window to watch the other babies. Still reeling from this miracle, he listened to Anna croon to his son.

And imagined what it would be like to lose the baby she held, his baby, when he was an infant, a toddler or even as an adult. Fury shot through him. Mackenzie had deprived this woman of her child. And, Ben knew in his heart, for her sake and for Emily's, that he had to find a way to reunite mother and daughter.

Another insidious thought sneaked in with the rest. Along with an unwanted sympathy for a man he hated. Mackenzie had a son he didn't even know about. Even though the whole situation was his fault, he'd lost his child, too.

Hell, Ben didn't want to feel sorry for the guy. But turning to watch grandson and grandmother, he couldn't help it.

IT WAS MIDNIGHT when Mac finally hurtled through the doors of Rockford Memorial Hospital. Though he'd talked to his daughter on the phone, in between the endless plane rides back to Rockford, he had to see for himself that she was all right. She'd told him she was in room 4333, so he rode the elevator up to the maternity ward. Thankfully his daughter had made it through the cesarian. And goddamn, *he* had a grandson. Even the fact that it was Cassidy's kid didn't diminish the joy he felt over the birth of this child.

Slowly, he opened the door to her room and tiptoed inside. He found her asleep, on her side, holding Cassidy's hand. Cassidy was stretched out on a lounge chair, asleep, too. No baby in sight. For a minute, he watched his daughter. She looked like an angel, lying there. Finally he left the room and went to the nurse's station. He explained who he was and asked after the baby.

The nurse smiled at him. "I think it would be all right if you went to the neonatal center." She told him how to get there. He found his way down the maze of corridors and reached the glassed-in nursery.

And there he was. Little Ian Cassidy. "Well I'll be

damned," Mac said smiling. He put his hand up to the glass. "Hi, little guy." He forced back a lump in his throat and felt his eyes sting. Staring at the baby, he felt such joy, yet such an abysmal sense of loss.

"Hello, Lammon."

His hand dropped from the window. He knew he had to be hallucinating, that his memories must have conjured the sweetest voice he'd ever known. But turning just in case, he saw his ex-wife standing three feet away from him.

He stepped toward her. "Annie? That can't be you."

"It is, Lammon. It's me. I'm back."

Mac was immobilized. So many emotions, already brought to the surface by Emily's baby, engulfed him. He swallowed hard. He lifted his hand then dropped it again. After long seconds, he opened his mouth to speak, but couldn't get words out.

"I'm sorry to spring my presence on you like this."

Still he couldn't answer.

Crossing so she was close enough to touch him, she pressed a hand on the sleeve of his sports coat. "Are you all right?"

Finally he was able to nod.

She pointed to a nearby couch and said, "Come sit. I know this is a shock." He let her lead him to across the room.

"How did you know about the baby?"

She smiled. It was the same one that had sucker

punched him when he was twenty-one and saw her for the first time in the bookstore she was working at. "We have a grandson, Lammon."

No one else called him that. At the sound of her saying his given name, his heart began to beat fast. "I know. He's terrific." Mac studied her, seeing the evidence of age, marveling at how lovely she still was. "How, Annie?"

"Ben Cassidy hired a private investigator to find me. He'd just arrived at my bookstore in New York, when Emily called his cell to say she'd gone into labor. I couldn't resist coming back with him."

Reality began to dawn. "She *knows* what I've done?"

Anna shook her head. Though her hair was graying, it was soft and feminine and curled around her face. He'd always loved her hair, and had to resist the urge to reach out and touch it. "No, she doesn't know I'm here. I only got to hold the baby."

"You held the baby?" he asked stupidly.

An even broader grin. "Yes."

"Why didn't you see Emily?"

"Ben and I thought it best, not after a C-section."

He glanced at her stomach. "You had her the same way."

"Yes."

He was getting his wits about him. Was Anna here to destroy his relationship with his daughter? First Cassidy, now her. "What…what are you going to do?"

"Whatever's best for Emily."

"Even if it's to leave us alone?"

She raised her chin. "Yes, although Ben doesn't think abandoning her now is the right thing. Do you know she found my journal, the one I kept about my pregnancy and her birth?"

"No, she didn't tell me."

"Ben says she's been talking about me a lot." Anna drew in a breath. "If he believes it's wise, which is where he's leaning, I'm going to establish a relationship with her."

Feeling like a patient who'd been sick for a long time and sapped of strength, Mac leaned back on the vinyl and closed his eyes. He had no idea what to do. He tried to summon some manner of intimidation, but he couldn't.

"Lammon, I don't want to hurt Emily or you with the truth, but what we did will come out, and she won't be happy with either of us."

"She'll hate me."

"And me perhaps."

He opened his eyes. "Why would she hate you? I drove you away."

"Because I've done some awful things, too."

"By not coming back? I always thought you would, someday."

"I couldn't."

"Why?"

Anna's gaze hardened. "Because at first, I was afraid of you. Then, when I found out you told her I was dead, I thought it best for her."

"I wonder if she can ever forgive me for that lie."

"I hope so. Very much."

He frowned. "Why? Why would you hope so?"

"Because I lied to you, too."

"About what?"

"You have a son, Lammon. I was pregnant when I left here. And I told him *you* were dead, when he was old enough to ask."

Mac couldn't take it in. Then he felt fury burn inside him. Raw, unadulterated fury. "You *what?*"

"We have another child."

He stood abruptly and towered over her. "How could you deprive me of my *son?*"

Anna stood, too. She was a foot shorter than him, but undeterred. "Don't go holier-than-thou, Lammon. You did the same thing to me. You took my child away, too."

The stark words deflated him. Defused his anger.

"Now, sit back down and let's talk about how we're going to deal with all this. How we're going to do what's best for our children, this time, not necessarily for you and me."

Staring at the only woman he'd ever loved, he sat back down. "Yes, let's talk about that."

CHAPTER SIXTEEN

EMILY NESTLED HER TEN-DAY-OLD son in her lap and let him latch on to her breast. He stared up at her with wide gray eyes, watching her intently, as he took nourishment from her body.

"You're a little nighthawk, aren't you, sweetie?"

That was no exaggeration. In the week they'd been home from the hospital, Ian had slept most of the day and was awake most of the night. Because of the harrowing experience Emily and Ben had had in the hospital, and two nights of sleeplessness at their house, Jordan had moved herself in. She volunteered to take the night shift, either giving Ian a bottle or waking Emily to feed him, then sitting up with a pleasant but very wide-awake baby. She'd gone home this morning. Emily didn't know what they would have done without her best friend. It was times like these a girl needed her mother. She admonished herself for the thought and vowed to be grateful for what she had.

"So, are we going to get you on a schedule any time soon?" she asked the baby. He stopped sucking at the sound of her voice. She loved that he knew her. He seemed to respond to Ben's voice, too.

"I certainly hope so."

Her husband stood in the doorway, wearing only navy sweatpants and a night's growth of beard. But his eyes weren't as red-rimmed as before Jordan had come to help. "It's just seven. Why don't you go back to sleep?"

"No, I got a good eight hours. You go back when he's done."

"Maybe." She smiled. She couldn't believe how exhausted she was. Neither of them had had any idea one tiny baby could be so much work.

Ben dropped down into a chair and watched her. "I'll never get tired of seeing you do that."

"It's so intimate. I've never felt this kind of connection with anybody."

"You were a real trooper, keeping it up when you were sick."

She frowned. The day after the baby had been born, Emily had developed a fever that had spiked and plummeted for seventy-two hours, despite the antibiotic she'd taken. All she remembered from that time was feeding Ian, and images of people floating in and out of her room: her father, Trey and Jordan, nurses. "I didn't want to lose any ground. Breast-feeding Ian is the only thing I can recall as pleasurable during that time."

"I was worried about you."

"I know. I'm sorry. It seems like I was in the hospital forever."

"Well, we're home now."

"Mmm. Don't you have to go back to work soon?"

He rubbed a hand over his face. "I'm off till after Christmas. The people from work have called, though. They want to come over some time and see you two. So does Alice."

"They can visit whenever they like." Gray morning sneaked in through the slotted blinds. The primary colors she'd decorated the nursery with brightened up the dim light. They still needed wall decorations, but thankfully they'd bought all the furniture. "It's hard to believe Christmas is less than a week away."

"I know."

"What are we going to do about my father and the holidays? I really appreciated your letting him come over here to see us."

"I've given your father a great deal of thought."

There was something about his tone. "Is…is anything else, other than the usual, wrong?"

"No, why would you ask that?"

"Your tone of voice. Is he doing anything unethical with the company he's buying in Florida?"

"I don't know."

She rocked back and forth, soothing the baby. "I have to find out. I can't allow that to happen again."

Her husband came over to kiss her forehead. "You have to take care of yourself and our baby. You gave us all quite a scare." He straightened. "I'm going to get coffee, then come back and take this little guy so you can catch a few more winks."

"He'll probably go back down, too. Will you come and sleep with me if he does?"

"Then, and always, love." He started away.

"Ben?"

He glanced over his shoulder from the doorway. "Hmm?"

"You're a good father, and a good husband."

"I love you," was all he said, which was odd. He'd been acting odd lately, come to think of it.

Well, of course he was! His whole life had turned around in a matter of days. She'd gone into premature labor, then gotten sick, which she knew scared him. On top of all this, he was forced to accommodate a man he hated.

"He's not only a good father and husband, Ian," she whispered to his son after Ben left. "He's a very good man. Just like you'll be someday."

Ian patted his hand on her breast and stared at her. Damned if she didn't think he agreed.

HOLDING IAN, WHO FUSSED on his shoulder, Ben made his way into the downstairs den. He had to do some things today that would be hard, but necessary.

When Ian finally fell asleep, Ben placed him in the port-a-crib in the corner and crossed to his desk. From the locked drawer at the bottom, he drew out the folder with the information of what Mackenzie had done to get Ben's patent. Information Ben had indirectly promised his wife he wouldn't use against her father. She slept blissfully upstairs, unaware of what ammunition Ben held in his hands.

What to do? Trey had recently come to him with details about another Mackenzie takeover in the works. This time in Florida. The man was going to hurt other people unless he was stopped. Evidence of criminal activity given to the right people would halt his unethical tactics once and for all. But how could Ben do that to Emily? She still didn't know about her mother and brother. Anna, who'd had to return to New York to her job, was planning to come to town a few days before Christmas. Emily would have to be told about her and Dylan before that, and she couldn't handle two blows at once.

The baby cried out from the crib. Ben picked him back up and wandered to the great room to sit by the tree. As he rocked his child, he thought about Christmas and forgiveness and redemption. Could he put his feelings for Mackenzie aside, forever? Could he come up with some other way to stop the man?

When Ian continued to fuss, Ben adjusted the baby to cradle him in his arms and put a pacifier in his mouth.

He smiled down at this innocent child who'd shown him he could love like he'd never loved before. It hit him then, that Ian, along with Emily, had helped him feel like the man he used to be.

He whispered, "I hope I never let you down, buddy." But if he did, would his child forgive him? When he made mistakes raising Ian, which he would, how would his son react?

Again, the baby cried. Ben stood and walked him, realizing what he had to do.

THE BUZZER ON MAC'S DESK sounded. "Ben Cassidy's here to see you."

Oh, no. Something must be wrong with Emily. Without answering his secretary, Mac flew to the door. He whipped it open and found Cassidy standing there, a manila envelope in his hand, dressed casually in jeans, boots, sweater and a bomber jacket. "What's wrong? Is Emily all right?"

"She's fine. Jordan's with her and the baby. I need to talk to you alone."

Relief made Mac weak in the knees. All his emotions were heightened these days, all his reactions were off since he'd met up with Anna in the hospital ten days ago. Since he'd found out he had a son. And a grandson.

"Come on in."

Cassidy frowned.

Mac nodded to the conference table where a few short months ago he'd gone head-to-head with this man. When Cassidy had taken away his daughter.

Your daughter, Anna had said, *who, by all reports, has never been happier.*

He and Cassidy sat and, for a moment, just stared at each other.

Finally Cassidy spoke. "I've come to straighten out this whole mess with Emily and her mother. And Dylan."

At the mention of Dylan's name, Mac felt pain in his heart. Sometimes he couldn't handle the emotions elicited by the fact that he had a son.

He's back from Paris, Lammon, Anna had said on the phone last night when she'd called. *I'm going to tell him about you tomorrow after he catches up on jet lag.*

Cassidy interrupted his thoughts. "Mackenzie? I said I've come to talk about Anna and Dylan."

Mac's first impulse was to ask Ben who he thought he was, interfering like this. But he wasn't stupid. Cassidy was holding all the cards—personally with his daughter and professionally with the patent information. At one time that would have infuriated Mac. Now, he didn't know what he was feeling. The contempt he held for Cassidy had been diluted in the past week. Other pressing matters seemed more important. And there was the fact that Cassidy was his grandson's father. Somehow, that changed things.

Finally, Mac said, "Emily has to be told about her mother and brother. You should do it, not Anna. It would be too much of a shock for Emily and too hard for Anna."

"Anna and I aren't going to tell Emily. You are." Ben held up the manila folder.

"What's that?"

"Disks and hard copies I've accumulated about the crime you committed with the fuel-cell patent. It's yours, if you do two things."

"Not that I'm confessing to what's in there. But if I were to do what you want, whatever that is, why would you give this proof to me?"

"Because it's best for my wife and my son." Cassidy studied him. "And for *your* wife and *your* son."

"I don't understand."

"Emily needs to know the whole story about why her mother left. I want you to tell her, and try to make her understand your reasoning, your fears, your motives all those years ago. Tell her you never knew about her brother. Anna can deal with that. If you take responsibility, and tell Emily honestly, and gently, she'll handle it better. She'll forgive you." Cassidy looked away for a minute. "I'm willing to let you be a part of Emily's life, see her, see the baby, if you take care of this as best you can."

"I see." Mackenzie had never expected a concession like this or to be let off the hook. It set the world out of focus for a moment.

"But if you try to destroy her relationship with her mother, rage about not knowing your son, it'll come back to haunt you in the end, I promise." He shook his head. "Think about your past, and what it's been like. Is that what you want your future to be?"

Leaning back in his chair, he watched Cassidy for a minute. "This has overtones of the Scrooge story."

"Hmm. I guess it does. Consider me the ghost of Christmas future, then."

A chuckle escaped Mackenzie. Then his gaze narrowed. There had to be more to this. "What's the other condition?"

"You're not going to like it."

"Go ahead."

"I can't allow you to destroy other men like you did me. You've got to stop the way you do business."

"I'm not admitting to any wrongdoing."

"I have the evidence here." He held up the envelope.

"Which makes you think you can control my corporation?"

Ben shrugged. "I'm not asking you to forego acquiring companies. Just to do it aboveboard."

"Hypothetically, if I don't agree to those terms—and mind you I'm admitting nothing—what will you do?"

"I'll give this patent information to Emily. I don't want to, but I will when she's stronger. And she'll find a way to stop you, like she kept you from cutting jobs all those years. You know she will." He zeroed in for the kill. "And with hard and fast proof of real criminal activity, she'll feel differently about you, too."

"Are you saying you won't tell her about the information in that packet if I meet your conditions?"

"I am. Actually, I'd prefer it if she didn't know."

"Why not? It would destroy our relationship. That's what you wanted all along."

"It was. But I don't think that would be good for Emily. She's already lost too much." His smile was self-effacing. "Besides, I'm not the same man that I was when I married your daughter." He shook his head. "And maybe you're not the same man either."

"Maybe."

Ben stood. "So what's it going to be Mackenzie? A chance to reconcile with your son properly, and have your daughter's respect? Or continue on as you've been and end up a lonely old man?"

Was there really a choice? Still, he hesitated. "I'll let you know."

"You've got until tomorrow morning."

"I've heard that before." Right in this very room.

"Yes, I guess you have." Cassidy turned and walked out of the office.

Mac looked after him thoughtfully. In some ways, he was more confused than ever. And in some ways, the light was just beginning to dawn. Maybe he wasn't the man he used to be, like Cassidy had said.

EMILY WAS BAKING COOKIES in the kitchen, while Ben was in the great room with the baby and the dog, when the doorbell rang. The smell of spicy fruit bars filled the air, and the sound of Christmas carols wafted from the stereo in the other room. Ben must have answered the door because the noise stopped.

She turned just as her father, Ben and Ian came to the doorway. For a minute, the tableau startled her. Three generations of men that she loved—the baby in a navy-blue jumper, Ben in jeans and black sweatshirt and her father in slacks and sweater. She'd never seen them all together like this. Though her dad had been over several times to visit her and Ian, Ben had always made himself scarce.

"Hi, honey," her father said.

"Dad, this is a surprise."

"I'd like to talk to you."

She looked to Ben, who said, "I'll leave you alone."

And then Emily saw something she'd never expected to see in her lifetime. Ben put his hand on her dad's shoulder and squeezed it before he left.

Emily sucked in a breath. "What's wrong?"

"A lot." He nodded to the table. "Can we sit?"

"Yes, of course." She took off the towel she'd wrapped around her green sweatsuit.

They sat at the kitchen table and her father took her hand. "I have something to tell you, Emmy, that's going to be hard to hear. But you have to know now."

"Oh, dear Lord, please, you're not sick are you?" That would explain Ben's kindness. *Please, not that, not now.*

"Not in the way you mean. But I've been sick, emotionally, for a long time. Ever since your mother left."

"Oh, Dad. Though you never said so, I knew she hurt you when she abandoned us."

"No, you don't know. The whole story, at least. I lied, honey. Your mother didn't want to be my wife anymore, but she wanted to be your mother. I was the one to prevent that."

"What do you mean?"

"She was planning to leave me and take you with her. I couldn't allow that. I couldn't stop her from going, but I found a way to keep you with me."

"I don't understand." Her pulse sped up. "My mother wanted me?"

"Yes, before *and* after you were born."

Emily felt her whole body sag. "Now the journal makes sense." She glanced away. "How did you do it?"

"She had a breakdown. I used that against her. I had my lawyer bully and intimidate her into leaving you with me."

"That doesn't seem right, Dad. If someone tried to make me abandon Ian, I'd never do it. I'd stay and fight no matter what they said."

"There were two reasons she didn't stay, though I didn't know about the second at the time. She left you with me because she was too mentally and physically depleted to fight me. I played on that. Used it. Manipulated her to leave town without you."

"Still…."

"The second reason makes more sense." Here her father stood and began to pace. "I didn't know at the time…" His voice cracked. "I didn't know, Emily, that she was pregnant again."

Emily swallowed hard. "Oh, Dad."

"She left to protect that child from me."

"Did she lose the baby?"

"No." He drew in a breath. "She had the baby in New York and I never knew about it."

"She had the…you mean…I have a sibling?"

"You have a brother who's a little less than six years younger than you. His name is Dylan."

Emily gripped the edge of the table. "Oh, Lord. Oh, dear Lord."

Her dad put his hand on her shoulder.

Emily asked, "Didn't he ever want to know about his father?"

"Anna told him I was dead."

"She had no right to do that."

"Maybe not. But I'm as guilty as she is. When she recovered from being ill, she did contact me about getting you back. I said you thought *she* was dead and it was best for you to stay out of your life."

"You told her I thought she was *dead?*" This was incredible.

"Yes, I did."

Emily buried her face in her hands. "Oh, Dad."

"I'm so sorry. It's my fault, all of it."

Emily looked at him. "How did you find out all this? If she never contacted you."

"After you found the journal, your husband had a private investigator look for her. Ben went down to New York to see her the day you went into labor."

"*What?* Ben did all this without telling me?"

"Yes, he didn't know what he'd find. He was planning to tell you, but you went into labor, had the baby, got sick..." Her father shrugged. "There was no time to do it."

"I can barely take this in."

"Emmy, she was there, when you had Ian, in the waiting room."

"My mother? She was there?" It was too much. Emily felt the emotion gush out of her. "Sh-she was there. I wanted her with me, so much." She began to sob.

Her father dropped into a chair beside her and tugged her to him, held her close. "I'm so sorry, honey. It's my fault. No one else's. I only hope you'll forgive me someday."

Emily didn't know how long she cried into his chest. When she was done, she drew back. Her father's face was ravaged and, for the first time, he looked older than his fifty-nine years. She'd been deprived of so much because of this man's actions, he'd affected her life so much by his manipulation. Could she ever forgive him?

The smell of baking cookies and faint sound of carols in the background reminded her of the Christmas season. Then, through the door to the great room, she heard her son cry. Her father had a son, too. One he'd never seen. She stared at him. She'd never in her life seen him cry before. But now, tears coursed down his cheeks.

She took her father's hands in hers. "I forgive you, Dad. I don't like all this, and it might take time to get over it, but I do forgive you. Your life, in some ways, must have been hell."

She held onto him as she thought about all they'd lost. Mourned for it.

"Well, we've got to make plans. For me to see my mother..." She touched his cheek. "And for you to see your son."

Her father gave her a weak smile. "Your husband's already taken care of that. They're both ready to come up here, as soon as you were strong enough to hear this."

Her smile was genuine. "Oh, my, that's wonderful. Truly wonderful."

"I hope so, honey. I really hope so."

CHAPTER SEVENTEEN

EMILY DROPPED THE CUP she was holding and it smashed onto the floor, splintering everywhere. She was a wreck; so nervous, she was shaking. Ben rushed out into the kitchen, looking harried himself. She'd driven both of them crazy all morning.

"Here, I'll get that."

She raised her gaze from the shards at her feet to look at him. "I'm so...I can't...are you sure we shouldn't go to the airport to get them?"

"No, Dylan rented a car. He wanted to do it this way."

"*Dylan.* Oh, God, Ben, I'm going to see my brother. My mother. I can barely stand it."

He glanced at the floor then to her, the corners of his mouth turned up. "No kidding?"

She sighed and closed her eyes. He crossed to her, his booted feet crunching the shattered china, and lifted her up by the waist to set her on the counter. Standing between her legs, he kissed her nose. "You're about to get everything you want, sweetheart. Just be happy about it."

She studied her husband. His expression had softened since they'd had the baby and now his eyes were always filled with warmth. "Because of you. I can't believe you did all this—found my mother, arranged for her and my brother to come here."

"I thought you might be angry I did it without telling you."

Cradling his cheek in her palm, she shook her head. "No, of course not. You didn't know what you'd find when you went to New York, then the sky fell here, with the baby coming early and me getting sick."

"I'm glad you understand."

She gave him a watery smile and felt her eyes brim with tears.

"What?"

"Then you made peace with my father. Do you have any idea what a gift you've given me by doing that?"

"I think so."

She frowned. "He still won't tell me why, but I think you were responsible for his promise not to do anything like he did with Cassidy Industries in future acquisitions of Mackenzie Enterprises."

"I can only speak for myself, but it's easy forgiving past transgressions, when you've been given everything you want in life. When I think back to last year, I'm so grateful for what *I* have this Christmas."

Slowly, she slid her arms around his neck and pulled him close. He looked so sexy in his black slacks and gray shirt rolled up at the sleeves. She raised her lips to his and gave him a full, open-mouthed kiss that heated her blood. "Hmm, I miss this. Us, together."

He rubbed the back of her green velour dress. "Oh man, me too. The doctor said soon, though, right?" There was sexual promise in his eyes.

"Can't be soon enough for me."

He gave her one last hug, then retrieved the broom and dustpan and cleaned up the mess. Finally, the doorbell rang.

Still seated on the counter, Emily gasped. "It's them."

Ben glanced at his watch. "No, it's too early. That's probably your dad." He lowered her to the floor. "Go answer it. I'll bet he's a wreck, like you."

She flew to the front door and whipped it open. On the porch stood her father. She had to chuckle. His hair was wind-whipped, his face panicky, like hers. Even his usually meticulous clothes were rumpled. "Hi, Emmy."

His flustered appearance calmed her. "Come in, Dad."

He entered the room and began to pace. Alternately, he ran a hand through his hair and mumbled to himself.

"Give me your coat."

"Huh?"

"Your coat, Dad. Then we'll sit by the fire and wait."

"I'm as nervous as when I asked your mother to marry me."

Someday, Emily wanted to know all those stories about how her parents had met, what their young life had been like together. She hadn't asked because it was too soon. Taking her father by the arm, she led him to the couch. The fire spit and crackled, and the heat warmed them. Emily watched the flames, consumed with her own doubts but trying not to let her father see it.

"I wonder if he'll…"

She looked over at him. He was staring into the fire, too. "What, Dad?"

"Will he resent me, Emily? He should. I behaved badly. Still, if I'd known about him…" He hesitated. "Oh, hell, who knows what I would have done?"

The doorbell rang and they both froze, staring at the doorway to the foyer.

Ben entered the great room from the kitchen, assessed her and her father, and headed for the foyer before either of them moved. Emily heard voices. She stood. So did her father. She held his hand.

Finally, they came to the doorway. Emily battled back tears as she looked at them. Her mother was holding on to her brother's hand, like she held on to her father's.

Ben said, "Come on in, you two, I'll take your coats."

Instead, her mother strode across the room. Up close, Emily could see her own resemblance to Anna

McGee: the same color eyes, same high cheekbones, same shape of the mouth. "Hello, darling," her mother said shakily. The voice kicked into some unconscious part of Emily's mind, and she remembered it on a visceral level. "It's so good to see you."

Emily swallowed hard. Her father let go of her hand and nudged her forward. For the first time in thirty years, Emily touched her mother.

And promptly burst into tears.

Her mother drew Emily to her breast. A soothing hand slid down her hair. A gentle kiss on her head. "It's all right dear, we're here now. We're together now."

"I *missed* you."

"And I you."

So much was familiar. The scent of her cologne. The firm hold of her hand. For seconds, Emily reveled in it. Then she drew back. She saw her mother share a glance with her father before leading her across the room. "Come on, I'll introduce you to your brother."

Dylan still stood in the doorway. He was tall, broad shouldered and had hair a shade or two darker than hers. He had her father's dark eyes. "Emily, this is Dylan."

His face was sober. His gaze narrowed on her. Oh, no! What if he hated her? What if he *was* resentful of the whole situation, as her father feared?

And then he smiled—a beautiful, brilliant smile—

and grabbed her in a big hug. Oh, God, she had a brother.

He didn't say anything. Just held on. When he drew back, she saw that his cheeks were wet. She wiped at her own and cleared her throat. "Hello, Dylan."

"Hi, Emily."

She touched his jaw, his hair. "I can't believe you're real."

His hand smoothed down her arm. "Back at ya."

Looking over her shoulder, his gaze darkened. He was staring at their father. "Please, be nice," she whispered.

The room tilted as Mac watched his son and daughter come toward him. He could barely take it all in. The boy—*his* boy—looked just like him. He had the same confident gait. The sure set of his shoulders. Dylan never took his eyes off Mac. Waiting for a cue, for some sign of his acceptance, Mac just watched Dylan. When he could stand it no longer, when the hush in the room became smothering, he said, "Hello, son."

"Hello."

Mac swallowed hard. He extended his hand. Somehow, a simple handshake seemed inadequate, but he didn't know what to do here.

Dylan glanced down, then back up at Mac. He shook his head. "I don't think so."

Mac's heart plummeted. He didn't expect forgiveness, but damn, this hurt. "Well, I—"

The boy shocked him by dragging Mac into another huge bear hug. "Hello, Dad," he whispered. "I've really missed knowing you."

He was just like Emily and Anna.

Mac closed his eyes and held on. He'd bought and sold companies, altered the course of hundreds of lives, had almost as much money as Donald Trump. But never in his life had he felt more of a man.

When the emotional moment passed, Mac and Dylan both drew back. His son's look was sheepish. Mac sighed. He glanced around the room. He saw Anna and Emily holding hands. And Ben Cassidy standing in the background.

"I see we've missed introducing somebody," Mac said to Dylan.

Ben came forward. "I'm—"

But Mac cut him off. "Dylan, I'd like you to meet Ben." He drew in a breath and added, "My son-in-law."

Ben's jaw dropped, and Emily started to cry. Dylan shook Ben's hand. "Hey, Ben. Nice to meet you."

Mac was about to say more, when a lusty howl sounded from the den. A child's innocent cry, so appropriate for this Christmas season and for all the miracles in this room.

"Hey," Dylan said, his eyes lighting up. "Is that my nephew?"

"My grandson," Mac said.

Ben turned to Dylan. "What do you say I introduce

you to Ian?" He nodded to Mac. "You come, too. It'll be just us guys."

When Mac passed Emily and Anna, he squeezed Anna's arm and leaned over to kiss the child of his heart.

Then he followed the *guys* into the den to introduce the son he'd never known he had to the grandson who'd brought them all together.

"THIS IS SO WICKED."

Emily chuckled at her brother. "Wicked? You sound like your daughter."

Dylan smiled. "Yeah, she rubs off on you. It means great, by the way."

"Hmm. I'll probably learn a whole new vocabulary. I can't wait to meet her tomorrow."

Along with everything else that had happened, Emily had been further shocked to learn Dylan had been married at twenty and had a child before getting divorced. Seven-year-old Katie was with her mother today, on Christmas, but would fly out to Rockford tomorrow to be with her dad and his newfound family.

Dylan said, "She's thrilled to have a cousin."

Emily stood close to her brother as they watched Ben across the room at Cassidy Place helping Santa pass out presents. Trey and Jordan also assisted, the three of them wearing Santa caps, while Alice looked on, beaming with pride. "I'm so glad you came here with us today," Emily said.

As Dylan studied the soup kitchen, Emily saw it through his eyes. A twenty-foot tree dominated the end of the big room; greens hung on the walls; tables were decorated with white cloths and red poinsettias. Carols played low from the corner stereo. "This is a great place," her brother said.

"I think so. And it has sentimental meaning for me and Ben."

He laughed. "You're blushing. Must be some story. I want all the details."

"Maybe." She loved the brother-sister banter they'd fallen into the last three days. "If you tell me some of your deep and dark secrets."

Ben laughed at something Alice said and picked up a little girl so she could sit on Santa's lap. Dressed in black jeans and a red cable-knit sweater, he looked young and happy and healthy.

"He seems like a great guy, Em."

"The best." She grinned. "This is the first time we've been out of the house without Ian since he was born."

"Grandma and Grandpa will take good care of him." Her mother and father had insisted Emily and Ben follow through with their plans to serve noontime dinner at Cassidy Place. Anna volunteered to cook at Emily's home, and they both begged to keep the baby with them. Emily wanted to bring Ian to celebrate Christmas at the place his mother and father had met, but she thought Ian's grandparents needed him more.

Though it would take a while for her mother and father to forgive each other, they were making progress.

"Amazing, isn't it?" Emily said. "How things work out."

"Yeah."

"Do you resent them for what happened?" she asked Dylan.

He waited before he answered. "Yeah, some. Don't you?"

"Yep. But I'm not going to dwell on it. I'm going to think about you and Katie, and Ian and Ben, instead." She scanned the area, taking in all the homeless, hungry people at Cassidy Place. "We have so much, Dylan. We can't forget that. We shouldn't focus on the past and what we've lost."

He slid an arm around her shoulder. "All right, we won't."

Together, Emily and her brother watched the kids squeal with delight as they got presents from Santa. They watched as each guest was given boots Ben had provided. Finally, it was time for the meal. "Ready to go to work, little brother?"

"Uh-huh. Come on, I'll beat you to the kitchen."

Ben caught up to them just as they started away. "Not so fast." Alice was behind him, and Trey and Jordan were heading for the kitchen. "I want my wife for a minute."

Alice took Dylan by the arm. "Come on, young

man, I'll tell you all about your brother-in-law and how he started this place."

Ben was grinning broadly as he grasped Emily's hand and dragged her to the small enclosed alcove where Lady had delivered her pups.

Once they were obscured from view, he took her into his arms. Without saying anything, he kissed her thoroughly. It was both carnal and tender.

"Wow," she said, snuggling into him.

"Hmm." He hugged her tightly. He could see a slice of the dining room from where he stood. The green-and-red decorations, the smells of pine and cooking ham, the buzz of voices warmed him. The sound of Christmas carols made the setting perfect. Though Cassidy Place was no longer the *only* evidence of the good Ben had done in the world, it still meant a lot to him.

"I wanted a minute to savor all this with you."

"It's a wonderful day, here, Ben. This is a wonderful place."

"If for no other reason than it brought me you." He stole another kiss. "We're...blessed."

"The First Noel" began to play. Her head on his chest, his hand in her hair, Ben realized he'd never meant anything more. He *was* blessed to have her, their own child and the means to do something good for others.

Over her head, he could see the entrance to Cassidy Place. The picture of his father hung there, illuminated by tiny white Christmas lights. For a moment, he just stared at Mick Cassidy. Ben thought about the life he'd lived as a child, how hard his father's day-to-day existence had been, and how all those things had culminated in Ben establishing Cassidy Place.

Still staring at the picture, he pulled his wife even closer and made a silent vow never to take anything for granted again.

And, quietly, he whispered, "Merry Christmas, Dad."

HARLEQUIN *SuperRomance*

THE OPERATIVES
Sometimes the most dangerous people you
know are the only ones you can trust.

NOT WITHOUT
THE TRUTH
by Kay David

Lauren Stanley is afraid of almost everything.
Despite that, she goes to Peru to find a mysterious
man named Armando Torres. It's the only way to
discover the truth about her past. But before she can,
an "accident" has her forgetting everything
she once knew.

On sale January 2006

Watch for the exciting final book in Kay David's
trilogy *Not Without Cause* (#1338) in April 2006.

Available wherever Harlequin books are sold.

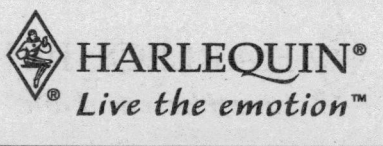

HARLEQUIN®
Live the emotion™

HARLEQUIN *Super Romance*

COLD CASES: L.A.
Giving up is not an option.

AND JUSTICE FOR ALL
by Linda Style

With three unsolved murders and only one suspect, Detective Jordan St. James demands justice. He's convinced the suspect, a notorious mob boss, also killed his mother. What St. James doesn't know is that he's putting his source, Laura Gianni—and her daughter—in terrible danger.

On sale January 2006

Available wherever Harlequin books are sold.

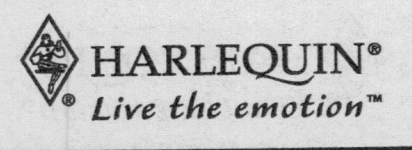

HARLEQUIN®
Live the emotion™

www.eHarlequin.com   HSRAJFA0106

If you enjoyed what you just read,
then we've got an offer you can't resist!

Take 2 bestselling
love stories FREE!
Plus get a FREE surprise gift!

Clip this page and mail it to Harlequin Reader Service®

IN U.S.A.	IN CANADA
3010 Walden Ave.	P.O. Box 609
P.O. Box 1867	Fort Erie, Ontario
Buffalo, N.Y. 14240-1867	L2A 5X3

YES! Please send me 2 free Harlequin Superromance® novels and my free surprise gift. After receiving them, if I don't wish to receive anymore, I can return the shipping statement marked cancel. If I don't cancel, I will receive 6 brand-new novels every month, before they're available in stores. In the U.S.A., bill me at the bargain price of $4.69 plus 25¢ shipping and handling per book and applicable sales tax, if any*. In Canada, bill me at the bargain price of $5.24 plus 25¢ shipping and handling per book and applicable taxes**. That's the complete price, and a savings of at least 10% off the cover prices—what a great deal! I understand that accepting the 2 free books and gift places me under no obligation ever to buy any books. I can always return a shipment and cancel at any time. Even if I never buy another book from Harlequin, the 2 free books and gift are mine to keep forever.

135 HDN DZ7W   336 HDN DZ7X

Name	
	(PLEASE PRINT)
Address	Apt.#
City	State/Prov.	Zip/Postal Code

Not valid to current Harlequin Superromance® subscribers.

Want to try two free books from another series?
Call 1-800-873-8635 or visit www.morefreebooks.com.

* Terms and prices subject to change without notice. Sales tax applicable in N.Y.
** Canadian residents will be charged applicable provincial taxes and GST.
All orders subject to approval. Offer limited to one per household.
® are registered trademarks owned and used by the trademark owner and or its licensee.
©2004 Harlequin Enterprises Limited

SUP04R

eHARLEQUIN.com

The Ultimate Destination for Women's Fiction

The ultimate destination for women's fiction.
Visit eHarlequin.com today!

GREAT BOOKS:

- We've got something for everyone—and at great low prices!
- Choose from new releases, backlist favorites, Themed Collections and preview upcoming books, too.
- Favorite authors: Debbie Macomber, Diana Palmer, Susan Wiggs and more!

EASY SHOPPING:

- Choose our convenient "bill me" option.
  No credit card required!
- Easy, secure, 24-hour shopping from the comfort of your own home.
- Sign-up for free membership and get $4 off your first purchase.
- Exclusive online offers: FREE books, bargain outlet savings, hot deals.

EXCLUSIVE FEATURES:

- Try Book Matcher—finding your favorite read has never been easier!
- Save & redeem Bonus Bucks.
- Another reason to love Fridays—
  Free Book Fridays!

— Shop online —
at www.eHarlequin.com today!

INTB204R

TheNextNovel.com

Available January 2006

HARLEQUIN®

N*xt™

Three friends,
two exes
and a plan
to get payback.

The Payback Club

by **Rexanne Becnel**

USA TODAY BESTSELLING AUTHOR

MIDNIGHT MARRIAGE
Victoria Bylin

Dr. Susanna Leaf was a woman of startling contradictions, and Rafe LaCroix found every one of them too intriguing for his own good. He was a powder keg of unpredictability and wore his secrets as close as his battered trail duster. Yet his raw masculinity compelled her in ways that reminded her she was a woman first and a physician second. And *that*—more than anything else—made him dangerous.

On-sale January 2006

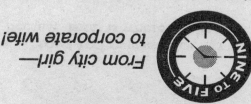

NINE TO FIVE

From city girl—
to corporate wife!

Working side by side, nine to five—and beyond...

HER SPANISH BOSS
by Barbara McMahon

On sale January 2006, #3875,
in Harlequin Romance®!

When Rachel Goodson starts working for Luis Alvares
he's prickly and suspicious. But soon they draw closer
and secrets spill out. Luis's heart is still with his late wife,
so Rachel is stunned when he wants her to pose as
his girlfriend. And then Luis makes it clear that he
wants more than just a pretend relationship....

Barbara McMahon creates stories bubbling
with warmth and emotion. Her captivating style
and believable characters will leave your
romance senses tingling!

Available wherever Harlequin books are sold.

www.eHarlequin.com   HRHSP

HOME TO LOVELESS COUNTY
Because Texas is where the heart is.

MORE TO TEXAS THAN COWBOYS

by Roz Denny Fox

Greer Bell is returning to Texas for the first time since she left as a pregnant teenager. She and her daughter are determined to make a success of their new dude ranch—and the last thing Greer needs is romance, even with the handsome Reverend Noah Kelley.

On sale January 2006

Also look for the final book in this miniseries
The Prodigal Texan (#1326) by Lynnette Kent
in February 2006.

Available wherever Harlequin books are sold.

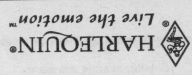

® HARLEQUIN® *Live the emotion*™

www.eHarlequin.com   HSRMTTC0106